To John
for 1989 Birthday
Love From Aunt
× × ×

Any Fool Can Be Independent

Any Fool Can Be Independent

JAMES ROBERTSON
Illustrated by Larry

PELHAM BOOKS
STEPHEN GREENE PRESS

PELHAM BOOKS/STEPHEN GREENE PRESS

Published by the Penguin Group
27 Wrights Lane, London W8 5TZ, England
Viking Penguin Inc., 40 West 23rd Street, New York, New York 10010, USA
The Stephen Greene Press Inc.,
15 Muzzey Street, Lexington, Massachusetts 02173, USA
Penguin Books Australia Ltd, Ringwood, Victoria, Australia
Penguin Books Canada Ltd, 2801 John Street, Markham, Ontario, Canada L3R 1B4
Penguin Books (NZ) Ltd, 182–190 Wairau Road, Auckland 10, New Zealand

Penguin Books Ltd, Registered Offices: Harmondsworth, Middlesex, England

First published 1989

Copyright © James Robertson, 1989
Illustrations © Larry, 1989

Printed and bound in Great Britain by
Richard Clay Ltd, Bungay, Suffolk

Typeset by Cambrian Typesetters, Frimley, Surrey

A CIP catalogue record for this book is available from the British Library.

ISBN 0 7207 1903 8

Introduction

NATURE IS not always red in tooth and claw; she has a kinder side. Look, for example, at the mole. They spend their lives underground, tunnelling through soil and stones to create dank, dark passages no wider than their own bodies. A certain recipe for claustrophobia, one would think, and yet few have been known to suffer from this condition.

In the midst of a twenty-foot square of lawn, primped and trimmed to the quality of the putting greens at Augusta, one mole was happy. It felt the sweet rip of the roots of the turf as it heaved the rich, black soil to the surface. Since it had last passed this way, the rocks had disappeared and the clods of sour clay had been transformed into a fine tilth, rich in nutriments. The worms promised to be plump and plentiful. It even poked its nose from the burgeoning mound of soil to risk a sniff at the spring air.

Had Mandy been a woman of greater imagination, she might have been able to appreciate the mole's point of view as she peered through the lace curtains shrouding the double-glazed window of the spare room, en suite with bathroom in slurry brown. After all, she and her husband, Keith, had only moved to Moorcombe five years earlier, whereas the mole and its forebears had already been resident for millennia when Mandy's skin-clad ancestors trekked across the isthmus which would become the English Channel.

But Mandy had the sensitivity of a Gila monster.

Her glossy, scarlet lips tightened and her ample bosom, carapaced in a whalebone-reinforced corset, rose against her pink, satin blouse.

'Keith!'

Moles are not deaf. Out in the garden, the animal found itself scurrying back along the entrails of the earth. Inside its velvet suit, its little heart thumped with terror.

1

Keith was preparing to settle on the downstairs loo with the *Reader's Digest* when the call came. In his mid forties, he was a small man with a London accent, a thin foxy face, dark hair and a scrubby little moustache. His career as a butcher in Reading, culminating in the presidency of the Meat and Offal Processors Club (South Central Division), had ended when Mandy discovered he made personal deliveries of sausages weekly, to four commuter widows on the nearby executive housing estate.

On a touring holiday in the West Country, designed to renew their marriage, they had fallen in love with the moor. Many visitors did, but few went so far as to settle there until retirement, but Keith, being a handy fellow with a substantial capital once they had sold up, had become a builder.

Being ignorant of the conventions of his new profession, he

began by giving written quotations and keeping to them. He turned up when he said he would, paid his assistant, Jason Loosemire, on time, in cash, while his finished barns, extensions and re-roofings were no more liable to collapse than anyone else's. By his second year, he had learned the proper way a builder should conduct himself but, by then, he had established himself.

Keith had learned that his only chance of a quiet life lay in instant, unquestioning obedience to his wife's slightest whim, so he re-fastened his trousers round his skinny waist and scurried up the stairs. 'Coming, dear!'

Mandy was holding a pink plastic pony, of which she had the best collection since Imelda Marcos's was broken up. On a table in front of her stood a sheet of plywood covered in moss, bits of twig and stones.

'What are you doing, dear?' asked Keith, as he came through the door.

'Never mind that. Look at the lawn.' She waved the pony towards the window.

'Oh dear, dear. It's a mole.'

Mandy spared a glance from the offending mound of earth to look at her husband. Very occasionally, a gossamer wisp of suspicion floated through her brain that Keith did not take her entirely seriously. 'Of course it's a mole!'

'It's made a hill. Oh dear, dear, dear, dear.'

'Do shut up. I told you we should have concreted the back as well as the front. Go out and kill the thing. When you've done that I want you to stuff the soil back down the hole. It cost a fortune and I'm not having it wasted. The peat was from King's Sedgemoor, you know.'

'How?'

'How?' Mandy looked at her husband again. 'Your flies are undone.'

'Sorry, dear.' Keith rectified the condition.

'How what?'

'How do I kill it?'

Putting her little pony back on the table, she picked up a feather duster and slapped viciously at a spider which dared to string a tentative strand between a couple of curlicues on a gilt-framed print of a well-honeysuckled thatched cottage. 'I don't know. Poison it or shoot it or something. I want it dead, though. Today!'

3

Keith sighed. 'Yes, dear.'

'Use the garden fork to stab it.'

'That's a good idea, dear.'

Once again the wisp tendrilled through her brain, but she turned back to the window and the modest pile of soil which dominated her field of vision.

The cottage, 'Pixies Laughter,' lay in a cul-de-sac at the bottom of the village alongside the river. Out the back, in the direction in which Mandy was looking, across a field bisected by a massive hedgebank, the tower of St Wilgeforts was visible through a gap in the centuries-old beech trees with their circling rooks. With crazily-paved paths, patio and neat rectangles of bare earth waiting for the annuals, the garden was lapped by an anarchic sea of squalid nature. The gardens on either side were thick with the skeletons of last year's thistles and nettles and, in the field between 'Pixies Laughter' and the lane by the church, a few scrofulous sheep belonging to Chairman of the Parish Council, Kelvin Morchard, bleated continually to maintain contact amid the gorse bushes.

With a sigh, Mandy turned back towards her husband, still waiting patiently to be dismissed so that he could return to 'It Pays To Increase Your Word Power'. 'I'll need you later on to hold "Frolic in the Forest" while I drive it round.'

'Sorry, dear?'

With a wave of her hand, she indicated the vegetable matter on the table. ' "Frolic in the Forest", my entry for the flower arrangement cup in the Horticultural Show.'

'Oh! Is that what it is!'

'It'll be clearer when I put in the ponies. I expect I'll come first this year.' Keith looked at the partially completed tableau with some doubt. 'If I win, I said you'd produce a plan for the new village hall without charge.'

'But . . .'

'Don't worry, I'll give you my advice. You can go and get rid of that mole now.'

'But . . .'

'Now,' said Mandy.

'Yes, dear.' Keith's sphincter wiffled its frustration as he ambled off.

4

Chapter One

'NEXT YEAR in the village hall, eh, Commander?' said Jimmy, staggering under the weight of a large cardboard box as he came through the door of the school.

'What've you got in there?' asked the commander, peering into the box where all that was to be seen was a blanket.

Jimmy placed his burden carefully on one of the low trestle tables hugging the wall of the room. 'Onions, Commander, onions,' he said with a sly smile. 'Onions the size of cannon balls. Onions the like of which you'll never see. Unblemished perfection. Best I've ever produced.'

'Mine are good, too,' said the commander. 'Look.'

Jimmy looked.

As he supplemented his pension by running a market garden, the commander had to take the Moorcombe Horticultural Society's Spring Show extremely seriously. Most villages held their show towards the end of the growing season in late summer, but Moorcombe's had to be first. A spring show made life complicated, entries having to be grown through the winter or preserved from the previous year, but it had been held in the spring for at least fifty years which meant there would have to be a very good reason for any change. Common sense and convenience were not sufficient.

Arriving at the school early, the commander had laid out his wares beneath the photograph of the Queen and the map of the world, showing the British Empire at its most sunlit, above the head mistress's desk at one end of the room.

Jimmy examined the produce with a critical eye. 'Not bad, Commander,' he said. 'You could do quite well with those. Nice pickling onions.'

'Pickling onions! How dare you! They're going to win the Shield today.'

Jimmy smiled, not a pretty sight. His long, thin face, topped

5

by a surprising thatch of greasy white hair, was deeply creased to counter the smoke which wreathed his head from the hand-rolled cigarettes he had used for sixty years. 'You said that last year and I won the Onion Shield. You said that the year before and I won the Shield. You said it the year before that and I won it then, too.'

'But I won it in 1984.'

'Only because I was away and didn't enter.'

'Well, I'll win it this year.' The commander defiantly picked up one of his onions and rubbed an invisible blemish against the sleeve of his blue combat sweater.

'Blood and bone. That's why you'll never do anything against me. You're afraid of it. Onions need blood. I go into town on the bus and bring back a couple of buckets from the abattoir to put in the onion bed when they're just beginning to sprout. Nothing like it.'

The commander shuddered.

When he had first arrived in Moorcombe, the casually organic lifestyle and decision-making processes of the village had offended his sense of order, inculcated by twenty-five years in the Senior Service. Once his market garden was in order, he set out to bring some discipline and efficiency into local institutions. He became secretary of the Conservative Association, of the Over Sixties Club, the leading light of the Parochial Church Council, a governor of the C of E primary school where the show was being held and always wore a tie since there was no need to let standards slip simply because one had left the Service.

Under the sardonic and phlegmatic gaze of the locals, he bustled round the community. They'd seen his kind before – reforming squires and curates, Cromwell's major generals, conquering Normans. If they stayed long enough, the torpor of the moor stole over them.

His wife, Elfrieda, who had loyally supported him in the role of naval wife for his career afloat, was the first to crack. Tired of neat ranks of sprouts, strawberries and courgettes, she declared her independence and developed an interest in feminism, Greenham Common and alternative religions.

One evening in the Hunted Hind shortly afterwards, the commander became drunk and fell off his barstool to be wheeled home by Kelvin and Jimmy in a barrow. Over the subsequent few months, he went native, spending most of his

6

time in the tap bar of the Hunted Hind gossiping with the regulars. He stopped wearing a tie and he bought himself a new wardrobe from jumble sales. His hair grew longer and whiter. He grew a moustache; his erect posture slouched, his belly swelled and his complexion became reddened and speckled with broken capillaries under the assault of the large amounts of barley wine he consumed each evening. In short, he became one of the select band of incomers who was indistinguishable in habit and appearance from the natives, unless he opened his mouth when his accent would betray him.

'Well, keep your revolting vegetables well away from mine.' He shooed Jimmy away from his table.

Moving down the room, Jimmy selected an empty table where he carefully peeled back the protective blanket from his treasured wares and began to lay them out.

Built in the middle of the nineteenth century, Moorcombe Church of England Primary School had never had more than forty pupils and never less than thirty, although now half the children were bussed in from neighbouring Swinehanger. Most of the natives of Moorcombe had, like Jimmy, received their entire education from one of the three mistresses who had run the school since 1921. There had been changes. The map was the same, but the cream-painted walls, above the four feet of brown varnished panelling, were now papered by examples of the pupils' work. Smiling black-and-white quadrupeds produced by the coming generation of cowmen, startled clouds with legs from embryo sheep farmers, tractors, combines and forage harvesters, each meticulously detailed and painted so that its manufacturer was immediately apparent, mingled with collages of dead leaves, dried wild flowers and the skulls of rodents and birds.

Today, tables and desks had been cleared and sheeted trestle tables lined the walls, which gradually filled with vegetables, flowers and flower arrangements, pots of jam from the Women's Institute and a proud rampart of pickles.

'When's the squire and his missus due to do the judging?' asked Jimmy, strolling down the room filled with the murmur of nervous conversation, of the commander who was smugly comparing his courgettes with those of his neighbour.

The latter looked at his watch. 'Half an hour, I suppose. Marcia and he usually turn up at eleven.'

'Here's Kelvin.'

'Oh God!' groaned the commander, turning towards the door. 'I didn't think he'd turn up until the pub was due to open.'

In the Byzantine social heirarchy of Moorcombe, Kelvin occupied an important place. Not only the latest in a line of Morchards, stretching far back into antiquity, to farm Northcott, half a mile downstream from Moorcombe bridge, but also Chairman of the Parish Council, Leader of the Emergency Volunteers and one-time special constable. The scruffy sixty-year old figure with a lantern jaw and ill-fitting false teeth, elbowing his way through the crowd in the entrance to the school, held a concentration of power that many local analysts considered dangerous.

'Ho ho,' said Kelvin, approaching the commander's display. 'Pickling onions again, Commander?'

'How's Brett?' responded the commander, frostily.

Kelvin's face darkened. Brett was his grandson – now two years old – by his middle-aged spinster daughter, Prudence. Refusing to marry the neighbour who had sired Brett, she had threatened to walk out on her father, leaving him to do the farm work, should he object to her behaviour. Kelvin was all for having an heir but . . . . 'The little bastard shows no respect for me,' he said bitterly.

'You shouldn't call Brett a little bastard, Kelvin,' reproved the commander.

'Well that's what he is, isn't he?'

'A child by chance,' said Jimmy, using the local euphemism. 'There but for the grace . . . I remember you at your parent's wedding. I was standing in the graveyard when your mother came out and you should've heard the crones cawing at the size of her belly. Looked as if you were a calf, they said.'

Kelvin looked bleakly at Jimmy. 'You should've called your boy Baaaaasil.' He drew out the 'a' in imitation of a bleating sheep, referring to an apocryphal amorous exploit in Jimmy's youth. As usual, it served its purpose.

'That's a lie!'

'Hush!' said the commander, looking round the room. 'Calm down, Jimmy.'

'He's got no right to say things like that. It's downright ignorant!'

'Who d'you think you're calling ignorant?' demanded Kelvin, belligerently.

8

'For heaven's sake! You two may be back at school, but you're not ten-year-olds now.'

'Huh!' said Kelvin. 'We weren't allowed to talk in here unless Miss Crabbe asked a direct question.'

'That's right. She used to keep her strap on a hook by the mantelpiece.' Jimmy gestured towards the wall where the skeleton of a long-boarded up fireplace could still be seen. 'We had to be tough in them days.'

''S'right,' agreed Kelvin. 'She'd never light the fire unless there was snow lying outside.'

'And I had to do two hours of chores every morning before walking three miles across the fields to school. I carried a piece of bread and dripping for my dinner.' The commander tutted his tongue sympathetically. 'It was the very best dripping, mind. My mother always made sure of that.'

'I'm sure she did.' The commander's attention drifted towards the doorway. 'Who's that?'

The heads of the other two swivelled in unison towards the door. A small, pear-shaped woman, about forty, with straight black hair and a face like an angry hamster was coming through, carrying a cardboard box.

Kelvin drew in his breath with a hiss. 'What's she doing here? That's Sheila Biss. She's from the other side of the moor.'

'She's the district councillor over there, isn't she?' asked Jimmy.

'That's right. When her father died, she took it on. Nobody else would. She's got the post office at Puddlewick and twenty acres of damn good land she lets to her nephew.'

'She's an odd looking woman,' said the commander.

'They say she's a witch,' said Kelvin. 'Lot of them over that way.'

'That's true,' agreed Jimmy.

'Ssh! She's coming over here,' said the commander, who had learned there were more things in the culture of Moorcombe than dreamt of in his philosophy.

With huge buttocks retained in blue Crimplene slacks, she waddled over to the table alongside the commander and moved a bunch of his courgettes in order to put down her box.

'Bloody cheek!' muttered the commander, moving towards her. 'Excuse me, madam, but you're spoiling my display.'

9

'You're taking up more than your share of room.' She had a
flat, whining voice.

'Oh, you're displaying something?'

'Yes. Onions. I had a good crop this year and I thought I'd
go in for the Moorcombe Onion Shield.'

The commander laughed, patronisingly. 'I'm afraid you'll
have a lot of competition. You might find a table down near
the lavatory door.' He indicated the least desirable spot in the
room, adjacent to eleven year-old Tracy Loosemire's display
of cacti.

Mrs Biss followed his pointing finger, her lips pursed like a
cat's anus. 'You can move down there if you want,' she said.
'But I'm putting my onions here.'

'I was here first!'

She gave him a pale, wet, ruthless smile. 'I'm here now.
Look after them while I park my car.' She waddled off.

The commander looked after her, his eyes popping with
outrage. 'I must say,' he expostulated. 'I've a good mind to
chuck her damned onions on the floor. They're going beneath
my courgettes at least.' He peered into the box. 'Good Lord!'

He looked from his own onions back to those in the box.

'What's wrong?' asked Jimmy instantly.

'These onions are quite impressive.'

'Let's have a look.' He looked. 'Bugger me! Where did she get hold of those? She can't've grown them over in Puddlewick.'

'Can't we nobble them?' asked the commander, dropping his voice to a nervous whisper.

'We could swop them round . . .' said Jimmy.

'That's a good idea,' said the commander, seizing a couple of his onions.

'. . . with mine.'

'Oh.' The commander's face fell. 'We seem to be faced with a bit of a problem.'

'Gentlemen,' said Kelvin with heavy sarcasm. 'I'm disappointed in you. You can't cheat.'

'I don't suppose we should,' said the commander.

'However,' continued Kelvin. 'If you just bruise them or cut them with a knife, the squire'd be forced to disqualify them.'

'So we could.'

'But then I'd have to tell the squire what you'd done and he'd disqualify you, too.'

'You wouldn't do that,' said the commander.

'It would be my duty,' said Kelvin with simple dignity. 'I swore an oath when I was a special constable to uphold the law and confound the Queen's enemies.'

'So did I when I received a commission, but it doesn't mean I have to tell the squire I've dropped an onion.'

'You might have your own standards of what's right and wrong, but we Morchards've always been honourable respected folk hereabouts. That's true, isn't it, Jimmy?'

'Yes. Always been one of the leading families of Moorcombe.'

'My grandfather was a Methodie lay preacher.'

'Look, Kelvin,' said the commander with anger. 'I'm not taking a lecture on integrity from you.'

'I don't blame you . . .' Unobserved, the owner of the onions had returned. 'He's got a shocking reputation on our side of the moor.'

'That's not true, missus,' said Kelvin. 'Some of my best friends come from the other side of the moor.'

'Who?'

11

'Well . . . er . . . Caleb Ridd.'

'Caleb Ridd! You've sold him sheep too often for him to look on you as a friend.'

'It's not my fault if he can't tell a top from a gimmer.'

'It's certainly your fault when you kicked his ram on the leg on market day and got it cheap because it was limping.'

'I never did!'

'Aha!' said the commander. 'I remember that!'

'Well, perhaps I might've done. But that was business.'

'And you trying to make out you're an honest man,' said Jimmy, shaking his head.

'Oh come on, Jimmy,' said Kelvin. 'Caleb comes from Puddlewick. It's not as if he was local.'

'True.'

Mrs Biss twitched her lips. 'Jackals of the moor. That's what we call you lot from Moorcombe. It's going to be a pleasure to take away the Onion Shield. I'll use it in Puddlewick to prop open the post office door. Get these marrows out of the way!'

'Courgettes,' snapped the commander. 'And you're going to leave them where they are.'

Mrs Biss ignored him. Picking up the courgettes, she placed them on top of the commander's best lettuce, snapping a leaf. 'Oh dear. Still, not to worry. It wouldn't've won anything.'

The commander recoiled from her tight, malevolent smile. 'Madam, as well as a competitor, I am one of the stewards at this event. I must insist.' He put his hand on her arm.

Shrugging it off, Mrs Biss turned to him. Her black eyes narrowed and the corners of her lips turned down. 'Violence. That's all your sort understand. Bullying a poor, weak woman. Go away! Go away!' She went back to her onions.

Beckoning to the other two, the commander led them towards the door. 'What a monstrous woman! We can't let her win.'

'No,' agreed Kelvin grimly. 'We'd better have a word with the squire about it. We'll catch him before he comes in.'

Pushing their way to the doorway, they went outside into the playground.

There, the squire, in a brown tweed suit and Guards tie, was solemnly playing hopscotch. Now in his sixties, the squire and Marcia, author of a pamphlet on roses published in 1959 at 1s.6d. and still staple fare of every jumble sale in the vicinity, had sent their children on to jobs in merchant banks and publishing. A vague, gentle man, he attributed the same standards of honour, duty and decency to everyone else. Moorcombe exploited his good nature and also protected him. They were proud of their squire; few villages could boast of having the same family in the great house for five hundred years. Nowadays the oddest people had sold their semis in Clapham and bought estates and Puddlewick's great house had even been bought by a foreigner, an Arab who was reputed to mastermind international terrorism.

'What are you doing?' asked Kelvin.

'Oh, good morning, Kelvin. I'm waiting till the clock strikes. I'm not due to arrive till eleven.'

'Where's Marcia?' asked the commander. 'I thought she was judging the jams and pickles.'

'She is. She's just dropping a dog in at the vet's.'

'One of those little ratty ones of hers?'

'Yes, I slammed a door on the creature and broke its tail.'

'We wanted to have a word with you before the judging.' Kelvin put his hand on the squire's tweed-jacketed arm.

The latter smiled encouragingly. 'Yes?' Long gone were the days when the squire owned the land and the lives in most of the parish. The current incumbent was still a magistrate, but otherwise his position was entirely symbolic.

'The Onion Shield. There's a woman who's next to the commander. We don't want her to win.'

The squire clicked his tongue. 'Come, come, Kelvin. You can't expect me to agree to that. The best onions will win the Shield. That was Arnie Bladderwick's intention when it was presented and that's the tradition of the Moorcombe Horti-cultural Society which I and my father before me have tried to uphold all our lives.'

'Don't be so feeble,' said the commander. 'She's a dreadful woman.'

'Who is she?'

'Sheila Biss.'

'From Puddlewick?'

'From Puddlewick,' confirmed the commander.

'I see.' said the squire. 'However, the fact remains. If she has the biggest onions, I shall have to award her the Shield.' He brightened. 'Of course, if there was any doubt about which were the best, I would use my own judgement and you can rely on that.'

'There ain't no bloody doubt, Squire,' said Jimmy. 'If there was, we wouldn't've needed a word with you.'

The squire sighed. 'I appreciate the confidence you have in me, but I really don't see what I can do if things are as clear cut as that.'

'She must've cheated, Squire,' continued Jimmy doggedly. 'There ain't no way she could've grown onions that big over in Puddlewick.'

The squire sighed again. 'She might well've cheated, as you say, Jimmy. From what I hear of the lady, it's quite likely. But if we disqualified cheats, we wouldn't have a show at all.'

'That's a lamentable assertion', said the commander.

'It's true, though, isn't it?'

'I don't cheat.'

'Nor do I,' said Jimmy.

'I'm not suggesting that either of *you* cheat,' said the squire, to the accompaniment of a disparaging snort from Kelvin. 'But one can't say the same about everyone. Last year, one competitor even left the manufacturer's label on the jar of one of her entries into the jam competition. I don't think disqualification on grounds like that are my responsibility anyway. It should be up to the Show Committee to vet entries.' The church clock began to toll out the hour of judgement from the creeper-cloaked tower fifty yards away. 'Incidentally, who is on the Show Committee?'

The commander and Jimmy looked at each other blankly. Then at Kelvin.

'You should know, Squire,' said the latter. 'Who asks you to do the judging each year?'

'Nobody. It's the first Saturday in May and always has been. After my father died, I just came along as usual. Nobody seemed to mind.' He looked anxious. 'D'you think I should've waited to be asked?'

'No, no,' reassured Kelvin. 'You were quite right.'

'Who takes entries for the show?' asked the squire. 'That ought to be a clue.'

'I don't think anybody does. People just know to come along,' said the commander.

'Well, where are the rules? Who's got the constitution? That sort of thing.'

14

'I don't think there are any rules, are there?' asked the commander.

'There must be. What classes are there, for instance? I don't have to judge any gooseberries, so presumably there isn't a gooseberry class.'

'Nobody's ever presented a gooseberry trophy, that's why,' said Jimmy. 'There'd be no point in bringing any gooseberries round if there wasn't anything to win.'

'And look at the Snodgrass Cup,' said Kelvin.

'The Snodgrass Cup? Which one's that?' asked the squire.

'You remember Dr Snodgrass?'

'No.'

'He were an incomer. Retired. Lived in the bungalow behind the post office. He used to chop up bodies for the police.'

'Oh yes. He died years ago.'

'That's right. His widow gave the cup in his memory. But it's for the best strawberries. And nobody's ever got any strawberries till June, so there're never any entries.'

'Right! So where's the Snodgrass Cup? Whoever holds that is obviously in charge.'

'That won't work,' said Jimmy. 'When the widow sold the bungalow and went to live with her daughter in Bristol, we sold the cup and drank the proceeds.'

'Tsk, tsk' tutted the squire. 'Who sold the cup?'

'Jethro Bidgood and he's been dead ten year or more.'

'Twelve years,' said Kelvin. 'He dropped dead chasing Sharon Loosemire round the churchyard during the street party on the Queen's Jubilee.'

A face appeared round the door of the school. 'Aren't you coming in, Squire?'

The squire turned. 'Ah! Mrs Baggins. Just waiting for Marcia.'

'My flower arrangement is the one with the cupid doll in it, Squire.'

'Good, good.' The squire gave an approving smile and a wave of the hand. 'I'm sure it'll do very well.'

'It had better,' snapped Mrs Baggins. 'If you want your drains unblocked.'

'What did she mean?' asked the commander, as the face disappeared.

'Her husband's the only person who knows where the

15

sewers go at the manor,' said the squire with gloom. 'Anyway, I suppose I'd better go and do my duty. Marcia can join me when she turns up.' He turned to enter the school.

'But what about the onions?' cried Jimmy.

'In the absence of any rules or constitution, I have little choice. The best onion I see will win the Shield.'

'Sometimes he's too much of a gentleman for his own good,' said Kelvin, as the squire disappeared through the door into the babble of excited villagers. 'I'd better help him out.'

'What are you going to do?' asked Jimmy.

'This and that,' replied Kelvin evasively. 'You two'd better get inside. I might see you later on.'

'He's up to no good,' said the commander as they watched Kelvin, hobnailed boots clattering on the tarmac, walk across to his battered Land Rover.

'I hope you're right,' said Jimmy.

Shortly after midday, the squire took his station at the desk on the dais at the end of the schoolroom and began to read out the long list of those who had been given trophies, had been second, third, fourth or fifth, been specially commended, highly commended or merely commended, and Marcia gave out the appropriate rosettes and trophies.

Mandy took the WI certificate for 'Frolic in the Forest'. The commander won the Veal Memorial Bowl for parsnips and the William Isaacs Cup for isaacberries, a cross betwc loganberries and raspberries, the only surviving colony c which grew next to his compost heap, but the Onion Shield, the big one, went to the cuckoo who had forced her way into the midst of his courgettes.

Apart from the coveted Shield, most people were just as pleased to win a rosette as a trophy. Like the medal ribbons on American servicemen, most houses on the moor had a fine array of rosettes. They were distributed at the horticultural shows, at gymkhanas, hunter trials, dog shows, point-to-points and pony club meetings, at ploughing matches, stock judging events and quizzes for Young Farmers. All rosettes were put on display which meant that those households with litters of horsey, agricultural offspring could cram the walls of room after room with fragile, dusty scraps of coloured card and ribbon, recording the triumphs of entire generations.

Unable to tolerate their disgrace, Jimmy and the com-

16

mander chose to wait outside in the playground during the presentation. The former laboriously heaved himself to the top of the climbing frame and perched there, hands on knees like an ancient gibbon to stare moodily into the middle distance.

'Are you going home?' asked the commander, on a swing a few yards away. The seat, a tubular metal cage, had been built for bottoms considerably smaller and younger than his and it embraced his hips in a tenacious hold.

'I will when I can get my entries out.'

'Why are you sitting up there, by the way?' asked the commander, shading his eyes against the sun as he looked up.

'I thought I might be able to see over the Jarrett's wall from here, but I can't.'

'Ah!'

Stephanie Jarrett, who, in considered local opinion, had the most delectable breasts and thighs in Moorcombe, had once let slip that she sunbathed naked in the back garden of the cottage where she lived with her husband, Malcolm, a lecturer at the local College of Further Education. So far, the top of the church tower had been found by Jimmy to provide the only vantage point in the village from where an observer, particularly when armed with a good pair of binoculars, could profit from this information. On sunny Saturday afternoons, sometimes in the company of the commander or Kelvin, he would make the ascent when the Hunted Hind closed after lunch, carrying cushions and bottles of beer which kept cool in the stone bell chamber below.

'Blast the woman!' said the commander.

Jimmy grunted. 'You can't expect her to take off her clothes in the garden in April.'

'No, I was talking about Mrs Biss.'

'Oh. Here's Kelvin back.'

Kelvin was almost running as he approached the school. 'You can't see over the wall from there, Jimmy.'

'I know.'

'Has the judging finished?'

'I don't know.'

'I'd better get in there.' Kelvin hurried through the grey stone porch, past the heavily-coated pegs, into the school room.

'What's he in such a hurry for?' asked Jimmy. 'D'you think we should go and see?'

'No,' said the commander.

'Aah!' In craning round to follow Kelvin's progress, Jimmy had overbalanced. The commander watched dispassionately as his windmilling arms eventually grasped a bar and he regained his equilibrium. 'I might've been killed!'

'Yes,' said the commander.

'Why didn't you come to my aid?' said Jimmy, accusingly. He carefully lowered himself back to the ground.

'I'm stuck in this swing.'

'Serves you bloody right,' said Jimmy, hobbling over to examine the commander's predicament. 'Your arse is too fat.'

'No, the seat's too narrow.'

They had the bones of a gentle squabble to which they could have added flesh over the next few minutes had not a sudden rise in the volume of the conversational roar coming from the open door of the school caught their attention.

'That must be the Biss woman giving a speech,' said Jimmy. 'I think I'll go and jeer.'

'Wait for me!' shouted the commander, struggling to escape from the unyielding grasp of the swing.

Leaving the back pocket of his corduroy trousers as a tribute to the tenacity of the swing, the commander hurried across the chalked hopscotch squares to the school. An interested crowd was lined up on one side of the room, watching Kelvin as he attempted to wrestle the Onion Shield from Mrs Biss. She had the trophy clasped to her chest and was trying to kick him on the ankles. From his eyrie on the dais, the squire was ineffectually flapping his hands.

'What's happening?' asked the commander.

Kelvin looked up from his work. 'Here, Commander. Come and help me. She's trying to make off with your Shield.'

'It's not his. It's mine!' shouted Mrs Biss. With a sudden heave, she wrested herself from Kelvin's grasp and skipped between the produce-laden tables. Before Kelvin could make a further move, she had picked up an onion and hurled it at him.

The commander was outraged. Not only because the missile had unerringly hit him in the centre of his tweed cap before ricocheting to damage a collage made from small yellow rubber rings, normally used to castrate lambs, pinned to the wall, but it was one of his own onions.

He decided to take charge.

Pushing Jimmy aside, he strode towards the fracas. On his way, he had to sidestep his very best onion which struck Jimmy on the knee. Pausing only to pick up the rosettes which had fallen from it – as well as being given second prize, it had been specially commended by the squire as he tried to mitigate the disappointment of losing the Shield, he grabbed Kelvin by the shoulder.

'What on earth do you think you're doing? Leave the poor woman alone!'

'I'm trying to get the Shield off her. You won it. Ow!'

'Will you stop throwing my onions at him, madam! If you must, throw your own.'

'I won it,' shouted Mrs Biss. 'He can't take it away!' The commander recoiled from her expression of understandable fury. Red blotches of rage throbbed in her cheeks and she had bared her yellowing teeth in a snarl.

'He's not going to take it away,' said the commander, soothingly.

'It's not quite as simple as that, Commander,' said the squire, tentatively descending from the dais now that relative peace had been restored. 'You see Kelvin has discovered the constitution of the Horticultural Show and it only allows entries from residents of the parish.'

'It's all lies!' shrieked Mrs Biss.

'It's not lies,' said Kelvin. 'Look!' He thrust a dirty hard-backed notebook at the commander.

'What's that?'

'It's the minutes of the Parish Council meetings for 1901.'

'Very nice. But what about it?'

'Look there!' Kelvin put his grimy forefinger beneath a line.

The commander pulled out his half-moon spectacles and read out a line. 'Mr Henry Doubtfire – heavens! – Higher Barton, said a short prayer for guidance for the meeting . . .'

'No. Further down.'

'It was agreed that entries for Horticultural Show can only be accepted from inhabitants of the Parish . . . Oh, I see.'

The squire shook his head unhappily. 'Mrs Biss, I'm most desperately sorry. It's a very unfortunate mistake.'

'Mistake!' She turned her outrage towards the squire. 'You rob me of my trophy and you call it a mistake!'

'But, you heard the entry in the book . . .' Not being a man who enjoyed confrontation, the squire turned towards his wife for assistance, but she had retired to the far end of the room to discuss catering arrangements at the forthcoming Hunter Trials with the rump of the WI.

'Let me see it,' demanded Mrs Biss.

'Certainly,' said the commander.

Tucking the shield behind her, she edged towards him. The commander placed the book on the table and stood back to avoid startling her.

Mrs Biss looked down. 'Where is it supposed to say what it says?'

'The bit in blue biro.'

Mrs Biss read the offending passage. 'Huh! I don't think much of that! There's nothing about them being a properly constituted governing body of the Horticultural Society. It doesn't say what the voting figures were. It doesn't say what parish entries are restricted to and it's not even in the same handwriting or ink colour as the rest of it.'

'Let me see,' said the squire.

20

Mrs Biss made a fatal error.. Putting the Shield down amid the commander's remaining onions, she picked up the minute book to pass over to the squire.

Kelvin pounced.

Spinning on her heel, Mrs Biss dropped the book and lunged towards Kelvin, but he had already lobbed the Shield across the table to the commander. 'Run! You've won it! Quick!'

With Mrs Biss, her face screwed up in determination, speeding along the wall towards him, the commander needed little encouragement. He sprinted out of the door while Mrs Biss was still enmeshed in Mandy's abuse for rocking the table on which 'Frolic in the Forest' rested.

'That'll teach you!' jeered Kelvin. 'You can't come to Moorcombe and steal what's ours.'

Mrs Biss stopped, looking round at the smug natives like a badger cornered by terriers. 'You won't get away with this. I'll get you. I'll get you all!'

Her reputation and the knowledge of strange practices on the other side of the moor raised a tingle of apprehension inside both Jimmy and Kelvin, but others were oblivious.

'Get out!' said Mandy. 'Go to your own damn show!'

She had no choice. She went. But she did manage to upset the trestle table of jams on the way out.

21

Chapter Two

THE LATCH clicked, the hinges creaked and the door of the Hunted Hind opened. 'I've brought the plans,' said Keith, ducking his head to avoid the stone lintel.

The inmates turned to look at him, their faces showing the mild enthusiasm that a herd of bullocks might show towards a couple of ramblers pausing to copulate beneath their field hedge.

The most striking aspect of the tap bar was its silence. The buzz of conversation, music from the juke box, electronic cadences from the fruit machine, all the usual noises of the sophisticated modern licensed establishment were absent. Only the tick of the station clock on the wall opposite a stuffed, decaying stag's head and the burble of the aerator in the tank of tropical fish in a dimly lit alcove broke the silence.

Keith tried again. 'I've got the plans!' he repeated. 'The plans for the village hall.'

Since the success of 'Frolic in the Forest' at the Horticultural Show, the responsibility of designing, as well as building the new village hall had fallen on his shoulders. The community had raised the money by itself and intended that as much of it as possible would circulate within the local economy. Individual farmers were providing timber. The Loosemires, a large family of poachers and ne'er-do-wells produced by the postman and his gargantuan, monosyllabic wife, were providing the labour as well as most of the building materials which, Keith had been promised, would fall off the back of a lorry as they were required.

'It's taken you long enough to produce them,' said the commander from a stool by the bar. 'I suppose you'd better bring them over here so's we can have a look at them.'

'I'm not putting them on the bar. They've got to go up to

the district council in triplicate and they won't like them with beer stains on them.'

'Stick them on the bench over here by the window.' The speaker was Annie, the white-haired widow of a farmer. In her declining years, she had swopped her farmhouse and her Methodism for a bungalow in the village and schooners of sherry.

Keith crossed the sawdust-scattered lino towards the mullioned window.

'Hold one end,' said Keith, taking the sheet of cartridge paper from beneath his arm. Grabbing a couple of ashtrays from the neighbouring tables, he weighted the ends and then stood back. 'There!'

'Oh!' exclaimed Annie. 'That's lovely! What's that?'

'The moat.'

'What?' The commander turned from his dominoes.

'The moat.'

'What've you got there?'

'I told you,' said Keith, patiently. 'The plans for the village hall.'

The commander and Kelvin exchanged looks. 'I think we'd better have a look.'

'That's what I brought them in for,' said Keith, with the bright tones of a tour guide.

With a scraping of stools, those round the bar came over and examined the plans in silence.

'The leat gave me the idea,' said Keith. 'We'd've had to put a bridge across it, so I thought I'd make it a feature and Mandy decided a castle would look nice.'

'What's it made of?' asked Kelvin.

'Concrete blocks. They're very good for crenellations – they're the craggy bits at the top. I'm very pleased with the turrets too.' Keith pointed to them on the plan.

'How much'll it cost?' asked Kelvin.

'No problems at all. There should even be a surplus. Our costs should be unusually low. The actual roof of the hall is below the level of the battlements. I've drawn it in cross section there.' He pointed again. His eyes darted from face to face. 'What d'you think?'

'Well . . .' started the commander.

Kelvin lifted his head to look at Keith. 'I think you're a genius. It's wonderful. Right beside the church, too. Moor-

combe's very own castle and its moat. It'll be a tourist attraction and they'll make postcards out of it. There isn't a proper castle like this for miles.'

'Hmm.' The commander rubbed his chin thoughtfully. 'It's certainly original. Perhaps a bit too original?'

'Not for a castle it isn't,' said Annie. 'I've seen lots of castles that look like that. Some, anyway.'

'Yes, but this is a village hall.'

'You'll be able to see it from the road the other side of the river,' said Kelvin. 'It'll be right on the skyline.'

'I thought of that,' said Keith. 'From the village, it'll be silhouetted against the setting sun.'

'Don't see how,' said Annie. 'Not with the hillside behind it.'

'Well, it would be silhouetted if the hill wasn't there.'

'I suppose you're right. I'd never thought of it before.'

'What do you think?' repeated Keith.

'I think it's marvellous,' said Kelvin. 'A real asset to the village.'

'The kiddies'll love it,' agreed Annie. 'They'll be using it a lot. Mothers and toddlers is on Wednesdays. They have to go

24

over to Swinehanger now and mix with the riffraff over there.'

'Commander?' Keith had pinpointed the one possible dissenter in the room.

The commander bared his teeth in an embarrassed grimace. 'Well. I'm not really very sure about it. Don't you think it might be just a little over the top? There's a school of thought which believes that buildings ought to be either entirely functional or else blend unobtrusively into their surroundings.'

'Nonesense!' said Kelvin. 'Look at the church. D'you think that's functional or blends?'

'It's functional.'

'No, it ain't. What d'you need the tower for?'

'That's to hang the bells,' said Jimmy. 'They've got awful long ropes. If the tower had been any lower, the ringers wouldn't've been able to reach them.'

The commander frowned. 'I'm not altogether sure I follow that.'

'What're those letters in the corner of the picture?' asked Annie.

'Oh . . . er . . . they're our initials,' replied Keith.

'Ours?'

'Mandy's and mine. She said she deserved it as she thought of the castle theme before me.'

'M.P.B. What does the "P" stand for?'

'Plantagenet,' said Keith. 'What about my castle?'

'Plantagenet!' said Annie. 'What kind of a daft name is that?'

'It's a family name,' said Keith. 'Look . . .'

'And how about yours K.M.B. What's the "M"?'

'None of your business.'

'Go on. Tell us.'

'Well . . . er . . . it's Mary.'

'Mary!' Nobody's called Mary!' jeered Kelvin.

'My mother's called Mary,' said the commander, stiffly.

'No, you fool. No man is called Mary. How the hell did you get landed with that?'

'If you must know,' said Keith. 'My grandmother's name was Mary and she owned the family butchering business. My father was made a director on condition that his first child was named Mary. It's just bad luck it happened to me and that I was a boy.'

'You poor bugger!'

'Your middle name's Azor,' said Annie.

'That's totally different,' said Kelvin. 'That's a perfectly respectable name from the Bible.'

'Yes . . . well . . . do you like the design?' repeated Keith. 'It took me three days to get it right. The main problem was getting the water from the roof, because I couldn't use gutters.'

'I saw the gargoyles,' said the commander. 'They're very decorative.'

'They discharge straight into the moat. I know where we can get them in fibreglass.'

'I think you can be sure the whole village'll be behind you,' said Kelvin. 'I like it. I think it's going to be wonderful.'

A murmur of agreement ran through the pub.

'Commander?' Keith knew Kelvin's agreement had ensured the support of the natives of the village. The commander's approval would carry most of the incomers.

The latter sighed. 'I think it looks like a stage set for an *Ivanhoe* film . . .'

'Great!' said Mick, who ran the café. 'We can have a jousting tournament on the August bank holdiay.'

'. . . however, if the Parish Council goes along with it, I shall not demur.'

'I'm glad about that,' said Keith.

The castle came before Moorcombe Parish Council for official approval on the second Tuesday of the month.

In the damp church rooms, where spiders picked a meagre living from the mosquitoes hatching from the buckets left to catch the drips coming through the roof, Kelvin brought it up as item four on the agenda. Item three considered the possible purchase of a new broom, to be used to clear autumn leaves from the path to the church as well as from the gutters outside the pub and the post office. Both the Parish Council and the Parochial Church Council agreed on the need for a broom, but disagreed on the way to split the £6.54 it would cost.

'So we propose that the matter of the broom should be referred back to the Parochial Church Council for their considerations?' said the chairman. He looked round his council, a full turn out, save for the squire who was always voted on to the council but never attended the meetings. 'Mark it down, Clerk.'

'I mark everything down, Kelvin. It's what I'm here for.' Malcolm had seen that the position of clerk to the council fulfilled an ambition from which he had thought his sex precluded him – power without responsibility. In writing the minutes, it was he who decided what the decisions of the council had been, sometimes adjusting those of which he disapproved. The elected members never noticed.

Kelvin gave him a cold stare. 'Just do as you're told, Clerk. No need to give any backchat. Item four. Planning applications. First we have Willie Beasley wanting to put up a shed for his motor mower. No problems there. Agreed?'

'He doesn't need permission for a shed,' said Bill.

'That's true,' said Kelvin. 'Perhaps he was just doing it out of courtesy. But anyway we've agreed to allow it.'

'I think we should reject the application.'

'No,' said Kelvin. 'We get precious little to do as it is.'

'It's the thin end of the wedge,' said Bill, solemnly.

Kelvin looked grave.

'Why?' asked Lindy, since nobody seemed inclined to ask the question.

Lindy, the district nurse, was the only woman present, but otherwise the council was generally representative of the population. Mick ran the café. Bill was a farmer, a native-born yeoman like Kelvin. Ivor was a farmer too, but he had bought his farm in the early sixties rather than inheriting it and was a gentleman. The commander represented the growing constituency of the retired.

'We'll be expected to apply for permission to raise agricultural buildings next,' said Bill. 'And we're not having that.'

'But . . .' began Lindy.

'Damn right,' said Kelvin crisply. 'The application is rejected. I move on to the plans for the village hall. Have you got them back from the district, Clerk?'

'Yes, Mr Chairman.' Malcolm produced them from his briefcase on the floor. His ownership of a briefcase was one of the reasons why he won the job over the claims of Jimmy.

'Thank you. Any reasons why we shouldn't approve them? Mick.' Kelvin acknowledged Mick's uplifted hand.

'I'd like to put it on the record, Mr Chairman, that Keith has done an excellent job in the design for the village hall.' Rumbles of approval came from those round about.

'It's a very striking design, but are we sure it's safe?' asked Lindy. 'I'm not an expert builder, but those walls are very high. They wouldn't topple over in a gale, or anything?'

'No. I don't think that'll be a problem,' said the commander. 'I'm just slightly concerned about its appropriateness in an upspoilt area like this.'

'It's perfect,' said Kelvin, firmly. 'And kindly remember to address your remarks to the chair, Commander.'

'Sorry, Mr Chairman.'

'I think the commander's got a point,' said Malcolm.

Kelvin spun in his seat, the splinters tearing at his trousers. 'You keep your mouth shut!' he spat. 'You have no right to speak your opinion in the council chamber.'

'Sorry,' said Malcolm.

With a sniff of disgust, Kelvin turned back to his cabinet. 'I want this vote to be unanimous. I think that's the best tribute we can give to the design. I might even go so far as calling it a work of genius.'

'Hear, hear,' said Mick.

'All those in favour?'

The ayes were unanimous.

'Mark it, Clerk' Kelvin banged the gavel. 'I now suspend this meeting of the Moorcombe Parish Council and call a meeting of the Moorcombe Village Hall Committee.' Malcolm shut his notebook and Lindy opened hers. The only difference in the composition of the two committees was the change in clerks. Kelvin continued, 'I would like to thank the Parish Council for their generous tribute to the design of the new hall. I think we can look upon it as a tribute as well to us on this committee who gave the job to Keith.'

'Hear, hear,' said Malcolm.

'I propose we now authorise Keith to start building.' He swiftly scanned the faces round the table, one of those recently used in the school for the Horticultural Show. 'We're all agreed. Mark it down, Clerk and convey the decision of this committee to the appointed contractor.' Kelvin banged his gavel again. 'I now declare this meeting of the Village Hall Committee closed and reconvene the meeting of the Moorcombe Parish Council. Any other business?'

The commander raised his hand.

'The chair recognises the commander.'

'I would like to propose that this council appoints a sub

committee to look after the affairs of the Horticultural Society Show and draws up a clear set of rules to prevent a repetition of those disgraceful scenes last week.'

'All those in favour?'

Hands were raised throughout the room.

'Carried unanimously. I further propose the sub committee be set up under the charge of the commander and he can write the rules himself and not bother anyone else with them.'

Ivor cleared his throat, 'I think we ought to ask the commander to show us the rules before they come into effect, Kelvin.'

'Why?'

'There'd be nothing to prevent him drafting them so that nobody who wasn't a retired naval officer with a market garden could win the Onion Shield.'

'Good point, Ivor,' said Kelvin.

The commander thought otherwise. 'I must . . .'

'Kindly address the chair,' said Kelvin, banging his gavel.

The commander reddened. 'Mr Chairman, I take great

exception to Ivor's remark. You know perfectly well I'd never do anything like that. I'm a retired officer and a man of honour.'

'You've also lived in Moorcombe for five years, Commander,' replied Ivor. 'I've lived here for twenty and I know the effect it can have on a man. Weren't you selling avocados from Israel last summer, claiming you'd grown them in your greenhouse?'

The commander pulled at his moustache. 'That was different.'

'Not different enough, in my opinion,' said Ivor.

'I withdraw my offer to draw up the rules,' said the commander frigidly.

'Right!' said Kelvin. 'Then you can do it, Ivor, and bring the draft to the next meeting. Mark it down, Clerk!'

'Here . . .' began Ivor.

'Anything else?'

Malcolm diffidently raised his pen.

'Yes?' said Kelvin.

'I wonder if I might beg your indulgence, Mr Chairman, and say a few words.'

Kelvin considered. He looked at his subordinate councillors. 'What d'you think? Shall we let him talk?

Malcolm smiled and decided to show a glimpse of the power he could wield. 'With respect, Mr Chairman. Under the 1974 Act, clerks to parish councils have the obligation to address the councils on matters pertinent. Failure to do so will result in the dismissal of the clerk and the impeachment and disbarrment from office of the chairman.'

Kelvin frowned. 'Is that true?'

'I'd be pleased to lend you my copy of the handbook to council clerks so's you can read it yourself. I think it was in section thirty-two a, sub-section fifteen or sixteen, in brackets somewhere.'

Kelvin shifted uneasily in his chair. His hand went down to remove a sliver of wood which had taken the chance to bite into his backside. 'All right. What is it that you wanted to say?'

'I've been asked if Moorcombe would be willing to twin with another village.'

'Twin! Didn't we go into that once before?' Kelvin looked across the table at Bill who, after himself, had had the longest service on the council.

'We did. Someone from County Hall came down and said we should do it, but he only offered French villages and Arnie Bladderwick didn't like foreigners and said he'd shoot any Frenchman on sight if he came to the village.'

'This isn't a village in France. It's in Bulgaria,' said Malcolm.

'Bulgaria! Where the hell's that?' asked Kelvin. 'Are they Christians?'

'More so than we are, I should think,' said Malcolm. 'A colleague at work married a Bulgarian girl and her family comes from there. It's a village very like Moorcombe, she says. It's called Botograd on Vit.'

Kelvin frowned. 'We can't have anything to do with a place with a barbaric name like that. Why don't you shut up and I'll close the meeting and we can get over to the pub.'

'I think it's rather interesting,' said Lindy. 'I know nothing about Bulgaria and I think it would be nice to be twinned with them. All the other villages have French twins. It would be a bit different.'

'But they're communists!' said the commander.

'So what? That'd make it even more interesting.'

'I believe they grow tobacco there,' said Malcolm. 'The women are supposed to be extremely beautiful.'

'Really?' said Mick.

'So I'm told. They still believe that men are better and wiser than women, and women do most of the work on the farms.'

'Just like Northcott, eh?' said the commander.

'My Prudence is a good daughter to me,' said Kelvin with smugness. 'I've always admitted it.'

'What would be the next step if we did want to twin?' asked Bill.

'I'd tell the twinning committee in County Hall and we'd have a chap down from the embassy to tell us about it,' said Malcolm.

'I propose we do that, then.'

'I second it,' said Lindy.

'I don't suppose finding out a bit more can do much harm,' said Kelvin. 'I'll vote in favour, too.'

'I'll abstain,' said the commander.

'Don't be so wet, man!' said Kelvin.

'If Arnie Bladderwick could shoot the French, I am allowed

31

to abstain when it comes to communists. I am on the committee of the Conservative Association.'

'Carried unanimously. Mark it down, Clerk, and then Malcolm, you can buy me a drink.'

'Mr Chairman,' said the commander.

'What?'

'Can I call a meeting of the Parochial Church Council to discuss the broom?'

'No,' said Kelvin. 'You need the vicar. I declare this meeting closed. Malcolm, you can buy me a drink.'

'It's time you grew up, Jimmy,' said Kelvin, wiping his face with a grimy khaki handkerchief.

'I am grown up. I've been grown up for fifty years.'

'Wasting your money on a squirting flower at your age!'

'I got it in a cracker at the Darby and Joan Christmas party last year. You're the first person who's been stupid enough to sniff it.'

'I wasn't sniffing it. I was just leaning over to get a peanut and you squirted my ear.'

A few days after the council meeting, the patriarchs of Moorcombe had plodded their weary way to the Hunted Hind at the end of the day's work. The approach to the bars lay along a low-ceilinged, narrow, cobbled corridor which plunged through the centre of the ancient thatched building from the street outside. The first door on the left led to the tap, the second to the lounge, the one at the far end led into the garden where patrons sometimes passed summer evenings, and those on the right of the corridor led to the urinals. Little light came down the corridor either from the nicotine-darkened mullion windows or the dim light from the shaded lamps, so it was not always easy to recognise new arrivals until they stepped into the dingy illumination of the bar.

'Do you know what the saddest day of my life was?' said the commander.

'Tell us,' said Jimmy.

'I was fourteen. I bought a copy of the *Beano* and found it boring. I realised I must be growing up.'

'I remember the first time I was allowed to plough a field on my own,' said Kelvin. 'Behind French and Haig. They were the last shire horses we had at Northcott.'

'I can't think of anything these days that used to give me as much pleasure as the weekly *Beano*.'

'It was *Comic Cuts* in my day,' said Jimmy. 'But that sort of thing happens all along. You wait till you find you no longer want a woman.' The commander did not look sufficiently appalled at the prospect. 'Not just your wife, but any woman,' emphasised Jimmy.

'Not even a sheep?' asked Kelvin innocently.

Jimmy's face darkened. 'Bastard!'

Kelvin smiled happily. 'On that subject, I hear Dickie Venn died in his sleep a couple of nights ago.'

''bout time,' said Jimmy. 'His son's not far short of your age. He's been the boy for nigh on half a century.'

'On which subject?' asked the commander.

'It was the old squire, see?' said Kelvin, settling himself comfortably on his stool. 'He brought down the first Border Leicester ewe ever seen in these parts. Dickie eloped with her.'

'Shocking, it were,' said Jimmy, a gleam of relish in his eye. His arthritic hands massaged the arm of his Windsor chair in his excitement.

'He stole her, you mean?' asked the commander.

'Elope was the word,' said Kelvin. 'Judiciously chosen. He left his wife and kiddie and set up house with the ewe in a caravan at the bottom of the farm. The squire was proper cross. That ewe'd cost him a pretty sum of money.'

'What happened?'

'The squire had him charged with indecent rustling,' said Jimmy. 'But he got off.'

'How?' demanded the commander, playing the role of straight man as was expected of him.

'No evidence,' replied Kelvin with relish. 'By the time the police'd caught up with him, he'd gone back to his wife.'

'Good Lord!' said the commander. 'And was the ewe . . . er . . . all right?'

'That's why there was no evidence. Dickie'd tired of his passion and taken 'er home and eaten her. They say his missus served him lamb every Sunday dinner till the day she died.'

The door to the tap bar opened. The new entrant was Malcolm, fresh from his fifteen-mile commute home.

'You're early,' said the commander by way of greeting.

Malcolm went behind the bar to pull himself a glass of beer and placed his money in the till. The landlady, Helga, left the natives to themselves which allowed her to concentrate on the tourists who liked the bright lights, foam benches and the juke box in the lounge.

Malcolm slammed the till shut. He took a long draught from his glass. 'That's better.' Placing the glass on the bar, he pulled himself on to a vacant stool. 'Never work in education. If the kids don't break you, the system will.'

'I'll remember that,' said Jimmy. 'If I ever feel like working in education. Have you smelled my flower?'

'I bought the crackers for the party,' said Malcolm, after a brief glance. 'I got you with it back at Christmas.'

'Spoilsport,' said Jimmy.

'I thought I'd better pop in before supper,' continued Malcolm. 'I had a couple of letters this morning from the council.'

'Which one?' demanded Kelvin, sitting straighter on his stool as he assumed the mantle of his office.

'Well, both, actually.'

'The County?'

'Yes, that one was from the county twinning officer asking us if we'd reconsider our selection of a Bulgarian village and think about one in Brittany instead. He'd got a rather nice little fishing port looking for a home.'

'Well, it can keep looking, can't it? We decided on that Botty place didn't we?' said Kelvin.

'I thought you'd say that so I phoned him from college. All the other villages on the moor have twinned with French places. If we don't do the same, he said we'd be unlikely to get any grants and things.'

'I didn't know they gave out money. Is there much?'

'He talked of perhaps helping towards a fare out there or something.'

'You wouldn't get me agreeing to deal on the basis of a commitment like that! He can bugger off. We'll raise a rate of our own.'

Jimmy gave an exclamation. 'You wouldn't dare!'

'Raise a rate? Why not? We can put on a tu'penny rate if we want to.'

Even the commander knew why that was a bad idea. 'When the council tried that back in the forties, they stoned the church hall during the meeting. I don't think it would be a good idea at all.'

'P'raps you're right,' agreed Kelvin. 'It was just a suggestion. But I'm not having someone at County Hall interfering with the democratically arrived-at decisions of my council.'

'That brings us to the other letter,' said Malcolm. 'It's from the District Council, the planning officer. It's about the application for the village hall. They've turned it down.' Malcolm found himself facing astonished silent faces. 'Er . . . he said we could appeal to the Minister if we disagreed with the decision, but it might take some months before we heard the result and he's likely to reject it.'

'I don't believe it!' said Kelvin. 'The District Council? They've never done anything like this before. What was our councillor up to?'

'There we have it, I'm afraid. Mrs Biss. She's actually deputy chairman of the planning committee and it was she who insisted the plan be turned down.'

'Mrs Bloody Biss! Commander!' The commander jumped. 'It's your bloody fault! If you hadn't made a fuss about your damned onions, this wouldn't've happened!'

'It most certainly is not my fault! It was you who produced that phony entry in the council minutes. Come to think of it,

you're probably guilty of some heinous crime. It's like altering a Bill just before the royal assent is given . . .'

'Stop wittering, man! Malcolm, they can't legally do this, can they?'

'Well yes, they can, actually. Planning is normally one of their main jobs. It goes along with yellow lines and refuse collection. The only thing we can do is appeal. But it'd take months and, judging by the noises I hear, the council feels quite strongly about it.'

'What do you hear?'

'Well, I thought I'd phone the planning chap from college. Apparently Mrs Biss started thumping on the table and demanded they wake up and look at the plans for once. When they did, most of them started to laugh.'

'Laugh?' Kelvin frowned his puzzlement. 'What was there to laugh about in the plans? They were the right ones, I suppose?'

'Oh yes. They were the right plans all right. But they weren't very impressed with them. Deleterious to the ambience of the area. Incongruous. Grotesque. Disneyland on the moor. Those are the sort of comments they made.'

'It's unbelievable!' said Kelvin. 'Apart from the Biss woman, there's nobody on that council who even lives on the moor. They've got no right to tell us what to do.'

'Well, they have done,' replied Malcolm. 'And it's up to us to decide what to do next.'

'I suppose we'll have to appeal,' said the commander gloomily.

'I doubt if it'll do much good,' said Malcolm. 'Those plans would've only gone through if nobody had bothered to look at them.'

'What's it to them? That's what I can't understand,' said Kelvin.

'There's a grant available towards the hall. It's up to them whether they give it or not.'

'There're always bloody grants and it's always up to some damn bureaucrat who knows nothing about anything who decides whether they should be given.'

'What're we going to do?' asked the commander.

'This is a big thing for Moorcombe,' said Kelvin, thoughtfully. 'It'd be nice to get a grant, but we've got our own money. It's the first time they've ever tried to cross us, but we don't need them at all.' He took a pull on his pint. 'I think we should call an open meeting for the whole parish and we can thrash everything out. Then the entire community can decide what to do.'

'There's nothing we can do,' said Malcolm.

'There's always something you can do,' said Kelvin. 'We'll all have to think about it till Tuesday.'

'We'll have to get the word round,' said the commander. 'We can get the vicar to announce it to the congregation on Sunday.'

'Huh!' grunted Kelvin. 'We'll want more than deathwatch beetles and bats coming to the meeting.' He turned to Malcolm. 'Tell Maud at the post office. She can pass the word on when people come in for their pensions on Thursday. The will of the people will not be denied.'

Chapter Three

ORIGINALLY ALL those who lived in a village would make their livelihoods within walking distance. The communities thus created existed for centuries. Generations of the same families intermarried, stamping common features on to the faces of the inhabitants and common surnames on gravestone after gravestone. Such communities survived the First World War and only began to collapse after the Second. Now, they are virtually extinct. No village without a council estate can be anything but a ghetto for the retired, holiday-makers or, if near enough to an employment centre, for commuters. The economic strength of these groups has priced natives out of the housing market in areas where incomes are based on the minimum agricultural wage, a sum which a yuppie would sniff up one nostril in an evening.

Moorcombe's community had survived to a remarkable extent. Incomers there had been, but the miles of minor roads and country lanes to be negotiated before one hit a railway station or a motorway deterred many would-be immigrants. By chance, many of the original families still farmed the land round the village and they supported the old infrastructure of casual farm labourers, builders, and agricultural mechanics.

The essence of such a community lies in the extent that it looks inward. The natives of New Guinea were said to have known of no other people outside their own tribe. Obviously then, nothing of the remotest interest could happen beyond the surrounding rim of the mountains where their world stopped. To an extent, the same feeling existed in Moorcombe. Intellectually, the natives knew that there was a bigger world out there whose incomprehensible doings were reported on their telvision screens, but *Dallas* and *Eastenders* were equally foreign and exotic, while Bristol tended to blur into Brussels, both being down the valley road and then on for quite a bit.

The omnipresent summer proof that there were people out there beyond the county boundary were the tourists, but they were not proper people; they did not do the same things as normal people. They clogged the lanes with their crawling progress to nowhere. They walked up and down eating ice creams, gaping at things like the church or the river which had always been there and were of no interest to anyone.

They looked different too, with their bright colours and skimpy clothes exposing strange pale limbs, broiled pink and red towards the end of a summer day. They said stupid things in accents which, Kelvin had once observed, sounded like a pig talking through its hams.

Was that the manor? When everyone knew it was the commander's house.

Was it a Norman church? When it said Church of England clearly on the notice-board.

Which way was the moor? When there was only one road out of the village and the moor dominated the high horizon. And some of them couldn't even understand simple English, looking baffled or even giggling when an older native gave them directions. The Moorcombe accent may have been different from their own, but it should be perfectly clear to the tourists if it could be understood by the bloody sheep-dogs.

On Tuesday evening Jimmy carefully shut the rusty iron gate to the garden of his cottage opposite the church and walked down the lane towards the school. As he approached the school, the light flooding from the windows showed the playground packed with battered Land Rovers, vans, rusty pick-ups and even a couple of tractors, as well as the squire's Range Rover with its silver hedgehog mascot.

Jimmy pushed open the door into the brightly lit interior. Most of the chairs, set out for morning assembly and prayers, were full. On the dais was Kelvin, the rest of the councillors flanking him. Opposite sat most of the adults of the parish, farm-hardened necks bursting from shirts unusually topped by ties; raw-boned women with red faces and calloused hands. A sprinkling of quilted waistcoats and Barbours covered occupants sweltering in the unaccustomed heat of the school's central heating. Many were used to the frigidity of unmodernised farmhouses with yards which funnelled gales from the moor through cracks in doors and between floorboards, floating rugs an eerie half inch above the floor.

As usual, the crowd looked like a gathering of munchkins, as people perched themselves on chairs designed for five-year-olds. Only Kelvin, having appropriated the head mistress's chair, still maintained his dignity from the platform.

Coughing his unlit cigarette into his hand, Jimmy pushed his way through a gaggle of leather-jacketed youths, many of them Loosemires who now occupied all three of the parish council houses, towards the piano where he hitched himself on to the lid, just in time to see Kelvin rise to his feet and survey the rows of squatting parishioners.

Apart from the councillors, who included the squire, the rest of the local luminaries were in the first few rows. Mandy and Keith sat directly beneath the dais with a gaggle of notables on either side of them. Frank Mattock, the most efficient and prosperous farmer in the parish. The Mowbrays who kept sheep and ran one of the local packs of hounds. The post mistress, Maud. The proprietors of the Olde Tea Shoppe and café, Mick and Beryl, representing tourism and the commercial interests of the village. Alongside Beryl, sat Helga and Lindy, the latter with her arms folded across her ample bosom, and Kelvin's daughter, Prudence.

With a smirk of satisfaction at the turn out, Kelvin banged his gavel on the table.

'Good evening fellow parishioners. I'd like to welcome you to this open meeting of the Moorcombe Parish Council. We have a very serious situation to contend with. I'm first going to ask our clerk to state the current position in simple terms and then I'll ask for suggestions and advice which can be acted on by your council in a session later on.' A rustle ran round the room. Kelvin's smile disappeared and a frown took its place. 'I know it's opening time, but the pub's shut till after the meeting.' He waved his gavel at the front row. 'Helga's here. It shows the importance of the occasion.'

'She ain't got a right to do that.' The speaker was the oldest of the Loosemire farrow, Winston, now a council labourer, but famous for wearing the only pair of winkle-picker shoes ever to have been seen in Moorcombe. 'The law says a pub's got to be open when it says it is.'

'Shut up, Winston. If you want to take it up with the law, Percy's right behind you.'

40

Winston was sitting in the back row. All sixteen stone of the local policeman loomed over him, a great blue jersey swelling out to enclose his abdomen.

'Don't make a nuisance of yourself, Winston,' said Kelvin. 'Just sit there and keep quiet. You're wrong, anyway. The law changed last year.' He looked down at Malcolm. 'Clerk?'

The latter, pleased to vacate his tiny chair to the side of the dais, rose briskly to his feet and put a sheaf of papers on the desk in front of Kelvin. As a practising college lecturer, Malcolm had no fears of facing an audience, so he took a few seconds to arrange his paperwork before lifting his head to look at the audience.

'We've got two main topics to bring before the meeting. The first concerns the proposed twinning of Moorcombe with Botograd on Vit.' Malcolm paused, but his audience received this piece of information in silence. Only those most closely involved in the politics of the village knew what he was talking about, the rest were content to allow further pieces to be added to the jigsaw before forming an opinion. 'At this stage all I need to say is that the county authorities disapprove of the idea and would prefer us to twin with a village in France.'

He put down the first paper and picked up the second.

'Can we twin with one in another star system?' Howard, tall, thin and intermittently bearded, was a long term inhabitant of the commune, a shifting colony of eccentrics, hippies and drop outs, which had survived for nearly a decade in a large decaying house a mile north of the village. He supplemented his social security benefit with earnings as a jobbing gardener.

'No,' said Malcolm.

'Where is Botograd on Vit?' asked Marcia, the squire's wife, from the front row.

'It's in Bulgaria. But can I leave this subject and get on?' Malcolm turned to Kelvin.

'Oh yes! Sorry.' He banged his gavel on the table. 'All remarks should be addressed through the chair and everyone can shut up till Malcolm's finished when we can have questions and ideas. Carry on, Clerk.'

'I wish you wouldn't call me Clerk, Kelvin,' said Malcolm. 'I don't call you Farmer.'

'Well he's not one. He hasn't done a stroke for years!' shouted a wag from the audience. This brought the first laugh of the evening and, as Kelvin pounded the desk to restore his control, Prudence, seated in the front row with Brett sleeping in her arms, permitted herself a thin-lipped smile.

'You call me Chairman and I call you Clerk,' explained Kelvin. 'It's the proper way to do it when we're doing council business.'

'Get on with it or I'll take over myself!' said Mandy from the front row.

Both Kelvin and Malcolm knew it was no idle threat and they exchanged a hurried glance. Malcolm picked up the next letter on the table. 'I'll briefly summarise the current position. I think we all know of the plans for the village hall.' He nodded to a copy of the plans, pinned to the blackboard. 'This is the building in question. It has been approved by your council. In fact a motion of thanks was passed on the quality of the design. We have also got ample funds for its construction, which will be carried out by the architect with local labour and materials wherever possible. The plans were then sent to the district council who turned them down.' Although this was known by all present, a murmur of disapproval and outrage still ran round the room.

'Do they want us to make changes to the design?' asked Mick.

Kelvin banged the gavel. 'That's not the point. The point is whether we allow them to interfere in our own affairs when they know nothing about it and it's none of their business anyway.'

'Thank you, Mr Chairman,' said Malcolm. 'In fact, Mick, it's not changes they want. They insist the whole design be scrapped. It's all Mrs Biss's fault, of course, but there doesn't seem much we can do about it.' The hiss from the meeting would not have disgraced the appearance of the pantomime villain. 'Now, that's not all. I got another letter this morning from the district council.'

'You didn't tell me about it!' said Kelvin.

Malcolm turned to him. 'I only got it at lunchtime.'

'But I might not've wanted it to be made public.'

'Get on with it!' shouted Mandy again.

Malcolm cleared his throat as Kelvin grumbled into silence. 'The district planning officer says that the land on which the hall was to be built is common land and planning permission could never be obtained for a building on that site.'

Kelvin uttered a great snort of disgust. 'Why not?'

'Lots of reasons to do with policy and things. He says we would also need to get permission of all the commoners before anything could happen.'

Kelvin frowned. 'I don't know what he's on about.'

'It's very simple. He's saying we can't have a village hall there, whatever the design. We have to find another site and then produce a completely different plan.' Malcolm sat down amid rising anger from the groundlings.

Kelvin frowned down at him. 'What do you suggest we do?'

'There is only one option. Appeal to the Secretary of State for the Environment. From what I can understand, we haven't got a chance in hell of being successful.'

Percy put up his hand.

'The chair recognises Constable Green', said Kelvin.

'Would I be right in saying that we can't build the village hall then?'

'You'd be right in saying the District Council would rather we didn't.'

'That's fine for them,' said Percy, 'but we want to get it finished by late summer.'

43

'I know,' said Kelvin.

Ivor, a parish councillor of long standing who prided himself on his diplomatic skills, rose to his feet.

'The chair recognises Ivor.'

'I think we ought to look at all the components of this little setback,' said Ivor. He was a small, thin man in his fifties with a sense of humour which had frozen at the age of eleven. 'Get to the bottom of it, as the bishop said to the actress.' The meeting knew Ivor, so waited patiently until he had stopped chortling at his own joke. 'It all goes back to the commander's onions. If that Biss woman had not come to the Horticultural Show, none of this would have happened. Anyway it has. Let us start with the common, do we know who owns it?'

'Er,' said the squire. 'I think it may be me. I think the manor used to own the whole of Moorcombe and it was all sold off over the years apart from the common which nobody wanted to buy because everyone had common rights on it. Grazing, firewood, thatching reed. That sort of thing.'

'Thank you, Squire. You would have no objection if the village hall was built on it by the church?'

'Of course not,' said the squire. 'I never think of it as mine anyway.'

'In that case I suggest you give it to the village. It would cut down your liability to inheritance tax.'

'Really? Thank you so much.' The squire smiled at Marcia. 'Good-oh, what?' Ivor was a tax commissioner and his opinion on such matters was generally sound.

'My pleasure. So the next thing is those who have common rights. Does anyone know who they are?'

'Daisy Webber used to graze her sheep on it,' said Kelvin. 'She was the only one who still exercised her rights. Now it's just used by kids to play on and people to walk their dogs. I suppose you must've inherited them, Frank. She was your aunt.'

'I was her heir,' agreed Frank, turning slightly red as he was unused to being the centre of attention. 'But I don't know anything about the common rights and I wouldn't want them even if I did.'

'Good,' said Ivor. 'Then we've decided the common is owned by the whole community as represented by the council and, if there are any common rights, they must belong to some of the people in this room and they relinquish them anyway.'

44

'All those in favour,' said Kelvin, banging his gavel.

The ayes thundered out, bringing a nervous outburst of caws from the jackdaws visiting their nest atop the chimney.

'Carried unanimously.'

Ivor smiled. 'Do we agree we want a village hall on the site?'

Kelvin, beginning to get the rhythm, banged his gavel. 'All those in favour?'

'Aye.'

'Do we further agree we want Keith's castle?'

'Aye.'

Kelvin banged his gavel. 'Wait for it! Wait for it! I hadn't asked for a vote. We'll have to have that aye again.'

'Aye.'

'No, wait until I've asked for the vote!'

'A point of order!' shouted Mandy.

Kelvin's gavel remained poised. 'What is it?'

'It's not Keith's castle. It's both of ours. I had a lot to do with the original idea.'

'All right, then. Keith and Mandy's castle.'

'Mandy and Keith's,' said Mandy.

'All right. Mandy and Keith's. All those in fav. . .'

'What are we voting on again, Kelvin?' asked the squire.

'Er . . .'

'If we want the castle,' supplied Ivor.

'All those in favour.' The audience was beginning to enjoy itself. Kelvin's gavel was drowned in the 'ayes'.

Ivor hurried on before Kelvin could declare the vote invalid. 'Do we further agree that it's nobody's business but our own?'

'All those in favour?'

'Aye.'

Bang! 'Carried unanimously.'

'Do we further agree to start work immediately?'

'All those in favour!'

'Aye.'

Bang! 'Carried unanimously.'

'And that you empower the Parish Council to make all further decisions necessary to ensure the execution of the wishes of this meeting?'

'All those in favour!'

'Stop!' shouted the commander.

Kelvin's gavel obeyed, half way to the table. 'What's up with you?'

'That last vote is ridiculous! It would let us declare war on behalf of the village if it helped get the hall built!'

'Don't be daft!'

'Well, it does.'

'You're wasting good drinking time.'

'I think it's important.'

'Right, just for the commander,' growled Kelvin, waving the gavel at the audience. 'You lot let the Parish Council do all those things Ivor said we could do except declare war. All those in favour!'

Bang!

'Aye.'

'Carried unanimously.' Kelvin looked expectantly at Ivor, but he took his place with the air of one having done a good job.

'Get on with it!' shouted Mandy.

'If you say that once more I'll expel you from the meeting! You have to show respect for the chair otherwise there'd be anarchy. Have you noted down the votes, Clerk?'

'Of course,' said Malcolm.

'In that case, tell us all what we decided.'

'You've forgotten already, have you? Sorry Mandy.' Malcolm forestalled the complaint. 'Well, we've given ourselves the common, taken away all commoners' rights and agreed to start building Keith's . . . sorry . . . Mandy's castle on it.'

'Well, I would think that's about it, then.'

'Haven't we forgotten something?' said Malcolm.

Kelvin frowned. 'I don't think so. Can anybody think of anything?'

Howard put up his hand. 'Will we still be allowed to have our ceremony on the common on Midsummer night?'

'I don't see why not. Just so long as you keep well away from the church. Some people get a bit funny when you lot hold your heathen rites too near hallowed ground. Anything else?'

'When will the hall be finished? Will it be in time for the Conservative wine and cheese?' asked Marcia.

'Keith?'

'If we make a start within the next couple of weeks, we should be done in plenty of time. There may be a problem with a portcullis, but we can always put that on later.'

'I think everything's under control', said Kelvin. 'Any other business, Clerk?'

'What about the planning permission and the appeal?' said Malcolm.

'I thought you said it wouldn't be worth appealing,' said Kelvin.

'It's not, but we ought to go through the motions.'

'All right. Appeal if you think we should.'

'The other little snag is that we're not allowed to go ahead until we do get permission.'

'We've been through all that,' said Kelvin impatiently. 'We've voted that it was just our business and it didn't matter what anyone else thought.'

'I know we have, but we'll break the law.'

'Is that right, Percy?' Kelvin threw the question across the heads of the seated parishioners who turned in their seats to hear the answer.

Percy considered. He was not a man to make hasty judgements. 'It'd be a civil offence not a criminal offence and it wouldn't become my business until a court order were issued.'

'There. Nothing to worry about then,' said Kelvin. He banged his gavel, catching the meeting unawares, jumped from his seat and ran towards the door. 'I declare this meeting adjourned.'

A significant part of the audience thundered after him in pursuit, but Kelvin was first in the queue when Helga unlocked the Hunted Hind a couple of minutes later.

Chapter Four

THE BRIEF ceremony to mark the start of the building of the hall took place a week later. Responsible for the foundation trench and the gap in the six-foot hedgebank, a JCB sat in a swamp of puddled clay as a small crowd, consisting of Keith, Mandy, the squire, Kelvin, the commander and five sheep, escaped from Kelvin's field a week earlier, watched the historic moment as Marcia tipped the contents of the concrete mixer into Jason Loosemire's barrow which he then emptied into the trench.

A passing car, which had been travelling slowly down the lane, paused in the gap to watch. The window wound down as the official party walked across the mud towards the road to disperse.

'What are you doing?'

'What's it to you?' asked Kelvin, bending to look inside the car at the occupant, a fleshy man in his thirties with red hair erupting over his shirt collar as well as sprouting from his ears, cheeks, nose and head. 'Here! Don't I know you?'

'Are you doing some building?'

'I'm talking to you. That's what I'm doing,' said Kelvin, straightening. 'And I've lots of better things to do than that.'

'Hold on!' Opening the car door, the driver emerged into the lane. 'You're building something in there!'

Kelvin stopped. 'I remember you,' he said accusingly. 'You're that building inspector. What's your name?'

'Partridge. Have you got permission?'

Chomping his plastic teeth ruminatively, Kelvin looked first at the JCB, then at the sky, then back at Partridge. 'Piss off.'

'You haven't got permission! Mrs Biss was right!' He turned to go round the car and enter the common.

49

'I wouldn't if I were you,' said Kelvin.

Partridge paused. 'Wouldn't what?'

'Go into that field. It would be a trespass and I would be authorised to use sufficient force to prevent it.'

The squire, while his wife was turning the Range Rover in front of the lych-gate of the church thirty yards up the lane, came over. 'What's going on, Kelvin?'

'It's the building inspector. I'm just warning him not to trespass in the field.'

Partridge pointed an accusing finger. 'They're building the village hall in there. I was warned by the planning officer that something like this might be going on. He asked me to take a quick look when I was passing.'

'I don't know what you're talking about,' said Kelvin. 'All I see is Keith digging a slurry pit.'

'A slurry pit? I don't believe you. Anyway it's within thirty metres of the road.'

'But it's a private road,' said the squire.

'A private road?' Partridge looked up and down. 'Don't be silly! It's one of ours. It's the main road to Swinehanger.'

'It isn't one of yours. It belongs to me. It was originally built by my grandfather when the adopted road went round the far side. When the council tarmacked the wrong stretch back in the twenties, it seemed easier to leave things be, especially when it saved us the cost of upkeep.'

50

'Nonsense.'

'Watch who you're talking to, boy,' growled Kelvin. 'That's the squire. He's a magistrate.'

'Is he now? Then he should be ashamed of himself, breaking the law.'

'Get out of here!' said Kelvin. 'Before I throw you out.'

'You can't I'm on the public highway.'

'We've been through that. The squire's handed the common over to the Parish Council and that means the road, too. Doesn't it, Squire?'

'I suppose so.'

'And I'm chairman of the council, so I have the right to chuck you off the land.'

Partridge's complexion almost matched his hair, but he returned to the car. 'I'll be back and then we'll see who's got the last laugh.' He disappeared up the lane in a flurry of loose grit and mud.

The squire looked after him. 'He'll be back I'm afraid. I hope our planning appeal goes through by then.'

Kelvin looked at him. 'Was it true about the road?'

'Probably not,' conceded the squire. A fine drizzle washed over them, spangling the Barbours worn by the two men with fine droplets of water. The squire sneezed as the engine of the concrete mixer started up on the far side of the hedge. 'Bloody man. Why couldn't he have kept away?'

'Not to worry. Nothing'll come of it. It's just Mrs Biss who'll stir it up and they'll all soon get tired of her.'

'It would've been better to have let her keep the Onion Shield!'

'That it would,' agreed Kelvin. 'But that's the advantage of hindsight for you. I've got to see a man about a pig. I'll see you.'

Over the next few weeks, Moorcombe got on with its business. The cattle were finally turned out from their winter quarters to gambol across the spring fields. The sheep were brought in to lamb, hay and silage crops grew apace and milk yields rose in response to the flush of new grass.

The beginning of the tourist year was marked by the sprinkling of ramblers, swathed in rustling cagoules of scarlet or blue, sheltering behind hedges or in copses and ditches from the soggy skirts of the gale-driven clouds sweeping down from the moor. Some sought refuge in Moorcombe to be served in the café by Beryl with the first cream teas of the season – cholesterol-stuffed scones, strawberry jam and thick clotted cream. More than two were guaranteed to induce nausea. The village hall rose above its foundations and Malcolm had a letter from the District Council.

'It's an enforcement action,' he explained to the Parish Council in the tap bar at lunchtime. 'It means that they're ordering us to stop building the hall and tear it down.'

'Tell them to go to hell,' growled Kelvin.

'We have the option of asking for a public inquiry and, if we find a point of law, we can even go as far as the House of Lords, but it would probably be rather expensive.'

'Tell them to go to hell,' repeated Kelvin.

'I'd put it a bit more diplomatically than that,' said the commander. 'Let me see . . . thank them for their interest but tell them that we've made our own decision and there's no need for them to worry about it any more.'

'That's very good, Commander,' said Kelvin.

'Thank you.' The commander smiled his appreciation before returning to Malcolm. 'You could also add something to the effect that they'd be wasting ratepayers money if they took things any further.'

Malcolm sniffed. 'I doubt if it'll put them off.'

'Well, just do it, Clerk,' said Kelvin, taking a pull on his pint.

The trio of councillors – the commander, Kelvin and Ivor were perched on stools round the horseshoe bar. The room was not full, a couple of tourists sitting at the oak tables and, in the black settle by the fireplace, an agricultural salesman, rustling noisily through his *Daily Express*.

'I made a phone call from college,' said Malcolm.

Kelvin turned to the commander. 'Are you growing strawberries again this year?'

'Yes. I made a fair profit last season.'

'You won't do any good this year. The winter was too mild to kill off the bugs and your plants are old anyway.'

'I'll get good currants anyway.'

'Jimmy's had big bud. You'll get it this season.'

'I think you ought to hear about my phone call,' said Malcolm.

Kelvin sniffed. 'You always come with bad news.'

'Look who's talking!' said the commander. 'You've just been telling me I'll go bankrupt.'

'That wasn't bad news. That was just a bit of friendly advice. You're new to Moorcombe, Commander.'

'I've been here for seven years!'

'Exactly!'

'About my telephone call,' said Malcolm.

Kelvin sighed. 'I suppose you'd better tell me about it.'

'Us, Kelvin. Us,' said Ivor. 'You're not the whole Parish Council.'

'I know. I know. But I am the chairman. It's me that really makes the decisions and takes the responsibility.'

The commander snorted.

'The District Council won't let it go,' said Malcolm.

'What do you mean?' asked Kelvin. 'We just tell them to piss off.'

Malcolm reddened slightly. 'Look! They can take us to court and then if we don't comply, we're in contempt and can be fined on a daily basis or even put in prison.'

'And remember, Kelvin,' said the commander, 'you did say that you made the decisions and took the responsibility. So you'll be the one to carry the can for all of us.'

'I'll just appoint you to run the village hall sub committee. Then it'll be your fault.'

'I wouldn't accept the post.'

'I'd kick you off the council.'

'You couldn't.'

'I bloody could.'

'You couldn't. You haven't got the power.'

'You forget I'm in charge of the Emergency Volunteers. In the event of a breakdown of civil administration, I have powers of life and death. And if you refuse to be sacked from the council, it would be a clear breakdown in Moorcombe and I could blow your head off with my shotgun.'

'You dare!' said the commander, sliding off his stool to confront Kelvin.

'For heaven's sake!' said Malcolm. 'I'm being serious.'

'So am I, sonny,' said Kelvin, thrusting his chin belligerently towards Malcolm. 'When I take over here, you'll be the first to go. I'll not have Moorcombe cluttered with Lefties like you.'

'When you think about it,' said Ivor. 'There's not a lot they could do if we all resigned from the council. Then there'd be nobody to fine and nobody to put in prison.'

'If we resigned, they could do what they like,' said Kelvin. 'Leave a power vacuum and they'd move in to fill it. Of course, if the council did resign, it'd be my responsibility to take over in the name of the Emergency Volunteers. But I must say, this sort of thing could make me very cross. It's interfering with the peaceful expression of the rights of decent English people. What right have they got to do this to us?'

'Right of Act of Parliament, I imagine,' said the commander. 'You could ask Malcolm to go back and look it up in his little book.'

'That's crap!' said Kelvin.

'Crap or not. They've got the full weight of the law, government and parliament behind them.'

'It's outrageous! What do we have governments for?'

'To govern?' suggested the commander.

'No. To carry out the wishes of the people,' said Kelvin.

'It depends, really,' said Ivor. 'You could hardly say that about dictatorships. And I don't think we've had a government since the war which has had a majority of the popular vote.'

'It's a damn scandal!' said Kelvin, smacking his hand on the top of the bar for emphasis.

'Oh quite,' agreed Malcolm. 'But I think it would be a good idea to call a halt to building work on the hall until we've sorted things out.'

'Never!' said Kelvin. 'You think Keith's going to stop building if you tell him?'

'Well, yes, of course. We're the ones who're paying the bills.'

'That hall'll be going up and it'll be staying up,' said Kelvin.

'It won't. It can't,' said Malcolm.

Kelvin smiled. 'You've forgotten something.'

'Have I?'

'This is the biggest job Keith has ever handled.'

'I know, but what's that got to do with it?'

'Who's going to tell Keith? Or rather, who's going to tell Mandy? It was her design after all.'

The silence round the bar spread to the rest of the room. The salesman stopped reading his horoscope and glanced curiously in their direction from the fireplace.

54

The commander sighed. 'He's got a point there. I'm damned if I'll tell Mandy. Bearers of bad news are not generally well received. She'd probably disembowel me.'

'She wouldn't find enough guts in you to case a chipolata,' said Kelvin.

'I don't hear you volunteering,' replied the commander.

'I'm not a fool!' said Kelvin. 'What are we going to do?'

'We could get the District Council to write and tell her,' said Malcolm.

'She'd still come and ask one of us if it was true,' said Kelvin.

The commander brightened. 'She'd come and ask you, Kelvin.'

A harsh bray of laughter came from Kelvin. 'And d'you think I'd tell her? I'll just say I know nothing about it and tell her to go and see Malcolm.'

Malcolm's hand jerked, spilling his half pint of beer on the counter.

'Watch it!' said Kelvin, looking at the wasted beer with concern.

'It was Ivor who said we should stop building. He can tell her.'

'Me? You're the clerk! You get paid to pass on the decisions of the council. It's your job.'

'I'd resign,' said Malcolm, quickly.

'I think we're in an impasse,' said Ivor. 'Anybody got any suggestions? She'll be in here in a few minutes. Along with Keith.'

'I know. We can ask someone else to tell her. Some outsider.'

'Who?'

'Someone from the District Council?'

Jimmy, who had been listening without contributing, suddenly came to life. 'I've got an idea!' Every stool creaked as the patrons turned to look at him. He jerked his head towards the salesman, who appeared to be doing the crossword. 'Ask him to tell her.'

'Why should he?' asked Ivor.

'He's a rep. He'll be selling to the farmers, sheep dip I should think. He's too scruffy to be selling fertiliser or insurance. Kelvin can give him an order. He might even buy us a drink.'

'That's a damn good idea, Jimmy,' said Kelvin. 'I'll go and ask him.' Sliding down from his stool, Kelvin walked across the room towards the fireplace. The salesman looked up from the remains of his ploughman's lunch – stale bread, fridge-dessicated mousetrap cheese, pickled onion and a piece of lettuce as limp as a royal handshake. 'Morning,' said Kelvin. 'I haven't seen you around before.'

The salesman put aside his paper, a wary expression on his face. In his thirties, he was a couple of stone overweight and going bald.

'Fertiliser is it?' continued Kelvin.

'What?' He had a strong London accent.

'Are you selling fertiliser?'

'No, I'm having my lunch.'

Kelvin sniffed in irritation. 'I'm one of the most important farmers hereabouts. Chairman of the Parish Council, too.'

'Bully for you.' The man ostentatiously turned back to his newspaper but Kelvin was not a man to take a hint.

'What're you selling then?'

'Mind your own business, mate. And leave me alone.'

Kelvin retreated towards the bar. 'Did you hear that? Bloody cheek! And I told him who I was.'

'Did he say he'd do it?' asked the commander.

'No. He was downright rude.'

'Try the other one, then.'

'Which other one?'

'The chap in the corner. The fat man.'

If the salesman was rather plump, the chap in the corner was gross. Spread along a bench, wearing a knitted cardigan which zipped up the front, he had a glass of lager in front of him and had been chain smoking acrid cigarettes.

'I'll go and ask him.' The salesman furtively lifted his eyes to watch, earning himself a scowl as Kelvin passed.

As Kelvin loomed over him, the fat man looked up, an apologetic smile appearing at the corners of his mouth. 'Yes?'

'I want you to do me a favour.'

'Plis?'

Kelvin's eyes narrowed in distaste. 'Are you a foreigner?'

'Yes.'

'I don't suppose it matters. Just passing through?'

'In a manner of speaking, I . . .'

'Good. You won't mind helping us out.'

'Well . . .'

Kelvin sat down on the chair opposite, turning to wink at his neighbours round the bar. He caught the eye of the salesman. 'Stop eyeing us! Mind your own business!'

'Ignore him,' said the other. 'He can do no harm.'

'D'y know him?' asked Kelvin.

'He has been following me all morning.'

'Has he? Is he some kind of pervert or a spy?'

His companion smiled, revealing a startling metal tooth. 'I would not be greatly surprised.'

'Hang on a minute.' Kelvin rose to his feet and returned to the bar. 'Has that fellow paid for his lunch?' He indicated the rep with a wave of his hand.

'I think so,' said Malcolm.

'In that case I'm chucking him out.'

'Why, for heaven's sake? And can you?'

'Of course I can. If Helga's not around, it's my duty to keep the peace. He's a pervert. He's been following that other bloke all morning. It's disgusting!'

The commander turned on his stool to look at the two strangers. 'I wonder what sort of pervert he is? I can't possibly see what he finds interesting or attractive about the other chap. I mean, just look at him.' They looked. The fat man's face was delineated by an Abe Lincoln beard. Without the line of whiskers, it would have been almost impossible to work out where one chin stopped and the next began.

'You can never tell with people like that. Perverts are attracted to the strangest things,' said Jimmy, sagely.

'You should know,' said Kelvin. 'Ha!' He slapped his thigh, raising a puff of powdered cattle dung from the grey serge trousers. 'You should know. You like a sheep.'

'Ewe,' said Ivor. 'Very droll.'

'I'm getting tired of that joke,' said Jimmy. 'I never did anything like what you're meaning I did.'

'I'm going to get rid of the nancy boy.' Kelvin slipped off the stool. 'We don't want any trouble when Mandy comes in.'

'I don't see why there should be any trouble,' remarked the commander, as Kelvin returned to the salesman.

'Have you finished your dinner?' asked Kelvin. The salesman, who had returned to his paper, turned a cold eye on him. 'If you have you can clear off.'

'Stop making a nuisance of yourself, dad. Go away.'

'You've been following my friend over there all morning.'

The salesman looked startled. 'How do you know?'

'None of your business. But if you must know, he told me.'

'Do you know him? What were you talking about?'

'I've told you once. Mind your own business. Come on, finish your drink and get out of here. We don't want the likes of you in Moorcombe. If you come back, remember tourists are more welcome in the public bar than here.'

The man pulled a wallet out of his pocket and flipped it open.

'Are you going to buy me a drink?' asked Kelvin.

'No. Look at it, doughnut.'

Kelvin looked. He was being offered a plastic card. 'What was that?' he asked as the wallet went back into the owner's pocket.

'It was my warrant card. Leave me alone.'

'What the hell's a warrant card?'

The wallet came out again and the card was proffered. 'Look at it inconspicuously,' said the salesman, trying to ignore the stare of the fat man who was taking a lively interest in their interchange.

Kelvin peered down. 'Hang on.' He took out his spectacles and put them on his nose. 'It's too dark. Bring it over to the window.'

'No! I said be inconspicuous.'

'For heaven's sake!' Kelvin turned towards the bar. 'Commander! Can you put the light on over here? He's trying to show me a dirty postcard or something.'

'Right oh!' The commander leaned over the bar and flipped a light switch. 'Let's have a look.' He slipped from his stool and crossed over, followed by the rest of the drinkers.

The salesman looked, aghast. 'I said inconspicuously!' Kelvin took the card. 'Here! What are you doing?' He tried to grab it back, but Kelvin held it from his reach.

'Now, now! Don't snatch!'

The salesman got to his feet, but the card was now in the centre of a curious group of natives. 'Heavens!' said the commander. 'It's a warrant card!' He turned to the salesman. 'You're a policeman!'

'What does it say?' asked Jimmy, standing at the back of the crowd as well as being virtually illiterate.

'It says he's a Sergeant Parrott of the Metropolitan Police Special Branch.'

'Coo!' The natives all turned to look at the unfortunate policeman.

'What are you doing in Moorcombe?' asked Malcolm.

'Give me my card back! Or I'll nick you.'

'Watch it, sonny!' said Kelvin. 'You're not in London now. Any nicking round here is done by us or Percy. Anyway, how do we know you didn't make up that card in your front room? You probably saw how to do it on the back of a corn flakes packet. It's just the sort of thing a pervert would have to keep himself out of trouble.'

'That's a point,' agreed the commander. 'The photograph doesn't look very much like him. He could've stolen it.'

'Let's have another look,' said Kelvin. He examined the picture critically. 'No, it doesn't. He's fatter and hasn't got so much hair.'

'It's not all that up to date,' said the policeman. 'I got four of them done in the booth at Victoria and this is the last of them. So it is three or four years old. Will you please give it back?'

'Not until you give a better explanation of yourself,' said Kelvin. 'Does Percy know you're here?'

'Who's Percy?'

Kelvin drew his breath sharply in. 'If you were a policeman, you'd know Percy Green.'

59

'Well, I don't.'

'He's our local bobby.'

'How the hell am I supposed to know that? Look, give me my card.'

'Are you here on business?' asked Malcolm.

'Give me my card back!'

'Why are you following that other bloke?'

'None of your business!'

'I'm not sure if that's really good enough,' said the commander. 'An innocent tourist comes into the pub for lunch, followed by someone pretending to be a salesman. When challenged, he produces dubious identification and refuses to explain himself.'

'He's a pervert,' said Jimmy.

'He could be a spy,' said Kelvin. 'That's what the other bloke said.'

'Did he? The bastard!' said the policeman.

'Does he know this man?' Malcolm nodded at the putative policeman.

'I'll go and ask him,' said Kelvin.

'No!' shouted the policeman, managing to wrest his card from Jimmy.

But Kelvin had already gone over to the corner. He jerked his thumb at the flustered Parrott. 'He says he's a policeman. Could he be?'

The fat man smiled. 'He could be. Excuse me. I could not help but overhear that you were the chairman of the council here. Might you know a Mr Jarrett as well?'

'Malcolm? Sure, he's over there.'

'Oh good. My name is Sodov.'

'What?'

'Sodov. I am here from the People's Republic of Bulgaria to tell you of Botograd on Vit.'

Kelvin looked blank for a moment or two before his memory rescued him. 'Oh yes! The twinning. Nice to meet you. Sodov? Is that really your name?'

'Yes.'

'Ah well.' Kelvin extended his hand and they shook. 'Now about this other chap.'

'The policeman? As a foreign diplomat, I sometimes find my movements are monitored by the authorities.'

'Really?'

'Oh yes. I have to inform them if I ever wish to travel more than fifty miles from London.'

'Huh!' said Kelvin. 'And I thought you lot could do what you like. Ignore parking meters and that sort of thing.'

'I find the police often make my work more difficult than it needs to be.'

'That's shocking! And this is supposed to be a free country! We might as well be in Russia. I'm going to have this out.' Kelvin stormed across the bar. Heaving himself to his feet, Sodov followed. 'You!' he said, 'Parrott, or whatever your name is. Is it true you're following this man because he's a foreigner?'

Parrott had had enough. He shot a poisonous glance at Sodov. 'I'm off,' he said, draining the last dregs from his drink and folding up his newspaper.

'Hold on,' said Kelvin. 'We haven't said you can go.' He turned to Sodov. 'Can you identify him?'

The Bulgarian flashed his metal tooth and wriggled his shoulders in satisfaction. 'We have photographs in our files of Fascist elements in the British police force. This man resembles one of them although he is fatter and has more hair.'

'That could have been one of the shots that were taken in the booth at Victoria Station,' said the commander.

'How did you get hold of one of those pictures, Sodov?' demanded Parrott.

Sodov smiled. 'We have friends in high places.'

'You cheeky bugger!' exclaimed Parrott. 'What are you doing here, anyway?'

'I am furthering the interests of my country, Sergeant.'

'Doing what?' Sodov pursed his lips and waggled his hand enigmatically. 'I haven't trailed after you all the way from London to leave here without finding out your contact.'

'Don't tell him!' shouted Kelvin.

'Do not worry. I have no intention of telling him.'

Parrott turned angrily on Kelvin. 'Whose side are you on?'

'I'm on his,' said Kelvin. 'Go on. Piss off out of here. We handle our own troubles in Moorcombe. We don't need any big city policeman, however special.'

'You're on the next plane home, Sodov,' snarled Parrott. 'And as for you . . .' He turned to Kelvin. 'You're going to regret the day you were born.' He picked up his driving gloves and stormed through the door.

'What an extraordinary chap!' said the commander. 'Did you hear that, Kelvin? He threatened you!'

'I should not concern yourself with him,' said Sodov. 'You are not a spy and his job is only concerned with those who are.'

'Oh,' said the commander. 'Does that mean you are one?' Sodov laughed.

So did Kelvin. 'No need to worry. Mr Sodov's down to tell us about Botograd on Vit. All the way from London.'

'Bulgarian, are you?' asked the commander. 'Hitman for the Kremlin?'

'Melodramatic exaggeration,' smiled Sodov. 'And very out of date. Let me buy you all drinks as a gesture of friendship between our two fraternal nations.'

'That would be right civil of you!' said Kelvin.

Even the commander's unease seemed assuaged when a fresh glass of barley wine appeared in front of him. 'How long are you down here?' he asked.

'I am booked in for two days at a hotel down the valley.'

'The *Fisherman's Arms*?'

'Yes. I am hoping to advise you on Botograd on Vit and then look round at your beautiful scenery and countryside.'

'It must cost you a fortune at the *Arms*,' said Kelvin.

'I am on expenses.'

'I've got an idea,' said Kelvin. 'We could put you up at Northcott. Prudence would cook you meals; it'd give you a chance to live with a typical British family and we'd charge you less.'

'It's very kind of you but . . .'

'I could give you receipts for £30 a night and only charge you £15.'

'Well . . .'

'Good! That's settled then.'

Jimmy broke the silence. 'If the weather brightens up, you've come to the right place for scenery. They say there's lots of it round here.'

'So I have heard. I am looking forward to seeing it. You have an airport if I wish to return quickly to London?'

'There's an airbase twenty-five miles away,' said Jimmy.

'Ah?'

'They're just the RAF. They've got an open day at the weekend.'

'I might then visit before I go back to London. Spotting aircraft is one of my favoured hobbies.'

'Mandy!' exclaimed Kelvin. 'I quite forgot! Here! Mr Sodov . . .'

'I beg your pardon? What was your name again?' asked the commander.

'Call me Boris.'

'Boris,' said Kelvin. 'We've got a lady coming in quite soon. Would you tell her that we've decided to stop building the village hall for a bit.'

'Is that all?' asked Sodov when it was clear Kelvin had said all he was going to.

'Yes. We've hit a bit of a snag with planning permission. Ah! Talk of the devil.'

Mandy, followed closely by Keith, came through the door from the lounge, pausing as she scanned those at the bar. In spite of her heavy make-up and rhinestone rings, sparkling on her fingers, the Medusa in her was revealed by the curl on her lip as she turned to snarl at Keith who bumped into her.

'Go on,' said Kelvin, nudging Sodov. 'That's the lady.'

'I can see why you wished me to inform her. She makes you afraid to talk to her?'

'Well . . .'

'Yes, she does,' confirmed Malcolm.

'Where I come from, we do not fear our women. They are our helpmeets in building a socialist society.'

'How very nice for you,' said the commander, politely.

Having pulled out a chair to seat Mandy at one of the tables, Keith approached the bar. Sodov went over to her. With the rest of the patrons watching silently, he clicked his heels and, spreading his chins like an amorous bullfrog, he inclined his head in a bow. 'Sodov.'

It did not get him off to a great start.

'If he's been in England for any length of time,' observed the commander, as Mandy slapped the Bulgarian resoundingly on the cheek, 'you'd think he'd've learned to introduce himself in another way. Keith, you'd better go and restrain your wife.'

'What's she doing?' Keith had been on his way behind the bar to pour their drinks.

63

'How dare you talk like that to me!' said Mandy.

Sodov backed away.

'Oh dear,' said Keith.

'The man's name is Sodov and I think she must have thought he was being rude,' said the commander. Having struggled free of the table, Mandy, hefting her make-up laden handbag, moved round the table to attack her abuser. 'He's down to tell us about twinning with Botograd on Vit,' continued the commander.

'I'd better go and help,' said Keith. 'It's all right, dear,' he called.

'It's not all right at all. This . . . this worm has just told me to sod off.'

'No dear. Sodov is his name.'

Mandy paused. 'What kind of a name is that?'

'He's a foreigner.'

'It is true,' said Sodov, backed into the corner by the fireplace. 'I am a Bulgar.'

'Huh!' said Mandy, lowering her arm. 'You said it!'

'You have stopped your violence?'

'For the time being.'

Pulling a handkerchief from his pocket, Sodov mopped his

brow. 'Please forgive my sweat. I am not accustomed to excitement. I was going to tell you a message from your friends. You must stop building the village hall.'

'What!'

'You must stop building the village hall.' Sodov looked uncertainly to the bar.

'Never!' shouted Mandy, advancing on him again.

Casting a despairing glance over to the bar, he edged hurriedly towards the exit. 'That was right, was it not? I think I must go outside for a little bit until this beautiful lady has calmed her passionate nature.'

'You won't get round me like that!' said Mandy, as she chased him through the door.

'Oh, I really hope he does,' said Keith.

'Giving you a bit of trouble, is she, eh?' said the commander.

'Nothing out of the ordinary. What's this about the village hall?'

Kelvin grunted contemptuously. 'Malcolm thinks we'll have it pulled down if we go ahead without permission.'

'That'd be a bit of a shame,' said Keith. 'I suppose it would give me a chance to get on with re-leading the church roof.'

'I think we should go ahead with the hall and tell the council to get stuffed.'

The pub door re-opened. 'What's Percy doing to your Land Rover?'

Kelvin looked up at Mandy, a puzzled frown on his face. 'What do you mean?'

'He's walking round it, writing things down in his notebook.'

Sodov, peace having been restored, was hard on her heels. 'I think the policeman is booking you.'

'He can't be!' said Jimmy. 'Not Percy.'

'He'd bloody well better not be,' said Kelvin, sliding from his stool and heading for the door.

'It was very kind of you to buy me a drink, Mr Sodov,' said Jimmy, looking at his glass.

'Ho! You are empty. Let me buy you another.'

'Kelvin's going to be very cross,' said Jimmy happily, as Keith filled up his glass. 'Missing a free drink.'

'Have no fear,' said Sodov. 'As a gesture from our people to yours, I will buy him one as well.'

Jimmy's face clouded. 'You don't have to do that.'

'It would be my pleasure.'

'You're a very generous person, Boris,' said Mandy, batting her eyelashes like vacuum cleaner brushes. 'Oh yes. Commander, what's all this about stopping work on the hall? I'm afraid I simply won't allow it.'

'We don't have much choice, I'm afraid.'

Mandy laughed. 'Keith won't stop the building unless I tell him to, will you, dear?'

'Good Lord no!' said Keith, twenty years experience of marital survival under his belt.

'And I can assure you I shall not tell him to,' said Mandy. She gave the commander the benefit of her sweetest smile. 'So you see it'll be finished, down to the last arrow slit.'

The door crashed open. 'I'm not standing outside in the pouring rain arguing with you, Percy Green!' shouted Kelvin over his shoulder. 'And you can shove your bloody ticket up your backside!' Kelvin stumped over towards the bar. 'How dare he!'

'What's wrong, Kelvin?' asked the commander.

'Percy's gone potty,' said Kelvin bluntly.

Percy was hot on Kelvin's heels. He took off his helmet as he ducked his head beneath the lintel. Red in the face and uneasy, he brushed a few drops of rain from his tunic. 'I'd like to continue this in private, if you don't mind, Kelvin.'

'Well, I do mind. Anything you have to say you can say here and now.'

Percy, now the centre of attention, looked miserably at the other patrons and cleared his throat. 'The law's very clear, Kelvin. That Land Rover of yours has no tax, no MOT; the tyres are illegal; the lights are broken and the rust makes it dangerous.'

'No, it doesn't.'

'It's got naked, jagged metal all round. In a collision with a pedestrian, you'd do serious injury.' He licked his lips, looking longingly at the glasses of beer on the bar. 'I'm afraid I'll have to report you.'

A gasp of astonishment ran round the pub. 'Are you serious, Percy?' asked Kelvin.

'I'm just doing my duty.'

'Percy,' said the commander, over the murmur of derision. 'Kelvin's been driving that vehicle for years. You've never taken any interest in it before, why should you suddenly do so now?'

'That's nothing to do with anything. The fact remains Kelvin's Land Rover is breaking the law and I'm reporting him.' He turned to Kelvin. 'It's up to the superintendent whether he brings any charges against you for these various offences. You don't have to say anything, but if you do, it may be used in evidence in a court of law. Have you anything to say?'

'Yes,' said Kelvin. 'Write this down!' Percy looked dubious. 'Go on! Write this down!' The policeman took out his notebook and pencil. 'On Thursday of last week . . .' Kelvin paused. 'Got that?'

'Of course I have.'

'On Thursday of last week Constable Percy Green was drinking in the Hunted Hind after hours. There are a dozen witnesses who'll say so.'

Percy looked up from his notebook. 'Damn you, Kelvin Morchard!'

'Temper, temper,' replied Kelvin, smugly.

'Unless you're careful, Kelvin. I'll add blackmail to the list of alleged offences,' said Percy, doggedly.

'For Christ's sake, be your age, Percy,' growled Jimmy. 'Go away and look for poachers or something. Or go back home and eat a scone. Stop being such a blinking nuisance.'

'I'm just doing my job.' Percy was too large and solid an individual to look comfortable whining.

'You've been supposed to have been doing it for the last five years, but why start now?' said Kelvin. 'You should know you're not in any position to start fussing about stupid little rules like that. You can't afford to go around offending prominent law abiding members of the community like me. I don't know what's come over you. Come on Percy. Just put your book away and forget about it.' Kelvin put an arm round Percy's shoulder, showing a gape of grey lining at the armpit of his jacket where the cloth had rotted away. 'I'll even buy you a drink.'

'Bugger me!' said Jimmy, with awe. 'The last time you offered to buy me a drink was in 1981.'

'Did I?' said Kelvin.

'Aye, you were drunk. But don't worry, it was only a half pint.'

'That's not too bad,' said Kelvin with relief. He turned back to Percy. 'How about it?'

'I can't.' Percy wrung his hands, a gesture sufficiently arresting for Kelvin to take his arm back and look concerned.

'Are you feeling all right?' asked Kelvin. 'You're behaving very peculiar.'

'I think I might have an answer to your puzzle,' said Sodov. Kelvin turned. 'You? What's this to do with you?'

Sodov ignored him. 'Constable, do you know who I am?'

'Yes,' said Percy, avoiding his eye. 'You're the foreign gentleman, Mr Sodov.'

'How the hell did you know that?' said Kelvin admiringly. 'He's only just introduced himself.'

'I suspect Sergeant Parrott may have been talking to you, is that not correct?'

'Yes,' replied Percy, hanging his head. 'I met him outside.'

'Here! What's going on?' demanded Kelvin. 'How did he know that?'

'It is simple,' said Sodov. 'I know how Sergeant Parrott and his kind can persecute those who cause them trouble.'

'Are you saying that this Parrott bloke told Percy to . . . to harry me?'

'Of course. People like him have a great deal of power and do not like to be thwarted.'

Kelvin turned to the policeman. 'Percy! Is this true?'

Percy shuffled his boots in the sawdust. 'He gave me a direct order, didn't he? I said I'd have to get on to the station to check it was all right and he said he'd make sure I was transferred or even lose my job if I didn't get on to it right away.'

'Percy! How could you?' said Kelvin, shocked to his core.

Percy raised his bloodhound face. 'I'm sorry Kelvin. But you should've heard him.' He gave a little shiver. 'Horrible bloke, he was. He used some shocking language for a policeman. I'm quite sure he'd've got me the sack, too. He had that sort of influential look about him.'

'Bit like the squire, I suppose,' said Jimmy. 'He's got that look.'

'Different sort of look. Nasty sort of look. The squire's influential sort of look isn't nasty.'

'I can assure you,' said Sodov. 'That Parrott and his kind are utterly without scruples. Had you disobeyed, he would have carried out his threat.'

'Even so . . .' began Kelvin.

'I can get my pension in another eighteen months, you see, Kelvin. I was going to start a little business here, selling tropical fish.'

'Not much call for tropical fish round here, I'd've thought,' said Keith.

'We need more shubunkin for the pond,' said Mandy.

'He'll need more trade than our pond.'

'I was thinking of doing them mail order,' said Percy.

'But how would you send them through the post?' asked Keith.

'I thought of watertight envelopes. Like that padded kind. If I sent them first class, they ought to get there all right.'

'Not sure that'd work,' said Keith.

'They send boar semen through the post these days. And I

should think that'd go off very quick,' said Jimmy. 'It travels in insulated containers. They should be able to do the same sort of thing with tropical fish.'

'So you agreed to hound and persecute me,' said Kelvin. 'I'd've expected a bit more loyalty from you, Percy Green.'

The animation in Percy died. 'I don't know what you did to him Kelvin. But when he heard you were a farmer he said he'd get the Health and Safety on to you.'

'You're trying to destroy me!' said Kelvin. 'I won't stand for it!'

'It's not me. It's him,' said Percy. 'I just carry out orders. Particularly when given by a right so-and-so like him.'

'I never thought this country could come to this,' said Kelvin, heavily.

'Ah yes. It is not like Bulgaria. Ours is a democratic Socialist Republic. All our people are happy and free.'

'So long as they don't disagree,' said the commander.

'Of course,' said Sodov. 'No one can interfere with the progress of the revolution. Those who do are enemies of the state.'

'Well, I'm no enemy of the state,' said Kelvin.

'I'm afraid that Parrott seems to think you are,' said Percy. 'That was the very phrase he used to describe you.'

'Why didn't you tell him otherwise?' asked Kelvin.

'I tried, but he wouldn't listen,' said Percy. 'He was in a right bate with you.'

'I can't understand it,' said Kelvin with a baffled shake of the head. 'Has the man no respect for my office? I told him I was chairman of the council.' He turned to Sodov. 'That's an important position to hold, you know.'

'I know,' said Sodov.

'You could complain to what's-his-name,' said the commander. 'You know, Seymour Bland MP.'

'That'll do no good at all,' said Kelvin, looking at the empty pint glass on the bar top in front of him. 'Bugger me,' he said, slowly. 'This all takes some thinking about.' The serious note in his voice brought a silence in the bar. 'What we have here is a threat to everything we hold dear. I don't suppose Moorcombe has known anything like it since the dark days of 1940.' He lifted his head. 'That was when the War Agricultural Committee started to tell us all what to plant and plough. Something has to be done.' He turned to Percy. 'Hold on to your tickets for a day or two, Percy, until we come up with an idea.'

'I might delay till after the weekend, Kelvin. But I'll not risk my pension for you. And if Mr Sodov stays around, I can tell you that Parrott won't be far away either. He's trouble.'

'I am going to the open day on Saturday at the airfield. And I am down here to convey fraternal greetings from Botograd to your council. I shall be here.'

'Don't do anything rash, Kelvin,' said the commander. The feeling that they were caught up in the plot of a Greek tragedy which would progress towards a grim conclusion with the inevitability of a hangover after a night on cowslip wine, had brushed the hearts of all at the bar.

'Whatever happens, freedom is our birthright,' said Kelvin. 'We may have some tough choices ahead, but I'll come up with something. It's my duty, after all. I am the elected leader of Moorcombe, sworn to protect your interests.'

'Oh dear,' sighed the commander, looking into the depths of his barley wine.

Chapter Five

IN THE COUPLE of days up to the weekend, tension rose in and around Moorcombe. Cattle gadded in the meadows, trout stayed sullenly at the bottom of the river, refusing to rise to anglers' flies, barn owls shrieked in the night, milk went quickly sour and Mandy broke a fingernail.

Keith was at fault.

'Look at it!' she shouted. 'It's ruined the set! I only got them last week.'

'Oh dear,' said Keith. They were gardening in front of 'Pixies Laughter'. While Keith had been giving the fence the annual coat of white gloss paint, Mandy had been scrubbing the concrete, scored to imitate crazy paving, which, dotted by tubs of plastic flowers and arcadian statues, filled the space between the house and the road. She had been rinsing the bleach from her scrubbing brush in the pond and caught her nail on the rod wielded by one of the plaster gnomes which stood sentinel over the limpid, dead water in the pool.

'It's you who should've been doing the gardening. It's a man's job. If you were a proper man, it wouldn't've happened!'

'Sorry, dear.'

'A fat lot of good it is being sorry! I'm going to see if I can glue the nail together again. I might be able to do it with Araldite. You'll have to cook supper as I won't be able to do anything till it dries. I suppose I'll have to watch *Gone with the Wind* on the video again. What a nuisance, it is!'

'Yes. Bad luck, dear.'

'I'll expect you to have finished the fence and sanded down the gate ready for its second coat by supper time.'

'Right, dear.' Having watched his wife safely through the front door, Keith crossed the lane to sit on the wall alongside the river. He took out a packet of cigarettes and lit up.

Eight feet below him the water lazily mooched past. Heavy rain on the moor could make the level rise five feet in a couple of hours, but, sustained by only the usual few hours of drizzle a day, the level was comparatively low for the time of year. Across the fifteen-yard river, its bed dotted with boulders, the side of the valley in which Moorcombe lay rose sharply upwards, three times the height of the church tower. The beech, ash and oak which covered the hillside were just stippled with green, as if a pointillist Nature was beginning to build the summer colours from her palette.

As the sun silently chased a shadow down the hillside, it brought the colours, textures and shapes sharply into focus. A single rogue cherry, its blossom not yet fully opened, scattered dabs of sugar-almond pink against the brown background of bracken and bramble covering the ground beneath the trees.

Among the trees, the nesting birds fought musical warfare from scores of vantage points, cascading, whistling and chirping defiance at each other against the rhythmic background chink of the chiffchaff, the first of the summer migrants. On the water, the half-tame mallards quacked through their squalid copulation, the drakes holding a frantically squawking duck beneath the surface as they lined up for their gangbang. On the wall, halfway between Keith and the bridge carrying the outside world across the river into the village, sat a jackdaw, adjusting a beakful of grass clippings which draped down across its chest like the beard of an Old Testament prophet. It launched itself across the river and up towards its nest on the crest of the valley as Kelvin's Land Rover crossed the bridge and turned left into the lane. It drew to a halt beside Keith and its owner emerged.

'Hullo, Kelvin,' said Keith, as the latter came to lean his arms on the wall beside him. Keith tossed his cigarette into the water. It landed with a soft hiss and bobbed off down the river.

Watching the cigarette go, Kelvin grunted in reply. He returned to his vehicle and hauled out a fertiliser bag, bulging with bits of twine, barbed wire and fragments of straw. Hefting it on to the wall, he toppled it into the river. It hit with a flat splash and, riding high, it swung round a large boulder and off downstream.

'What did you go and do that for?' asked Keith.

'Just getting rid of a bit of rubbish,' replied Kelvin.

'I can see that. Why didn't you leave it at the end o.' your lane for the binmen to collect?'

'They don't pick up there.'

Keith looked solemn. 'That's bad that. They ought to pick up from you. I wonder why they don't?'

' 'Cos there's never any rubbish, that's why.'

'Oh, I see. What do you do with it? Chuck it in the river?'

'The Morchards've always chucked their rubbish in the river.'

'Is that so? Can't be good. You must make a lot of pollution.'

'No, it doesn't. Look at it. It's nice clean water.' They looked down at the river.'

'That's true,' said Keith. Then a thought struck him. 'But Northcott's down river. The pollution wouldn't come up here. Why don't you put it in bags like everyone else for the rubbish lorry to pick up?'

'Because it doesn't stop. I've already told you.'

'Oh yes.' The rubbish had gone aground by the bridge. A passing dog paused to put a paw in the water to sniff, but the wind through the arches of the bridge caught the bag and it blew free to bump through the shallow rapids of the centre span and out of sight behind the stone piers. 'But why come all the way up here to drop your rubbish in the river?'

Frowning, Kelvin chomped his teeth. 'In the first place I didn't come up here just to dump rubbish. I came up to have a word with you. I just happened to have that bag in the Land Rover.' Kelvin parked his backside on the wall and looked expectantly at Keith.

'Would you like a cup of tea?' asked Keith. 'Or,' in response to Kelvin's hangdog look, 'I could probably find you a can of beer.'

'That'd be very civil of you,' said Kelvin. 'Beer, please. Is your missus out or something? I see you're in the middle of painting that there gate.'

'It's all right,' said Keith. 'She won't be out again. She broke a nail.'

'Ah! I see,' said Kelvin.

'I can go round the back to the kitchen. She's watching a video while she waits for the glue to dry.'

While Keith was getting the beer, Kelvin idly rocked his false teeth with his tongue and examined the cottage in front

74

of him. With the house martins not yet returned from the African sunshine, Mandy had taken the opportunity to rip down the nests she had tolerated beneath the gutters. Keith had been sent up a ladder to re-paint the pink walls and erect a coil of barbed wire, also painted pink, to discourage them from trying to rebuild.

Laden with early tourists, a coach warily halted before the narrow bridge and throbbed there for a few seconds before deciding it was wide enough to cross. Kelvin endured the stares of the passengers with indifference as he rooted in his ear with a little finger, scrutinising the resultant extraction. The coach passengers looked away.

Keith returned bearing a couple of glasses marked 'A Present from Longleat' and two cans of beer. Taking one, Kelvin stripped the tab and threw it over his shoulder into the river before filling his glass.

'Did you come out here just to muck up our bit of river?' asked Keith.

'No, I came out here to make sure you'd support me when I decide to take action on the hall and things.'

'I don't much like the sound of "and things",' replied Keith. 'It depends what you mean.'

'Make sure you have a hall to build and make you the second most important person in the parish,' said Kelvin.

'After you?'

'No, after Mandy.'

'Mandy! What are you talking about?'

'I've worked out a plan.'

'All by yourself?'

'I had a bit of advice on some of the details. I'm calling a secret meeting at the manor on Tuesday. You and Mandy'll have to be there. But first of all I want Mandy to have a word with Malcolm. There're just one or two things that need working out . . .'

From the outside, the crumbling golden brick of the manor still had sufficient charm to attract bids from tycoons passing overhead in their helicopters on their way to weekend retreats on the moor, but the squire would never sell. He believed fervently that his life's purpose was to provide guidance and continuity in the community which he served.

Fronting the ivy and creeper-clad house, with its pillared

portico, was a stretch of gravel and an acre of lawn across which the squire would putter in his mini-tractor. A ha-ha separated the lawn from a field where the pick of the manor herd of creamy Charolais cattle dreamed away the warm summer months.

The meeting was inside the library, where the atmosphere of ancient scholarship, created by two walls of leather-bound books of sermons and dissertations of the classics, gave gravitas to any discussion.

The squire hammered on the worn leather top of the desk with a gnarled countryman's fist to get the attention of the village elders. 'We all know about the crisis we face. I won't beat about the bush. Kelvin says he's come up with a solution and wanted to air it. Kelvin. I give the floor over to you.'

Seated in the front row, Kelvin slowly rose to his feet and surveyed his audience. Surprisingly, many farmers have few qualms about speaking in public. During their teens, they are members of the Young Farmers Club in which, as well as the formation of suitable marital alliances between adjacent farms, debating and the reading of reports plays a large part. 'Ladies and Gentlemen,' he began. 'We have a problem.' He pulled a sheet of paper out of his pocket, along with a pair of National Health spectacles which he placed on the end of his nose. A murmur of astonishment ran through the room. Kelvin was going to read, something at which his generation of agriculturalists was notoriously bad. He cleared his throat. 'I wasn't going to do a speech. You all know me. I'm a simple man who speaks his mind without any buggering about. But I feel this is an important day and a solemn occasion and I thought I'd write something down . . .'

'He's got a great deal of paper in his hand,' said the commander into Ivor's ear. 'I do hope he's not going to read it all.'

The squire looked severely over his spectacles. He had one of those spec/moustache/nose combinations which looked as if they might all come off as one to be parked by his false teeth at the side of his bed each night. 'Commander, I think it would be courteous if we all gave Kelvin our undivided attention.'

'Sorry,' said the commander, his ears turning pink.

Kelvin cleared his throat once more and shook his paper. 'When in the course of hu. . . human events it becomes necessary for one people to dissolve the political bands which have connected them with another, and to assume among the powers of the earth, the separate and equal station to which the Laws of Nature and Nature's God entitle them, a decent respect to the opinions of mankind requires that they should declare the causes which impel them to the separation.' Kelvin paused, the film of sweat from the effort bathing his face. His audience was stunned into incomprehending and inattentive silence. The unexpected mellifluous phrases, the eighteenth century setting and Kelvin's uncomprehending stumbling delivery produced instant narcolepsy, the birthright of every Anglican faced by a preacher.

The squire jumped. 'Er . . . very good, Kelvin. I wonder if anyone would care to comment?'

'I haven't finished yet,' said Kelvin, indignantly. 'I'm coming to the bit Prudence says was important.'

'Prudence?' queried the squire.

'She helped with the speech a bit. So did Mr Sodov. And they said I read the next bit well.'

'I see.' The squire looked at his watch. 'I suppose you'd better go on.'

Kelvin glared round his audience before returning to his notes. 'We hold these truths to be self evident, that all men are created equal, that they are endowed by their Creator with certain unalienable rights, that among these are life, liberty and the pursuit of happiness.' Faint frowns of recognition appeared on one or two of his audience, better educated and less comatose than the majority. 'That to secure these rights, governments are instituted among men, deriving their just powers from the consent of the governed. That whenever any form of government becomes destructive of these ends, it is the right of the people to alter or abolish it, and to institute new government, laying its foundation on such principles and organising its powers in such form as to them shall seem most likely to effect their safety and happiness. Prudence indeed will dictate . . .' Kelvin stopped, frowned and peered at his notes. 'What's she gone and writ that for? She's not going to do any dictating. Certainly not to me.' He looked up. 'There's quite a lot more, but I think that'll give you enough to chew on.' He turned to the squire. 'I'd like to thank you, Squire, for giving your support to this historic decision. Before we get down to the practicalities, I think I ought to give everyone else a say. Thank you.'

'Er . . . thank you for that most eloquent address,' said the squire with some bewilderment. 'I don't know what everyone else thought, but I was most impressed and found it quite fascinating. I . . . er . . . now would like to ask for any comments or questions that are felt to be relevant.' He lifted his head expectantly to the audience.

Beyond the window, there came a sudden burst of wails, snarls and yaps as Marcia took her horde of miniature dachshunds for their afternoon micturition. Inside the library, the audience studiously avoided their chairman's eye, concentrating instead on the ancestral portraits, many without frames, behind his head. On canvases from the beginning of the eighteenth century, the squire's large nose and myopic, benevolent eye looked mildly into the middle distance, fashioned by the hand of second-rate painters, many of whom had chosen to paint their patrons against the backdrop of the huge, gnarled oak still standing in the middle of the lawn in front of the house.

After a ten second silence, the squire cleared his throat again. 'Er . . . perhaps I had better start the ball rolling. I took a few notes during Kelvin's address. You mentioned safety and happiness . . .'

'Did I?'

The squire checked again. 'Yes. It was one of the last bits you said. In what way do you think our safety could be better?'

'Safety . . . safety . . .' Kelvin peered at his papers. 'Ah, here it is! Effecting . . . powers . . . safety . . . happiness,' he muttered. 'Well, you must remember it was Prudence who put in many of the ideas in this speech. I suppose she meant we need a new fire engine or something.'

'Oh, I see. Yes, I suppose we do. How old is the one we've got already?'

'It's a Dennis,' said Mick from the front row, a member of the team which fought the autumn barn fires, sometimes caused when farmers, dissatisfied with the quality and quantity of their hay, gave in to the temptation to light a match and claim on their insurance. 'I suppose we could do with a new one. It must be fifteen years old.'

'It's H reg,' said Jimmy from the back.

'There you are then,' said Kelvin. 'She just means we need a new fire engine.'

'I see,' said the squire. 'Is anyone taking minutes of this meeting?'

Malcolm raised his hand from the back of the room. 'I thought I'd better.'

'Very good,' said the squire. 'You have noted Prudence's point about the fire engine.'

'Yes, but what that's got to do with the American Declaration of Independence, I'm damned if I can see.'

The squire frowned as a stir ran round the room. 'The American Declaration of Independence? I don't understand.'

'The Americans rebelled against the British in 1776. Kelvin's just read out the Declaration of Independence.'

'Don't talk nonsense!' said Kelvin. 'I wrote that last night, with a bit of help from Prudence and Sodov.'

'If Malcolm's right,' said Jimmy, 'how did the Americans know about Prudence? Don't forget she wasn't alive in 1776.'

'I think you'll find that the Prudence in the text doesn't mean Kelvin's Prudence, but just being prudent.'

'How did they know our fire engine was getting old, then?' asked Kelvin. 'You can't tell me they could've predicted that. I bet they hadn't even got decent fire engines in those days.'

'You didn't say anything about fire engines,' said Malcolm.

'Yes, I did, you silly bugger. The squire's just asked you to note it in the minutes.'

'If you recall, it was you who mentioned fire engines.'

'I know. It was me that were making the speech.'

'But what you said about the fire engine was not part of your speech but just your interpretation of what you thought Prudence meant.'

'That's true,' conceded the squire after a glance at his notes. 'You originally just said safety and happiness.'

'All right, Mr Clever Dick,' said Kelvin. 'How do you account for the fact that I saw Prudence write that last night?'

'It's either a remarkable coincidence, proving that great minds think alike – Thomas Jefferson, George Washington, Benjamin Franklin on one side and Prudence Morchard on the other. Or she copied it out of a book.'

'It could be you're wrong,' pointed out the squire.

Malcolm looked round at the leather tomes covering the

wall. 'Haven't you got an old encyclopaedia here? We could easily look it up.'

'There's one over at the back, somewhere. I think,' said the squire.

'I believe Malcolm may be right,' said the commander. 'That bit about life, liberty and the pursuit of happiness struck a bell. So did all men being created equal.'

'If anything, that would surely be the Communist manifesto?' said the squire. 'After all Mr Sodov gave some help.'

Rising to his feet, Malcolm crossed to a six foot strata of shelves and selected a volume.

'What do you think, Ivor?' asked the squire.

'I'm afraid I wasn't listening,' confessed Ivor. Murmurs from the others indicated he had not been alone in this condition. 'I'm sure it was an excellent speech, Kelvin, whoever wrote it. But what exactly did you mean by it?'

'That's a very good question,' said the squire. 'I don't know how I didn't think to ask it myself.'

'It's perfectly obvious,' said Kelvin. 'Listen, whenever a government becomes a pain in the arse, it's the right of the people to alter or abolish it.'

The room was silent.

'So what exactly is it you propose?' asked the squire.

'I propose we throw off the yoke of oppression and declare Moorcombe independent,' replied Kelvin.

'I second,' said Mandy.

With a rustle of flaking leather, the room turned in the massive dining chairs in which they were seated to look at her. Her gaze, her jaw and her eyes were steely. She dug her husband in the ribs. Hard.

'So do I,' said Keith.

'Did you get that, Malcolm?' asked the squire. 'A motion has been properly proposed and seconded, although I'm not sure if we need two seconders.' He beamed at Keith. 'However we're all grateful to you, just in case we do. Malcolm, please read out the motion.'

'It is proposed that Moorcombe should become independ-ent,' said Malcolm, his finger on the pages of a large book. 'It was the Declaration of Independence.'

'Oh good. It's so nice to be proved right, isn't it? Anyway I call for a vote on the motion.'

The commander raised his hand.

'Yes, Commander?' said the squire.

'I think it would help if we had the implications of a "yes" vote explained.'

'Haven't we had it explained? Safety and happiness for all, wasn't it?'

Kelvin stood up. 'The motion means we throw off the shackles of the District Council and the County Council and, while we're at it, we repudiate the authority of parliament 'cos that MP Seymour Bland is a right idiot and anyone who did vote for him is sorry about it now.' Kelvin paused.

'That's a very interesting idea, Kelvin,' said the squire, staring up at him with intelligent interest. 'But can we repudiate their authority like that? It strikes me that there might well be legal difficulties and we've already got that blasted policeman making a nuisance of himself.'

'Don't you see?' said Kelvin. 'Moorcombe will become an independent country and we can rule ourselves.' He had the full attention of his audience. 'That'll mean we can twin with whom we like and we'll be able to tell Mrs Biss to get stuffed and get on with building the village hall and none of these damned outsiders'll be able to do a thing about it!'

The dumbfounded silence as the audience assimilated this glorious vision was shattered as the door to the library burst open, allowing entry to a seethe of yapping dachshunds followed by Marcia.

'I'm so sorry,' she shouted as the carpet of dogs fanned out beneath the chairs, sniffing and pissing on the agricultural legs, redolent with the scents of sheep, cow, silage or slurry. The interest of the audience switched from revolutionary politics to self preservation as they swatted at any individual members of the pack which paused within piddle or copulation range of their feet. 'I wonder if you'd all like some tea and biscuits?'

'Thank you, my dear,' said the squire who had lifted his feet to a stretcher on his chair as the ungodly horde entered. 'We seem to have come to a useful point to take a break. I suspend the meeting for fifteen minutes.' He banged on the table with his fist provoking ululating screams from the horde which flowed across the floor to coalesce round its mistress's feet.

'Really, Humphrey,' said Marcia, crossly. 'You know the animals don't like sudden noises.'

'I'm sorry,' said the squire. The windows shook as the

audience stamped their feet on the floor in unison. The dogs, eyes bulging, streamed round and through Marcia's legs and along the corridor, their screams and cries disappearing into the distance. The one remaining appeared to have suffered a seizure as it fell on its back with its legs sticking stiffly in the air.

Marcia gave the audience a withering look. 'They'll have peed all the way along the corridor.' She looked down at the creature at her feet. 'Get up!' she said, briskly. 'Come on. Don't be silly. They won't do it again.' She prodded it with her foot, shod in an old gym shoe. The animal, still on its back jetted an arc of urine into the air. 'Don't be disgusting, Peter.' The dog rolled over on to its legs and slunk out of the room. 'You hardly deserve anything after that,' she said, but, aside from the commander who blushed and looked at the floor, nobody else showed any remorse. Even the squire had a glimmer of bitter satisfaction on his face. Marcia gave a short snort of annoyance. 'Well, don't just sit there. Come and get it. I've put it in the billiard room.'

The bare oak floor of the corridor must once have been polished, but time and neglect had rendered it dull grey with broad seams of dirt between each board. The visitors stepped round the puddles and dribbles already being absorbed by the dry wood and walked in an untidy straggle towards the billiard room. Inside, the central table was shrouded in a dust sheet, upon which were laid bone china cups, plates of rich tea biscuits and a large pot of tea. The walls were oak-panelled and scattered with *Spy* cartoons. Round the room stood a set of heavy mahogany chairs, their seats, although many were split, covered in black, shiny horsehair. By the scoreboard in a corner stood a cue rack containing six assorted cues, three with their tips missing and one snapped in two and bound together with twine. A faded beige carpet was darkened in patches by the passing horde, three of whose members were clumped in front of the single bar electric fire. With their ears back and their brown eyes large with neurotic terror, the dogs could have been posing for a picture on an advertising calendar for thermal bedsocks.

'Two lumps, please,' said the commander, holding out his cup to Marcia. 'Thank you.' He turned to Jimmy, already chomping his way through his second biscuit. 'What do you think?'

'Not bad,' said Jimmy. 'It would've been nice if there'd been some chocolate ones, too.'

'I'm not talking about the biscuits, I mean what do you think about Kelvin's scheme?'

Jimmy stood chewing for a second or two. 'What scheme?'

'The scheme to make Moorcombe independent.'

'Oh. That scheme. I think it's grand. How can anyone but us know what's best for Moorcombe? It was much better in the old days. Then you knew the boss was the squire and so long as you kept on the right side of him, you were all right. Now you get all sorts of busybodies telling us what to do. And I don't think it's right.'

'Heavens!' said the commander. 'And our ancestors fought and died to create a democracy.'

'What's the point about a democracy if the bugger you elect don't know a damn thing about anything? If you had to have a yard of your guts removed, you'd want an expert who could do the job proper. Not some fellow who got the job because he could kiss babies better and got most votes.'

'It's a point of view,' said the commander.

'Damn right it is! The old squire used to look after the people of Moorcombe proper, he did. He didn't let all these new people in, buying up our houses and blocking the street with their shiny motor cars. Come to think of it, he can't've allowed any cars at all in the village. See that?' The commander followed the outstretched finger to a faded photograph of a young man, *sans* chin, standing by the portico of the manor beside a vehicle of the type driven by Mr Toad. 'That was the only car we ever saw. We'd've been one of the Thankful Villages if it hadn't been for him.'

'What do you mean?'

'They were the villages that didn't lose anybody in the Great War. He was the squire's uncle, went and got himself killed just before Armistice. He were a staff officer and had a chandelier fall on his head when he were having lunch. He's on the War Memorial in the church.'

The squire himself came bustling over. 'Commander. I wanted a word. What do you think about this idea of Kelvin's?'

'I think it's probably high treason.'

'Good Lord!'

'Yes. Once Percy understands the implications, Kelvin could be in trouble. Along with arson in a naval dockyard and enjoying illicit carnal relations with the daughter of the monarch, it's still a capital offence.'

'Oh dear!' said the squire, his tea cup tinkling against its saucer in his agitation. 'And Marcia does so want me to be High Sheriff the year after next. If I have to go along with this, it won't do my chances any good.'

'I wouldn't worry,' said the commander. 'When you restart the meeting, call me to speak first against the motion. It won't go through.'

'Oh good! I'm very grateful to you. I thought it was probably a bad idea, but I can never think of reasons why until much later. I'm not sure if the chairman's supposed to take sides anyway.' Glancing at his watch, he looked round the room. 'I promised Kelvin I'd finish the meeting before the pub opens.' He clapped his hands. 'I think we could return to the library now.'

'I'd like to propose a vote of thanks to Marcia for giving us tea and biscuits,' said Kelvin. 'Even if there weren't any chocolate ones.'

There weren't enough people present to raise much applause, but the three dogs by the fire squeaked in alarm at the enthusiastic rhubarb noises. Then the villagers streamed back towards the library to return to their seats and the squire re-opened the debate. 'A motion has been put to the floor and, before a vote, I call upon the commander to say a few words.'

'Thank you,' said the commander, rising to his feet. 'I'd first like to remind you of our power. Some of us here are on the council and have been given sweeping powers by our fellow parishioners. However, it is our duty to use those powers with responsibility and I most strongly submit Kelvin's suggestion as the height of irresponsibility.' Kelvin began to rumble from his seat a few along from the commander, but the latter was not to be intimidated. 'Kelvin wishes Moorcombe to be independent . . .'

Kelvin must have been doing some extensive lobbying during the tea interval as whoops and cheers erupted from many in the audience. The squire banged his fist. 'This is not a bear garden or the House of Commons. We must listen to the arguments or we'll be unable to make a balanced judgement.'

The commander waited patiently. His slightly bloodshot blue eye fixed each person one by one, a technique he had learned in a book, *How to Control Others and Change Your Life.* He started again. 'I was born an Englishman. I live as an Englishman and I intend to die as an Englishman. Kelvin's suggestion would mean that Moorcombe ceased to be an English village and became something entirely different. I shall tell you what some of those implications would be.' His eyes swept his audience. 'Jimmy.' Jimmy, dozily contemplating the digestion of his rich tea biscuits, focused his eyes upon the commander. 'You are a pensioner. Your pension is paid by the government. Percy, your salary is paid by the home office. Many people in Moorcombe receive state benefits – child allowances, family income supplement, housing benefit. All would stop if we were independent. The school is funded by

85

the County Council. It would close. Road maintenance would stop. The post office would close. Customs and immigration control would be set up on the other side of the bridge. Beer prices in the pub would go up to pay import charges . . .'

'Here . . .' began Kelvin.

'Keep quiet till I'm finished,' snapped the commander. 'As I was about to say, we would be vulnerable to invasion as we would no longer be part of NATO. On top of that, we'd need the permission of parliament to become independent which would not be given.' He had his audience. 'Percy, as a policeman, you must be aware that treason is one of the gravest crimes on the statute book. It would be your duty to uphold the law of the land and that would include the suppression of rebellion. Finally, I swore an oath of loyalty to Her Majesty the Queen. An oath which, as an officer and a gentleman, I have every intention of keeping.'

The commander sat down to a roar of comment from the audience. Stuffing a whisky flask back into his pocket, Kelvin was on his feet before anyone else. 'He's right, you know!' he shouted. This unusual support of his own case stilled the uproar. 'Jimmy, you will lose your pension. The school will lose its funding. So will the roads . . .'

'What the hell are you suggesting it for, then, you daft old fool!' shouted Mick.

'I'll tell you why. How much tax do you pay, Mick?'

'Too bloody much!' The café was one of the few businesses in Moorcombe which gave a reasonable living. In summer, the wholesaler replenished the freezer with scones and clotted cream twice a week.

'Right! Too bloody much. We all do. If we went independent, you could tell the Inland Revenue to go to hell. Petrol, beer and fags would halve in price 'cos there wouldn't be any duty or VAT.'

'Come off it, Kelvin!' said the commander. 'We get more in exchange. What about the post office, the school and our pensions?'

Kelvin looked down at the squire, but he did not seem to feel the authority of the chair was threatened by the interruption. Kelvin sniffed his contempt at such bias. 'I'm not a fool, Commander. D'y'not think Pru . . . er . . . I'd've thought it through first? We're all going to be rich. Duty on whisky is a couple of pounds. Would you buy yours in

Puddlewick or Swinehanger if you could buy it here at two quid off? We'd be a duty-free zone. People could come and buy cars, radios, perfume, videos and that kind of thing. You could start up a camera shop in your yard and make a fortune. And you wouldn't need permission from anybody. You, Maud. You'd sell foreign stamps. Moorcombe stamps. You'd get phil . . . philotell . . . stamp collectors wanting them from all over the world. You'd sell a million in your first year. We'd charge all the visitors entry permits to come through Moorcombe which'd pay for the school, pensions and everything. The bridge'd be a toll bridge and all the tourists who wanted to go up to the moor would have to pay us.'

The audience would have made an impartial jury. Having agreed with the commander, the force of Kelvin's argument was beginning to sway them.

The commander jumped to his feet, but Kelvin was not to be stopped.

'Of course, there's a whole other way we can earn money. Sodov said we could be a tax haven for companies. We could offer flags of convenience for the shipping fleets of the world. We'd be like Jersey, the Bahamas, Lichtenstein and Panama all rolled into one.'

The commander was still unconvinced. 'What about electricity, water and that sort of thing?'

'We'd pay our bills like everyone else.'

'How about policing and defence?' asked the squire.

'We've got Percy. His job is to serve the community. The only difference would be that he'd report to us instead of whoever he reports to now. We'd give him a pay rise of course. For defence we'd still have the emergency volunteers.'

'That wouldn't stop the Russians.'

'The British army would stop the Russians.'

'They could always do a parachute invasion.'

'Do you think the British would let Russian warplanes overfly their territory to attack us? Of course not.'

'We could ban them low flying jets,' said Jimmy.

This struck a chord. At any time of day or night, the world could turn into a gigantic strip of Velcro being ripped apart as the RAF practised bombing runs up the valley.

'And we could get some anti-aircraft missiles to make sure they kept away,' agreed Kelvin.

'This is lunacy!' said the commander. 'The government

wouldn't let us. And it's totally unconstitutional to take extraparliamentary action.'

'Unconstitutional or not, it still has to be done,' said Kelvin. 'How do you think countries happen in the first place? It's just like Sodov says. It's up to people to start them up when their existing rulers get out of line. That's how America got made. If the speech is the Declaration of Independence, they'd have to be on our side. Look at the Commonwealth. They were the Empire until they wanted to be Independent. I'm telling you. We'd have the support of virtually every member of the United Nations. You'd make a good ambassador for us there, Squire. That'd be better than just being High Sheriff.'

'Gosh, Kelvin. How exciting!'

'But we couldn't afford it,' said the commander. 'Even if this fantasy came true, it'd be months before our revenue built up and who'd pay the bills meantime? The bank'd call in all their loans so fast, we wouldn't know what'd hit us.'

'I've sorted that one out too,' said Kelvin, a smug look on his face.

'I don't believe you!' said the commander. 'You could be talking thousands. Even hundreds of thousands.'

'Grant aid,' said Kelvin. 'Me and Prudence sorted it out, didn't we?'

'How?'

'We've been given a gift of a million pounds as soon as we're independent.'

As the commander's jaw fell open, the room exploded.

Standing, arms folded, a grim smile playing about his lips, Kelvin watched the inhabitants of Moorcombe pound their knees in their excitement. Looking across at the dazed commander, he winked his triumph.

The commander, red-faced, had to wait to make himself heard. 'A million pounds!' he shouted. 'Bullshit!'

'Commander!' said the squire. 'I can understand your feelings, but I will not tolerate such language. Any repetition and I shall be forced to eject you from this room. I would remind you there are ladies present.'

'Damn right!' said Mandy. 'Chuck the bastard out!'

'Mrs Brown! Unless you're careful, you will go with him!'

'You wouldn't dare!' said Mandy. 'Just you wait and see!'

The squire looked puzzled, so the commander seized the

floor. 'Come on, Kelvin. Tell us who's stupid enough to give you a million pounds!' he sneered.

'It's a gift from the Democratic People's Republic of Bulgaria to the Kingdom of Moorcombe.'

Again the squire was forced to pound his fist upon the scrofulous leather top of his desk while the commander stared at Kelvin in confusion. Eventually order was restored. 'Commander?' prompted the squire.

Heaving a great sigh, the commander warily approached the problem again. 'So Sodov is giving a million. What have you agreed in exchange?'

'Just that we'll establish diplomatic relations with them,' said Kelvin airily. 'I've agreed they can build an embassy and an airstrip on my flat field.'

'They'll never get planning permission to build an embassy!' said the commander. He bit his moustache as he saw Kelvin's triumphant expression. 'All right. You'll be the one who'll be giving permission.'

'Exactly!' said Kelvin.

'But can't you see? Why do you think Sodov's doing this?'

'Because his country supports the democratic rights of people wherever they're under threat. At least that's what he said.'

'And you believe him? Do you honestly think Bulgaria is going to give you all that money without taking one hell of a lot in exchange?'

' 'Course I don't believe him!' said Kelvin. 'What kind of a fool do you think I am? He's interested in the RAF base up the road. He wants to put a dirty great wireless aerial on the roof of the embassy and fill the place with spies.'

'But why are you doing it then?'

'For a million quid, he can spy on whoever he wants for all I care. What's there to hide? If he wants to waste his money listening to those yobbos in their jets telling each other how fast they're going, he's welcome.'

'That's outrageous! The government would never allow it! I know,' said the commander, in response to a grin from Kelvin, 'it's up to us and not the government. But you know damn well the independent state of Moorcombe could be re-conquered by Percy and a couple of his colleagues in a squad car!'

'They'd face huge international pressure and a vote of

condemnation in the United Nations. Anyway, Sodov said he'd ask me over to Bulgaria for a state visit in order to sign a Treaty of Eternal Friendship. It should be a good holiday. Once I get back and clear his cheques through the bank, we'll tell him to get stuffed and break the treaty. That's what's so nice about making deals if you're a government. You never have to be honourable or keep your word.'

'You don't have to be a government if your name's Kelvin Morchard!' said Bill, experienced in dealing with the master of Northcott.

'And,' contributed Malcolm, 'by using the American Declaration of Independence, I'm sure the Yanks'd give us another million, especially if we broke off diplomatic relations with the Bulgarians. We could do very well indeed.'

'Huh!' said the commander. 'And what's all this about the Kingdom of Moorcombe? I'm damn sure you won't be able to go independent and expect the Queen to want to be head of state.'

'We'll have our income from duty-free sales and financial services, but there's tourism, too,' said Kelvin. 'We've got to think of people like Mick and Beryl who make their living from it. There's nothing like having our own royal family to bring in the tourists, so we'll have our own queen.'

The commander snorted. 'Her Majesty Queen Mandy the First, I suppose?'

'And what do you mean by that?' snapped Mandy.

'I'm just trying to show how ridiculous the whole thing is,' said the commander.

'There's nothing ridiculous about it at all!'

The audience was quiet.

'You mean you are to be Queen Mandy?' said the commander. 'Keith the king and you his consort?'

'Other way round,' said Mandy. 'It's me who's of the Blood Royal. He's just my husband.'

'I want to be ambassador to Washington,' said Jimmy. 'I want to meet some bimbos.'

'Stop it,' said the bewildered commander. 'Let's try to retain some shreds of sanity. Why choose Mandy, Kelvin?'

'I'll answer that,' said Mandy. She rose to her feet. 'I am the rightful occupant of the throne of England.'

'Oh God,' said the commander sadly. 'I think I'll call it a day. I don't see any point in going on with this conversation.'

Walking slowly back to his seat, he slumped down, his hands slack on his lap.

'You can't give up,' said the squire with alarm. 'Somebody's got to put the opposing argument.'

'Well it's not going to be me,' said the commander. 'Not any more.'

'Right,' said Kelvin. 'This gets us to the nitty-gritty of the whole thing. It was Mandy that gave me the idea. Her middle name, remember? Plantagenet. That's what she signed on the document and it's what the old kings and queens were called.'

'How the hell did you know that?' asked Jimmy.

'It's part of the common knowledge of an educated man,' replied Kelvin. 'Malcolm pointed it out.'

'He looked into my family tree,' said Mandy. 'And it turns out I'm descended from Edward IV.' After rummaging around in her capacious handbag, she pulled out a sheet of paper. 'He was my great-great-great-great-great-great-great-great-great-great . . .'

Jimmy shifted on the chair beside her.

'Sit still!'

Jimmy stilled.

'Great-great-great-great-great-great-great-great-great-great-granduncle. Isn't that right, Malcolm?'

'Yes,' said Malcolm.

'So you see. I should be queen. The Lancastrians wrested the throne from my ancestor and their successors have been illegally occupying it ever since.'

'That's right,' said Kelvin. 'So you see it won't be us who'll really be doing high treason like the commander said, but the rest of the country. They'll be in rebellion against their rightful ruler.'

Taking a large, red cotton handkerchief from his pocket, the squire dabbed his brow. 'I think I'd better give up the chair,' he said. 'I'm afraid I'm not feeling too well.'

'I can imagine,' said the commander grimly. 'But you might as well stay till the end.'

Kelvin stood up again. He clapped his horny hands together. 'Right!' he said briskly. 'I'll outline our system of government. I'd like to thank Malcolm for helping me draw it up.'

'Blasted pinko troublemaking teacher,' muttered the squire

91

in an uncharacteristic outburst of political and personal invective.

Kelvin affected not to hear. 'We're going to be a constitutional monarchy with Mandy as queen. The Parish Council will act as her parliament although we'll call fresh elections as soon as practicable after independence day.'

'Who's going to be Prime Minister?' asked Jimmy.

'I'm chairman of the council, so it's only right it's me.'

'Who's in charge of the money?' asked Keith.

'Me and Malcolm,' said Kelvin. 'He'll be Chancellor of the Exchequer and, as Prime Minister, I'm also First Lord of the Treasury.'

'I think the squire should be in charge of the money,' said Bill. 'He should be the king, too.'

'Heaven forbid!' said the squire fervently.

'He can't be king if Mandy's the queen,' pointed out Kelvin. 'Don't be silly. Both he and Mandy are already married. He's going to be the House of Lords and Foreign Secretary and Chief Justice. We'll have to do up the manor and pay for its upkeep out of the public purse, of course.'

'Did I understand you right?' asked the squire. 'You're going to repair the manor?'

'Of course,' said Kelvin. 'You'll have to do trials and things here and it's important that the dignity of the law should be upheld.'

'It'll cost a fortune,' said the squire. 'There's extensive dry rot, you know.'

'Not to worry,' said Kelvin. 'After the church, the manor's our most important ancient monument. We have to respect our traditions. I've earmarked £100,000 for the first year to look after it.'

'£100,000!'

'P'raps a bit more,' said Kelvin, looking round at the walls. 'This room could do with a lick of paint. We'll make it a couple of hundred thousand. Then you'll be able to buy a judge's wig, too.'

'Well,' said the squire. 'I must say that's a most generous offer.'

Percy rose to his feet with a frown on his face. 'I think the time has come, Kelvin, when we stop . . .'

'Ah, Percy! We've got you down to be Home Secretary and head of the police.'

'Me? I don't know,' said Percy. 'I don't think the inspector'll think it's a good idea.'

'Your duty is to the law, Percy, and not to your inspector. If our parliament changes the law, then you have to uphold it. I was thinking £20,000 a year might be fair if you're going to be Home Secretary.'

'If I was to be Chief Constable too, I'd need a bit more than that.'

'No problem. The sooner you order a new uniform, the better. In fact after we've voted, anyone who wants a job with our administration can come and see me.'

'Or me,' said Mandy. 'I'm queen, Kelvin, remember?'

'Of course. But you're just a figurehead. It's me that's got the power.'

'Huh!' said Mandy. 'Let's vote, anyway.'

'I protest!' said the commander. 'I was born a Briton and I'll die a Briton.'

'You can't be. If you stay here, you automatically become a citizen when we declare independence,' said Kelvin. 'I suppose you might be able to get dual nationality. Then you can be the British Ambassador!'

'A very good idea, Kelvin,' said the squire. 'This is a historic moment. I call upon Kelvin to propose the motion once more.'

'I propose Moorcombe dissolves its ties with the British Crown and Government to take its place amongst the world community of free and independent nations.'

'Who will second?'

Hands were raised throughout the room.

'All those in favour?'

'All those against?' Only the commander raised his hand.

'Passed unanimously!' said the squire.

'I was against!' said the commander.

'You're English, not a Moorcomber,' said Kelvin. 'And foreigners don't have a vote.'

Chapter Six

'IT IS ALL very confusing,' said Helga, the blonde licensee of the Hunted Hind, who was proof that mutton had no need to dress as lamb in order to look very tasty indeed.

'What do you mean?' asked Kelvin.

After the momentous vote at the manor, most people had gone home. Even if the country in which their cows and sheep lived was no longer Great Britain, they still needed to be milked and fed.

'I was born in Rumania, then I became British and now I do not know what I am. Is it a Moorcomber?'

'Yes,' said Kelvin. 'That's what you are. And you can drop your prices, too. We won't be charging excise duty on beer, you see.'

'Until the brewery drops his prices to me, you'll pay the same as always, Kelvin.'

'Well, don't order anything else until you've had a word with me.'

'What are you going to do now?' asked the commander. He had downed a couple of barley wines and was now beginning to relax a little under the influence of his third.

'What do you mean?'

'There's not much point in declaring yourself independent if you don't tell anyone about it.'

'That's very true,' said Kelvin. 'I think we'd better send a letter to the clerk of the District Council and he'll be able to pass the word on. We can give them a few days and, if they don't reply, we can just go ahead on our own and put up a customs barrier down at the bridge.'

'Drink up,' said Helga. 'I have to close in a minute. Otherwise that unpleasant policeman'll be trying to arrest me.'

Kelvin smiled. 'Don't you worry about a thing. You're not subject to English licensing laws anymore.'

'Is that so? And when did they stop applying?'

'I don't rightly know,' said Kelvin. 'When do you think the actual moment of independence was, Malcolm?'

'Interesting point, Kelvin,' said Malcolm, leaning forward on the bar. He was on a stool, the one usually occupied by Mick. He had not yet achieved the longevity in Moorcombe which would entitle him to a stool by right. Promotion was through dead men's bums, and Jimmy obstinately refused to join his peers in the churchyard which would have released the patriarch's windsor chair for Kelvin and thus free a stool for Malcolm. 'I suppose it must've been when the motion was carried.'

'No,' said the commander. 'There'll have to be a formality of some kind. An order signed by the Queen in Council, or something.'

'We could have an independence ceremony!' said Kelvin. 'Get Princess Di down to cut a ribbon on the bridge and lower the flag at sunset on the common. We could run a generator so's Mandy could play the *Last Post* and the *National Anthem* on her organ.'

'This is all very well, but if the licensing laws don't apply anymore, what time do I close?' asked Helga.

'What?' Kelvin had moved on to more important considerations.

'The opening times.'

'Ah! Well you see now we're independent, we can make our own.'

'That can't be right,' said the commander.

'Of course it is!' said Kelvin. 'The Parish Council is now the law maker for Moorcombe and we haven't made any laws yet.'

'Does that mean there aren't any laws, then?'

'How can there be if we haven't made any?'

'In that case I'll go and steal your tractor and you can't do anything about it.'

'Hm,' said Kelvin, rubbing his chin. 'I see what you mean. Course I'd come at you with my shotgun if you tried it. Perhaps we'd better make me the law.'

'I thought Percy was going to be the law.'

'Yes, but someone has to tell him what to do.'

'We're not going to let you be a dictator.'

'I don't see why not. I'd make a damn good dictator.'

'Remember Mandy is Head of State. She can dismiss the Prime Minister.'

'Like hell she can! This is my idea and my revolution.'

'If the people don't want you, they can get rid of you.'

'No chance!'

'We could organise a military coup to get rid of you when you get out of hand.'

'You'd have a job,' said Kelvin. 'As leader of the Emergency Volunteers, I run the army too.'

'I think we'd better enact a bill which makes all laws passed by Westminster our law unless we say otherwise,' suggested Malcolm.

'That'd be quite good. It'd mean Percy would be able to carry on enforcing the same sort of laws. We'd have to make a list of what we want to change.'

'All the finance bills, for a start.'

'The licensing laws, the planning laws, the laws of trespass . . .'

'What's wrong with them?' asked the commander.

'I've never liked every Tom, Dick or Harry wandering over my land. I'm going to make it a criminal offence. An instant fine of £500 which'll go to the landowner and jail after that. Hard labour which'll mean stone picking on one of my fields.'

'That'll cause trouble.'

'Tough.' Kelvin turned to Malcolm. 'By the way, I had a word with them hippies up at the commune. They'll give us full support if we legalise cannabis.'

'We can't do that!'

'We can do what we want. As far as I'm concerned they can smoke their reefers all day. They do it anyway and I said we'd tax them on it.' The door to the bar suddenly shuddered as some heavy weight crashed into it. Those at the bar turned to look with interest.

'You have to lift the latch!' called Malcolm.

A short pause, then the latch clicked open and Sergeant Parrott burst into the bar. 'Got you, you bastards! Drinking after hours.' Straightening from the defensive crouch he had adopted on entry, he made his way to the bar. 'Oh dearie me,' he said, surveying the commander's barley wine and the full beer glasses of the others. 'You are in a spot of bother. You should've been more careful with Frankie Parrott interested in your hide.' He looked across at Helga. 'You'll be closed down for a start, darling, and as for you lot . . .' He examined the patrons. 'You worzels are all under arrest.'

'Piss off,' said Kelvin contemptuously.

'Ah!' Clapping a hand to his belly, Parrott staggered back. 'Assaulting a police officer in the course of his duty.'

Kelvin frowned. 'What's he talking about?'

'He means he's going to say you hit him in the stomach,' explained Malcolm, taking a sip from his glass.

Kelvin turned to him in amazement. 'But I didn't! And you lot are all witnesses that I didn't.'

'Who d'you think the magistrate's going to believe?' jeered Parrott. 'A bunch like you caught red-handed in the commission of an offence? Or a sergeant of the Metropolitan police and your constable what's-is-name who'll say just what I tell him to in the witness box. If he wants to keep his job.'

'Percy's not here,' said Kelvin. 'How could he be a witness?'

'How you've managed to survive so long in this cruel world beats me,' said Parrott. 'Anyway, you're all nicked and you can stop drinking too.'

Jimmy took a pull from his glass. 'You do know the squire's on the bench here and he's known us all his life and you not at all? He'll believe any of us rather than you. Except Kelvin, perhaps. He might not believe Kelvin.'

'We'll see about that. Where's that Sodov?'

'Mind your own business,' said Kelvin. 'Prudence said it would be better if it wasn't generally known he was staying with us.'

'He got some lovely photos of the aeroplanes yesterday,' said Jimmy.

'He's going to be expelled from the country. Declared *persona non grata* and we'll have a team from the Customs and Excise and the Inland Revenue coming within the week to start teaching this village what life's all about. But you lot'll all be in court so it'll be your women who'll have all the awkward questions to answer.'

With a sigh, the commander drained his barley wine. 'You really are the most appalling fellow, Sergeant.'

'Watch your lip, Pugwash. Come on everybody out of here.'

'Fill me up, Helga.' The commander slid his glass across the bar.

Jimmy chuckled.

'You fill the glass up and I'll do you for obstruction,' said Parrott.

Helga looked at the commander. The latter nodded. Taking a bottle, she flipped off the top and passed it across the bar.

'Bloody hell!' said Parrott, starting forward, but he paused as the door creaked open and Mandy swept beneath the lintel with Keith, as usual, a few submissive yards behind.

Taking in the scene, she swept up to the bar, elbowing the startled Parrott out of the way. 'Stand up, you lot,' she snapped.

'What?' said Kelvin.

'Stand up when I come into the bar. You know who I am.'

'Oh yes. Sorry.' Even Jimmy creaked to his feet.

Helga frowned. 'I don't think I've been told who you are, Mandy.'

'Queen Mandy,' corrected Keith. 'Or your majesty.'

'That's wonderful!' cried Helga. 'I'm so pleased for you. How did you come to be chosen, your majesty?'

'By right. I am the rightful Queen of England. I'll have a brandy and passion fruit.'

'Here!' shouted Parrott. 'You silly old bag. You're under arrest, too.'

Mandy locked at him as if he'd been an incontinent corgi. 'Old? How dare you! Why are you still here? I banish you from my realms and dominions. Just bugger off!'

Parrott still did not realise he was on a losing wicket. Feeling in the pocket of his red nylon anorak and producing a pair of plastic handcuffs, he started towards her. Her eyes bulged with outraged fury but, before she could bring home to Parrott the error of his ways, the pub door ran through its tympanic repertoire once more and Percy entered.

'Ah!' said Parrott. 'Reinforcements.' He paused. 'What the hell are you wearing that for?'

As well as his uniform, Percy was wearing an army Sam Browne belt with polished brown holster from which protruded the butt of a large revolver. 'It's all right,' said Kelvin. 'I gave him permission. You always wanted to carry a pistol, didn't you, Percy?'

'Yes,' said Percy, gesturing to his belt. 'This used to be my

dad's. He was a policeman in the war and always wore it then. He used to let me play with it when he came off duty. He always took the bullets out first.'

'What's all this?' asked Parrott. 'Are you authorised to carry a firearm?'

'Yes,' said Kelvin. 'I've just told you. There's something else you ought to know too . . .'

'Shut your trap, you,' said Parrott. 'You . . . Constable. Help me book this lot.'

'Look . . .' began Kelvin.

'No, my son. You look. When Frankie Parrott tells you to shut your trap, it's safer to do as you're told. You're already being done for assaulting a police officer . . .'

'Percy . . .' Mandy brought her glass down on the elm counter with a sharp crack.

'Yes ma'am?'

'Get him out of here. He's becoming boring. See him and his car to the other side of the river and make sure he doesn't come back.'

'Yes, your majesty,' said Percy, touching his forehead with a finger. Turning to his erstwhile colleague, he put a hand on his arm. 'Come on, Mr Parrott. I'm afraid I must ask you to leave.'

Angrily, Parrott snatched his arm away. 'What're you doing?'

'I'm telling you to leave. I'm sorry, but I'm not a constable. I'm Chief Constable Green of the Moorcombe National Police Department. I'd be obliged if you'd put away those cuffs, sir. Otherwise I shall have to confiscate them.'

Parrott shook his head in bewilderment. 'Have you been at the scrumpy? Give me that firearm.'

'Mr Parrott,' said the commander. 'I'd better explain what's going on here.'

'Flagrant breaches of the law and probable mass insanity.'

'That's one interpretation,' agreed the commander.

'We've gone and made ourselves independent,' said Kelvin, proudly.

'And I'm the new queen,' said Mandy.

'Crikey! And you're the Prime Minister, I suppose?'

'That's right,' said Kelvin.

'And what are you, Admiral?'

'I intend to retain my British citizenship.'

'He's going to be their ambassador,' explained Kelvin.

Parrott put his handcuffs on the bar. 'Gimme a large scotch, darling.' He turned back to Kelvin. 'And what makes you think you can get away with this?'

'It's the right of free people to determine their own future,' said Kelvin.

'Not if you've got a wife, a boss and a mortgage,' said Parrott.

'And it so happens Mandy is the rightful occupant of the throne of Britain, but she's agreed not to claim it unless we're given any hassle.'

'Is that right?' Parrott accepted his drink and turned to Mandy, looking at her from head to toe. Wearing a long magenta skirt, split to the thigh, her scarlet satin blouse had spirals of sequins sewn over each breast. 'There's not much of a family likeness.'

'Our branch of the family is much older,' said Mandy. 'We're Plantagenets.'

'And you've rewritten the licensing laws?'

'You're a smart boy,' said Kelvin.

'You haven't done this just so's you can get a late drink?'

101

'No. It's more complicated than that. It's to do with a planning problem and all this fuss about twinning with Botograd on Vit.' Parrott looked blank. 'That's what Mr Sodov's down for, although I must admit he's also been very helpful in advising about our independence.'

'Mr bloody Sodov is down here to breach sections four and five of the Official Secrets Act.'

'No, he ain't,' contradicted Kelvin. 'We don't have an Official Secrets Act yet in Moorcombe. He's down here to give us a million quid. I think it's quid.'

The bar was hushed.

'I don't think you should've said that,' said the commander.

'A mill!' Parrott's eyes sparkled. 'And what do you have to do for that?'

'It's foreign aid. A gesture of solidarity between our peoples.'

'Well . . .' Parrott drained his drink. 'This is all very interesting but I think I'd better get on my way. Sodov's at your farm, you say?'

'You know what he's going to do,' said Malcolm. 'He's going to go and arrest Sodov and then come back with a van load of his chums and make a thorough nuisance of himself.'

'Guard the door, Percy,' said Kelvin. Percy moved casually into place, his hand unbuttoning the flap over the butt of his gun.

Parrott looked and laughed.

'I reckon he might keep his mouth shut for a few thousand pounds,' continued Kelvin. 'But I don't see why we should give any of our money to outsiders. Once we've organised a customs barrier in the middle of the bridge, he can do what he likes, but until then I think we'd better keep him under arrest.'

Parrott laughed again, so Jason Loosemire, winner of the welly throwing at the annual village sports day since he was fifteen, moved alongside Percy and looked menacing. Percy shot him a surprised but appreciative glance. Just emerging from his misspent youth, Jason usually met Percy over the carcass of a poached deer or pheasant, across the bonnet of a joy-ridden motorcar or in the midst of a fracas after the pub had closed or the disco was over. But, captivated by the gamine qualities of Sharon Bladderwick, he was proving again that the love of a good woman, fairly good anyway, could redeem the most hardened young recidivist.

'I thought the cellars at the manor would make the best jail.'

Malcolm and the commander exchanged an uneasy glance. 'I don't think it would be wise to lock him up,' said Malcolm. 'It's all very well declaring ourselves independent, but I'm not sure it would be a good idea if our first act was to lock up a policeman.'

'Needs must be,' said Kelvin briskly. 'What do you think, your majesty?'

'I'm not sure either . . .'

'Aren't you? That's a pity. It doesn't matter what you think really 'cos you're just symbolic but it'd be nice if you agreed with me. Sodov thinks we ought to abolish the monarchy, him being a Communist. I haven't made up my mind myself.'

'Keith! Get me another brandy and passion fruit,' said Mandy.

Having put aside his handcuffs, Parrott had ordered himself another whisky. 'Have it on me, love. It'll be on expenses.'

'Thank you,' said Mandy, accepting the first of the gifts and tributes which would shortly pour in from foreign potentates and grateful subjects.

'You buying?' said Kelvin.

'Not for you, chum.'

'How about me?' asked Jimmy, pushing his empty glass across the bar.

Parrott considered briefly. 'Yes, I don't see why not.'

'Why won't you buy me one?' demanded Kelvin.

'You've just put me under arrest.'

'Hmph! I don't see what that has got to do with it.'

'That's because you're a stupid man.'

'Bread and water,' said Kelvin. 'And the cellars of the manor are swarming with rats.'

'If I took you at all seriously, I'd ask to phone my solicitor.'

'That's a good point,' said the commander.

'It's a lousy point. He'd have to use a lawyer licensed to practise in Moorcombe and there aren't any.'

'I suppose habeas corpus doesn't exist either?'

'Certainly not!' said Kelvin emphatically. 'We've never gone in for that sort of thing round here.'

'You know you really should've got your act worked out

before you went independent,' said Parrott. 'Here am I, a trained police officer, karate expert, with a .38 revolver under my jacket, and I'm arrested without any charge and have no recourse to the law for protection.'

'It's a hard life,' said Kelvin. 'You can't be much use as a copper, though. You've just told us you're carrying a gun.'

'Oh Christ!' Parrott slapped his forehead. 'You trapped me into letting it slip out.'

'We're just too smart for you,' said Kelvin complacently. 'Percy, take his gun away. You should have searched him when he was arrested.'

'I wouldn't do anything silly,' said Parrott calmly as Percy began to haul out his pistol.

Percy paused. 'Hand over your firearm.'

'No.'

'Oh.'

'Shall I take it off him?' asked Jason, stepping eagerly forward.

Jimmy shook his head sadly. 'Loosemire's always were a bit dim.'

'You stay where you are, Jason,' said Percy. 'We don't want any trouble.'

'Come on, Percy,' said Kelvin. 'Do your duty. I order you to confiscate his weapon.'

Looking over at Parrott, Percy sucked his teeth reflectively. 'I resign my new job.'

Jimmy tittered. 'D'you remember, Kelvin, how you always like to tell us how you disarmed Gilbert Snow when he was drunk and waving around his gun?'

'Yes,' he said, with a curl to his lip. 'These two aren't man enough.'

Jimmy tittered again. 'You do it, Kelvin. Show us all how brave you are.'

'Yes,' said Percy. 'You do it, Kelvin.'

'I only wish I could,' said Kelvin. 'But I'm the Prime Minister. And it'd be downright irresponsible and unpatriotic if I followed my natural inclination and took risks.'

'It's all right, Kelvin,' said Mandy. 'I release you from your obligation. I could easily find a new Prime Minister. Keith would be very good.'

'Hear, hear, your majesty,' said Jimmy.

'I might even make you a Duke,' continued Mandy.

Kelvin brightened.

'Posthumously.'

'What'd be the good of that?' asked Kelvin scornfully. 'No, I think it'd be best if we let him keep his gun. He could never use it. It'd create a major diplomatic incident if he did. It could even be considered an act of war. And junior policemen are not encouraged to embroil the country in foreign wars.'

'I'll tell you what,' said Parrott. 'I'll give you my parole.'

'What does that mean?'

'I promise not to escape for . . . oh, say two days.'

'What makes you think we could trust you?' asked Percy.

'I'm a police officer.'

'You're a bloody funny sort of police officer. You've threatened, blackmailed, insulted half the community since you've been down here, and you dress like a football hooligan,' said Kelvin. 'That anorak! Who ever saw such a thing on a bobby? And proper policemen wear boots, not those trainer things. You'll be off to the authorities as soon as we let you out the door.'

'I might do rather well here, if I stick around. So far we've got resisting arrest, assaulting a police officer, wrongful arrest, wrongful imprisonment, possession of a firearm in a public place, threatening behaviour, conspiracy, various breaches of the Official Secrets Act, treason, high treason and drinking after hours. I'll get promotion out of this and maybe even a transfer to the vice squad. A smart policeman can make a good living on the vice squad.' He gestured to Helga to refill his glass. 'And then there's talk of a million quid. That's a lot of money for guys like you to look after. What the hell makes you think you're going to get rid of me? Especially with a couple of crackers like those two.' He nodded towards Mandy and Helga.

Mandy smiled at him. 'If Kelvin can have Sodov as an adviser, I can have one too. I'll be needing a bodyguard. You look and sound as if you know how to handle yourself. I'd be willing to give you a trial for the job.'

'You're on, darling. Undercover work, I call it. It's a deal.'

'You have to swear the vote of allegiance.'

'Certainly not!'

'Swear!' said Mandy.

'Swear!' said Keith.

'Swear!' agreed Kelvin and Jimmy.

105

'Shit!' said Parrott. 'I've already had to swear an oath of allegiance when I first went into the force. To the Queen, I think.'

'We're not asking anything different,' said Kelvin. 'If you've done it already, I don't see what your problem is in doing it again.'

'Oh, all right,' said Parrott on whom the double scotches were having an almost instantaneous effect. 'It's all in the course of duty.'

In the dim brown lighting created by the flickering candle-effect bulbs and the nicotine encrusted forty-watters round the wall, the ancient ceremony of fealty was enacted. With some prompting, Parrott knelt on one knee before his queen. As the stern faces of the natives looked on in grim approval, she proffered a pudgy hand, fingers heavy with diamonds – 'Even

106

a jeweller can hardly tell the difference!' – and Parrott gently touched her finger tips to his lips.

'I swear,' said Mandy.

'I swear.'

'– to serve the body and person of Mandy, my queen . . .'

'– to serve the body and person of Mandy, my queen . . .'

'– with all my might and all my manhood . . .'

'– with all my might and all my manhood . . .' Parrott looked speculatively at the mottled fleshy block of Mandy's thigh visible through the slit in her skirt a few inches in front of his eyes.

'– till death do us part.'

'– till death do us part.'

'Amen,' intoned Kelvin.

Chapter Seven

THERE WAS a knock at the front door.

Leaning against the Aga in the kitchen in his vest and long johns watching his early morning tea bag brew, Kelvin started.

With flagstoned floor and black oak beams across the ceiling, studded with wicked hooks, used to hang joints of bacon or maturing poultry and venison, the bleak wood-smoked room had a deep china sink with a single brass tap in one corner. At the pine table, spooning pork and apple sauce into Brett on his high chair, with one hand, Prudence was scanning the pages of a two-day old copy of *The Guardian*. Her other hand held a feeding bottle towards a cardboard box from which protruded a piglet whose lusty enthusiasm for breakfast was spraying the table top with milk.

'Who could that be?' asked Kelvin. His thinning grey hair stood up in chestnut-like spikes, his chin was stippled by Desperate Dan stubble and the fishbelly skin on his flabby arms and torso abruptly stopped at the weather-beaten brown of his neck and the grimy grey of his wrists and hands which rarely encountered soap and water or a nail brush.

'It's probably Boris. Go and find out,' said Prudence.

'I can't. I'm not properly dressed. It won't be Sodov anyway 'cos he'll still be in bed.'

Prudence lifted her head from the paper. 'In that case go and find out who it is.'

'You go,' said Kelvin. 'It might be important and, with me being Prime Minister, I have to look respectable 'cos I've the good name of Moorcombe to consider as well as my own.'

'Your good name!' snorted Prudence.

'I had a good name until you disgraced it with that little bastard.'

The little bastard pounded his tray and crowed his delight at the taste of his breakfast. Brett had become a fat cheerful child with a cast in one eye, a thatch of brown hair and a lantern jaw which stamped him as his grandfather's grandson. In Prudence's case, the jaw gene had alarmingly inverted to produce a profile that would be a hangman's nightmare.

The rapper rapped once more.

'Answer it, you lazy old goat!'

'You do it.'

'I've milked the cows, checked the ewes and I'm still a bit busy.'

'You haven't cooked me any breakfast, yet.'

'I'm not going to either!'

The pounder pounded. 'Kelvin!'

'That's Father Loosemire,' said Kelvin. 'It must be a registered letter. It won't be a summons 'cos they usually come by second post.'

'Well, go and get it! He won't mind what you look like.'

Grumbling, Kelvin crabbed his way through the kitchen door and into the hall. 'All right! I'm coming!' Turning the handle of the front door which scraped open against the stone floor, he peered out suspiciously.

'Bloody hell, Kelvin! What a horrible sight!' exclaimed Father Loosemire, stepping back from the porch. The Loosemires had been in Moorcombe almost as long as the Morchards, occupying, over the past few centuries, a social substratum of their own. They had been flogged, transported, clapped in the poorhouse, turfed from their hovels, fined and jailed, but the family had stubbornly survived with a bit of potato-picking here and a bit of poaching there.

Father Loosemire, the postman, and his elder brother Fred, had been their clan's last representatives until Fred had bedded and married a stout girl from Puddlewick of remarkable fecundity. A decade later Fred had died under the wheels of a milk tanker but his brother had moved in with the bereaved widow who continued to produce children. Now Mrs Loosemire's offspring were breeding in their turn and the family occupied several caravans as well as the three village council houses. A slight man, Father Loosemire's most prominent characteristic was a glossy brown wig, so startlingly bad that he was famed as much for that as the amount he received in state benefits.

'What do you want?' asked Kelvin with a scowl. Looking warily at Kelvin, the postman held out a letter. 'What's that? It's nothing legal, is it?'

'No, it's from Mandy. I've been made the Queen's Messenger.'

'Have you now?' said Kelvin, stretching out his arm to take the document. 'She's got no right to make any appointments without clearing them with me first.'

'I'm her messenger, not yours. I wouldn't want to be yours anyway.'

'Why can't she use the phone?' grumbled Kelvin. 'Or she could see me in the pub at lunchtime.'

'Don't ask me,' said Loosemire. 'Are you going to open it?'

'Not in front of you, I'm not. Communications between the Monarch and her Prime Minister are secret.'

'I've got quite a lot of these to deliver. I got one myself.'

'In that case you'll know already what it is.' Kelvin tried to slam the door in the postman's face, but the effect was spoiled as the door caught a raised flag before it was half shut.

'Don't you want the rest of your mail? There's another of

these letters from Mandy for Sodov. You've a final demand from the feed merchant and Prudence's got a letter from the book club.'

'Shove them through the letter box,' said Kelvin, putting his shoulder to the door. 'That's what it's for.'

'What was it?' asked Prudence as he re-entered the kitchen. The piglet had drained the bottle and was now lying in digestive sleep in its box on top of the Aga.

'It's a letter from Mandy,' said Kelvin, wandering towards the table. 'Have you seen my glasses?'

'Is that all the post?'

'No, there was something for you. From the book club.'

'Where is it?'

'On the floor by the letter box, I suppose. Where're my glasses?'

'Why didn't you bring it to me?' Prudence sighed. 'Give me the letter, Dad. I'll read it for you.' She held out her hand.

'No!' said Kelvin, hiding the letter behind his back. 'It's my private mail. Have you hidden my glasses?'

'You usually leave them by your bed.'

'Huh!' Kelvin clumped up the narrow wooden stairs in the corner of the kitchen leading up to the floors above.

'Old goat,' said Brett, precocious in both speech and perception.

'Now, now, dear. That's very rude,' said Prudence, with an absent look before plunging into the correspondence columns.

'Old goat, old goat, old goat!' shouted Brett, banging his bowl on the table. Some of its contents slopped over the edge to slither between the grey pine planks of the table top and drip sullenly to the floor.

Brandishing his specs, Kelvin came back into the kitchen. 'I've found them!'

'Oh good,' said Prudence, her eyes on the paper. She poked the spoon towards Brett's food.

'Old goat,' said Brett.

Kelvin scowled. 'You watch your step, you little bastard!' He shook his fist at the child.

'Leave him alone, Dad! You'll frighten him.'

Indeed Brett did screw up his chubby cheeks in the preliminaries of a wail but decided instead to take the spoon from his mother and flick its contents towards Kelvin. The latter was already examining his missive with the care he might bestow on a letter bomb and failed to notice the missile drop short at the base of a milk bottle.

'Huh!' grunted Kelvin. 'She's gone and written OHMS – that means On Her Majesty's Service – on the envelope in red ink. It's addressed to Mr Kelvin Morchard esquire and escort.' Ripping open the envelope with a calloused thumb, he pulled out a silver-edged square of pasteboard. A low rumble came from his throat as he carefully deciphered the script. His bushy eyebrows shot up. 'Do you know what this is?'

Prudence lifted patient eyes from the paper. 'It's a letter from Mandy, you said.'

'No. Yes. I mean it's not a letter, it's an invitation. It's an At Home. Listen to this. "Mandy and Keith, 'Pixies Laughter', Moorcombe, have much pleasure in inviting you to an At Home to celebrate" – all that bit's printed – "the coronation of Queen Mandy at 2.30pm. RSVP." And at the bottom she's written "NB. This is a Royal Command. It's today." '

'Bum!' shrieked Brett, bouncing up and down.

'I think it's a bit of a liberty to make it a royal command. Especially to me.'

'It is her government and you are her Prime Minister.'

'Even so. I suppose you're going to have to be my escort.'

'I can't. I've got half a dozen late ewes that look as if they're about to drop their lambs. Take Sodov instead.'

'For heaven's sake, daughter! This is an afternoon you'll remember all your life. It's a rare privilege to attend a coronation, especially this one when we're crowning a brand new monarch for a brand new country.'

'All kings and queens are brand new when they're crowned.'

'True.'

'And if I go with you, who's going to look after the ewes? They could get into trouble and we could lose a lamb. D'you think going to one of Mandy's parties is worth it?'

'Hmm. It's a very special party. I could go with Sodov. He's got an invitation too.'

'You go with him, Dad. I've got Brett to look after. I'll write her a note.'

'Note!' shouted Brett. 'Goat! Old goat!'

Kelvin looked at him with distaste. 'Can't you do something about him? If you talked to me like that when you were his age, I'd've thrashed you and you'd've spent the rest of the

112

day locked in with the pigs. He's old enough to learn discipline and manners.'

'We've talked about this before, Dad. You lay a finger on Brett and I'll kick you out and you can go and live in the pub. You spend most of your time there anyway.'

'You can't kick me out. It's my house.' He took the tea-bag from his cup and, adding two dessert spoons of sugar, he swirled the liquid for thirty seconds before removing the spoon and depositing it on the table. He sipped and smacked his lips. 'Anyway, I can't sit round all day just to amuse you. I'd better work out what to wear. 'Tin't every day there's a coronation. What're you going to do?'

'Take Brett to playschool, check the ewes again and I want to put fertiliser on the fifteen-acre field for silage.'

'I keep telling you, you should've stuck to making hay.'

'Yes, Dad.'

'It's just you're too idle to turn it and bale it.'

'Yes, Dad.'

'Hmph!' Kelvin looked suspiciously at his daughter, but she had re-immersed herself in the newspaper. Brett stuck out his tongue. Kelvin returned the compliment with the added, devastating refinement of projecting his top teeth on the end of his tongue.

Brett's face crumpled. 'Yech!' he said. 'Old goat!'

Kelvin smiled. Victory was his as Brett had yet to evolve a defence to his teeth-tongue gambit. 'Well, I suppose I'd better go and try to find a clean shirt and give Sodov a kick.' He heaved himself up from the bench. 'Did you clean my boots?'

'Which pair?'

'My good boots.'

'No. I haven't cleaned any boots.'

Kelvin shot an exasperated look. 'Why did you ask which pair if you haven't cleaned any of them?'

'How am I supposed to know which pair you were asking about?'

'But . . . oh, never mind. I'll have to do it for myself as usual.' He stumped off up the stairs.

'Old goat,' said Brett, but the enthusiasm had gone out of the words, now his grandfather had gone.

Father Loosemire having done his job, the Hunted Hind was

packed at lunchtime. From far-flung farms on the edge of the parish and remote cottages in outlying districts, an hour's travel on foot from the capital, the nation's citizens came to pay homage to their monarch. The trouble was nobody quite knew what to expect.

'Was this your idea, Kelvin?' asked Mary Mowbray who, with her husband, ran several hundred sheep on the fringes of the moor.

'Don't know nothing about it,' said Kelvin, an unaccustomed collar and tie already sawing a fiery band across the back of his neck.

'Has she any right to do it?' continued Mary. Red in the face, broad in the beam, she was usually found either on or round a horse. 'I mean it's all very well going independent, but we don't want it to take up too much of our time. The hunt doesn't meet today, but it could well've done.'

'The price of freedom is never cheap,' said Kelvin.

'It's eternal vigilance,' said Sodov.

'What?' asked Kelvin.

'Eternal vigilance,' repeated Sodov. 'That's the price of freedom.'

'How have you got on over the last day or two?' asked the commander.

'Very favourably,' said Sodov. Wearing a neat grey suit with a single medal, a red-ribboned star, pinned to his breast pocket, he was drinking a half pint of beer, dabbing his lips dry with a white handkerchief between each sip. 'I have taken many photographs of English aeroplanes.'

'Any trouble?'

'No. Since Sergeant Parrott has the duty of following me, he drove myself and Jimmy to the airfield. He was able to show his identification when I was interrupted trying to examine an aircraft too closely.'

'He was trying to remove some kind of computer from the cockpit of a Harrier,' explained Parrott. 'I'm not surprised they got a bit twitchy. If it hadn't been for me, your feet wouldn't've touched the ground until you'd hit Sofia.'

'We don't go in for hitting women round here,' said Kelvin. 'Who's . . . ?'

'Sofia's the capital of Bulgaria, Kelvin,' interrupted the commander. 'Mr Sodov would have been expelled for espionage.'

'I knew that!' said Kelvin. 'I'm not ignorant.'

'Oh good,' said the commander, turning back to Sodov. 'I must say it was very irresponsible of you to try to steal.'

'I was just doing my job,' replied Sodov. 'My job is important to me.'

'You ought to defect to Moorcombe,' said Kelvin. 'I could put you on the public salary as prime ministerial assistant.'

'Alas, it is not possible. Still living in a village in the mountains above Blod is my white-haired old mother. By her bedside she has a picture of me, her son, and, when the snows of autumn creep down from the peaks, she looks at my picture and smiles.' Sodov bared his teeth at his attentive listeners to show how she smiled. 'I am my mother's happiness. I send her gifts of fine food and she gains honour because others in the village can perceive that I, her son, have sent her gifts.'

'That's a very moving speech, Mr Sodov,' said Kelvin. 'I used to have a mother of my own. She loved me, too. I could sell you some lambs if you like. Your peasants might like a bit of fine English lamb.'

'That is most thoughtful of you,' said Sodov.

'When d'you think we should go down to Mandy's?' asked the commander.

'Not till closing time,' said Kelvin. 'I reckon we might all be grateful for a few drinks inside us this afternoon.'

'Closing time?' said Jason Loosemire, almost as respectable as Kelvin in water-slicked hair and a tight, high-waisted suit with flared trousers. 'Here! I only voted for independence because the pub could stay open all day.'

'It's very disappointing, I agree,' said Kelvin. 'But Helga says it's up to her what hours she keeps and she isn't changing. She could've stayed open all afternoon before, if she'd wanted to.'

'We ought to pass a law making her stay open or else she loses her licence.'

'You know that's not at all a bad idea. I could confiscate the pub on behalf of the state and take over myself,' said Kelvin.

'Kelvin, you naughty man,' said Helga, suddenly appearing behind the bar, the lunchtime *Neighbours* having finished. Her birthplace was in misty, Grimm-filled mittel-Europe where her ancestors had probably been subjects of the same Hapsburg emperors as those of Sodov. Naughty, rhyming with spotty, was one of her favourite words.

115

'Ah! Helga!' said Kelvin. 'We were just talking about you.'

'I heard.' Picking up a notebook which hung on a piece of string from the till, she turned to the first page. 'You owe £38. You can settle it and then get out. I am banning you from the pub.'

'Helga!' gasped Kelvin. 'You can't! I was only joking. You wouldn't.'

'I most certainly could and I would,' replied Helga. 'A publican can serve whom she likes.'

'In England,' said Kelvin. 'Not necessarily in Moorcombe.'

'Out!' said Helga.

'No, I didn't mean it,' said Kelvin. 'You must be going to the coronation too. You're looking really smashing in that frock.'

'Flatterer,' said Helga, in a Liberty-print silk suit. 'All right. You can stay.' She disappeared through to the lounge bar where some of the locals had spilled over from the tap.

'You've got to admit I really know how to handle the ladies,' said Kelvin proudly. 'Eh, Sodov?'

'A smooth operator? You do much copulating with the ladies here in Moorcombe?'

'What?'

'Copulate? Is that not the word? When a man and a woman take all their clothes off . . .'

'Yes, yes,' said Kelvin, looking furtively round to see who was within earshot but, apart from the other patrons, they were alone. 'You don't say things like that.'

'It is the code of the gentleman, is it? You copulate much but do not speak about it? But which of the ladies of Moorcombe do you think would copulate with me during my sojourn here? It is not easy for me to tell. Now that lady there,' he pointed a precise forefinger at Stephanie. 'I would enjoy copulating with her.'

'You shouldn't talk like that. Anyway, she's a respectably married woman.' Kelvin, now red in the face, sneaked a glance at Stephanie. So did the commander, Bill, Sodov, Jason and Parrott. 'Mind you, she's got very fine bosoms.'

'My old mother has fine bosoms,' said Sodov. Just when Stephanie was becoming aware she was the centre of attention, interest shifted. Puzzled eyes studied Sodov. 'She incubates the egg of geese in their midst. This is a custom amongst the ladies in our village.'

'Isn't it difficult at night?' asked the commander.

'Many of the ladies are widows or unmarried maidens and are chaste,' explained Sodov. 'So they do not move much at night. They are not like the women of England.'

'I'm glad ours aren't like yours,' said Jason with fervour.

'Ah!' said Sodov. 'You know they are not, do you? You have the experience which I was seeking. Which particular ones are most not like ours in this glorious new nation?'

Kelvin opened and shut his mouth. The question was shocking and outrageous, but the answer might prove to be extremely interesting.

'None of your damn business!' said Jason stoutly.

Approval of Jason's answer outweighed the disappointment in everyone but Kelvin. 'Don't be so disrespectful! He's the Ambassador of a friendly power, you treat him proper and give him a straight answer.'

'An answer to what?' asked a fresh voice.

'Lindy!' said Kelvin. 'You're in uniform!'

'Of course I am. I'm supposed to be Minister of Health or something.' A brisk and capable woman, now approaching forty, Lindy was the district nurse. She cheerfully admitted to have put on thirty pounds since she was a teenager, but most of it had ended up in acceptable places. 'What's the question you want answered?'

Even more stoutly, Jason supplied the answer. 'Kelvin was trying to get me to say who were the girls who like a good time hereabouts.'

'No, no,' said Sodov. 'That is not quite correct. It was those ladies who most enjoy copulating that I wish to meet.'

'You are a dreadful little man, Kelvin,' said Lindy. 'And the rest of you should have known better.'

The others had the grace to shuffle their feet, not Kelvin. 'You shouldn't've interrupted.'

'Of course, it's a question I've been asked in my time, too,' continued Lindy, ignoring his interruption.

'What do you mean?' asked Kelvin.

Lindy smiled. 'Who are the good lovers among the Moorcombe men. I've known all the young mothers over the past twenty years and it's amazing what we discuss.'

'Twenty years?' asked Kelvin.

'Oh, don't worry. I know about you, Kelvin. Word gets round. Meals on wheels. The WI. We girls will chatter.'

'That's shocking!'

'You'd be amazed if you knew just how inconsiderate some of you are. Once a month, drunk out of your minds if you're lucky. There'd be precious few of you lot going to stud if you were stallions.'

'You know for a fact? You have tested them?' asked Sodov with eagerness. 'Could you be the lady I seek?'

'Don't be disgusting. Of course I haven't tested them. I've heard,' said Lindy. 'I've got a perfectly reasonable husband of my own. You don't think I'd want to involve myself with any of these?' She waved a disdainful hand round the assembled drinkers. 'Except, perhaps, Jason.'

'Here!' said Kelvin. 'Why pick on poor Jason?'

'Now Jason might make it at stud,' said Lindy. 'Or so I've heard.'

'I be a handsome bugger. There's no doubt about that,' admitted Jason complacently.

' 'Course, I was widowed years ago,' said Kelvin. 'You didn't know my missus, did you, Lindy?'

'No.'

'Well then,' said Kelvin with a relieved smile.

'But Nellie Webber often drops in on me on the first Thursday of the month after she's done her rounds on her bike. Poor old thing, she's nearly past it now, but she still has

118

her gentleman friends, even if they aren't up to much. Eh, Kelvin?'

Her announcement created a rustle of alarm amongst some of the older men. Bill nearly choked on his beer and even Ivor, contentedly married for twenty-five years appeared uneasy.

'You talk to Nellie?' asked Kelvin.

'She talks to me,' said Lindy.

There was a silence.

'Should be a good crop of silage this year,' said Kelvin. 'I told Prudence to cut the fifteen-acre field this morning.'

Warm sunshine was gleaming on the shower-soaked tarmac of the street when the patrons of the tap spilled out of the door for the walk down through the village towards the river; the solid cob walls of the cottages washed pink, cream, pale blue or white. They turned right, just before the bridge, along the cul-de-sac towards 'Pixies Laughter.'

As they approached, Vidor's *Tocatta* on the electric organ was tootling away through the sitting-room window. Draped from the television aerial on the roof down to the front gate, a string of bunting, usually untangled for the village sports day, sagged across the concrete paving of the front garden. The gnome, crouching with a fishing rod over the pellucid, bleached water in the small pond, sported a small Union Jack.

'Does anyone know what exactly the form is here?' asked the commander.

'No,' said Kelvin. 'According to Loosemire, Mandy's thick with Jimmy. The two of them have worked it up between them.'

'Jimmy!' said the commander sombrely. 'Anything could happen.' He swung open the garden gate and Kelvin led the way up the path towards the door. It was opened by Jimmy in his Sunday suit. Draped round his shoulders was a red velvet curtain.

The skeleton of 'Pixies Laughter' was a typical mid-nineteenth-century slum cottage, jerry built to house the agricultural labour force. Most such cottages are now sold for tens of thousands to holiday-makers who carefully study the country magazines before restoring them. Mandy and Keith had arrived in Moorcombe just before the countryside became fashionable and the style of their restoration was more personal. Externally, 'Pixies Laughter' sat uneasily among the

rude architecture of the village. The pink paint and the double glazing were not remarkable, but the same could not be said for the fibreglass thatch, the white-painted shutters and the plastic honeysuckle round the door.

Inside the mood was maintained. From the wall, elephants charged against an African storm cloud, white horses plunged through the surf, an urchin's tear mirrored an intricate world alongside a collage in brass and plastic of a veteran motorcar. The countryside had been rigorously excluded by white shag pile, white paint and lace curtains, creating an interior worthy of a showhouse on any executive housing estate.

'Why are you wearing that?' asked Kelvin, peering at the

curtain round Jimmy's shoulders as he squeezed past into the hall.

'It's my robe,' said Jimmy. 'Will you go through to the back garden?'

'Why?' asked Kelvin.

'Because that's where Her Majesty's said you're to wait.'

'What are you wearing a tablecloth for?' asked the commander, the second through the front door.

'It's my coronation robe,' said Jimmy. 'Go through after Kelvin.

'Why do you wear a rug?' asked Helga, the first guest sufficiently intimidated to brush her feet on the doormat.

'It's not a rug,' said Jimmy. 'It's a robe. For the ceremony.'

'You look a damn fool,' said Bill, on her heels.

'Malcolm said I ought to wear it. Peers always wear robes at coronations.'

'Peers?' said Lindy. 'What do you mean?'

'I'm an earl now,' said Jimmy with pride. 'The Earl of Church Lane.'

The line of people shuffling through the narrow hall came to a domino halt as Kelvin pushed his way back. 'What? You're an earl? Has she gone and made you an earl?'

'Yes,' said Jimmy, squaring his shoulders beneath the robe. 'She said she wasn't really in favour of hereditary peerages but because my son's in the oil business in Canada and not going to come back to Moorcombe, she'd make me an earl. If I'm good, she might turn me into a marquis. That's even more noble than an earl, she said.'

'It's not fair!' said Kelvin. 'If you're an earl, I should be a duke! I'm the Prime Minister after all.'

'Then you've got to be a commoner,' said the commander. 'You can't have a Prime Minister who's a peer. Don't you remember Lord Home? He had to disclaim his peerage and become Sir Alec.'

'If I was a duke, I could do the same and end up Sir Kelvin. I wouldn't mind. Come to think of it, it's the Prime Minister who draws up the honours list anyway. So I'll get her to do it.'

'Fat chance!' said Jimmy. 'Will you move forward into the garden?'

'I hope you've got some drink out there,' said Kelvin.

'Not before the ceremony. Hurry along please.'

The back garden was not as sterile as the concreted front.

The lawn was tiny, immaculate as a billiard table and seedlings were in neat ranks in the beds of black peat against the white-painted wooden fence. Beyond the boundary the seedy anarchy of Kelvin's outlying four-acre field lapped at this oasis of order and civilisation. There buttercups, thistles, rushes and nettles almost hid the few hunched sheep, their wool interwoven with brambles, and their dung-tailed offspring.

Moorcombe tiptoed on to the lawn and stood in an uneasy group. Jason, seeking to kill his cigarette, stubbed it out against the sole of his shoe before tossing the butt across the fence where it landed on top of a molehill.

Kelvin frowned at him. 'Don't you litter up my land.'

Jason looked over the field. In its midst, a listless lamb flushed a snipe which zigzagged across the jagged corpse of a corrugated iron shed. 'Sorry.'

'Well, go and pick it up.'

'Piss off.'

'I reckon that poor brute's not long for this world,' said the commander, nodding towards a sheep, legs astraddle, coughing hopelessly into a clump of weeds.

'Needs worming,' said Bill. 'I'm surprised at Prudence having stock like that.'

'Prudence?' said Kelvin. 'What's it to do with her? It's my land and they're my sheep.'

'You manage this field yourself?' asked Bill.

'Yes!'

'Well, that explains it. I knew Prudence wouldn't let land get like this. Northcott's a tidy little farm now she runs it.'

'Look here!' began the indignant Kelvin.

'Calm down, Kelvin,' said the commander. 'This is no time for a quarrel.'

'Oh, I dunno,' said Kelvin. 'We've got to do something to pass the time.'

'If she's going to be crowned, she'll need a crown,' said the commander, seizing on a fresh subject. 'Where's she going to get one?'

'Are there other foreign ambassadors present?' asked Sodov.

'There's Gloria Field-Hay,' said the commander. 'Perhaps she's representing Puddlewick.'

Draped in a brown tent-like garment, Gloria filled the doorway. In her fifties and the widow of an Irish baronet, her face was a cross between Easter Island and Henry VIII, framed by lank, shoulder length blonde hair. 'Good afternoon, dear people,' she boomed. 'An auspicious day for your little community.' She suddenly lurched forward on to the path, crazy-paved with multicoloured ceramic tiles. 'Will you stop pushing, Jackson!' She turned, furiously, back to the doorway.

'You're in the way.' A mousy little woman in a sensible grey suit, Jackson was Lady Field-Hay's companion/housekeeper.

'That's still no reason to push like that! I could've fallen down and done a grave injury. Did you see her push me?' She turned to the lawn for support. Little was forthcoming. She turned back. 'I've a damn good mind to dismiss you.'

'You know what happens when you fire me.'

'I wouldn't make the same mistake twice.'

'Try it!' said Jackson. 'Go on, my lady.'

'What do you think happens when she's fired?' whispered Kelvin to the commander.

'I can't imagine. Why don't you ask her?'

'Which one?'

'Which one do you ask? I shouldn't think it matters. Both of them ought to know.'

'You exploit my good nature, Jackson!'

'How could I since you haven't got one!'

'You viper! You can walk home!'

'I've got the car keys.'

'Well give them to me!'

'No.'

'Brute! I shall refuse to talk to you for at least half an hour.'

'Praise the Lord!' said Jackson as her employer swept across the grass towards Kelvin.

'Afternoon, your ladyship,' said Kelvin.

She smiled. The village had speculated about a possible *tendresse* between the two of them, but this bizarre potential liaison had not yet had a chance to reach fruition. 'You are one of Nature's gentlemen, Kelvin.'

'I know,' said Kelvin. 'What happens when you fire Jackson?'

'She demands a pay rise before she agrees to be re-employed. So I simply can't afford to dismiss her any more.'

'That's blackmail.'

'Terrible isn't it?'

'You shouldn't let her get away with it. Prudence tried that sort of thing on me when she had Brett. I tried to do the right thing by her but she threatened to walk out.'

'And what happened?'

'He gave in,' said the commander.

'I didn't!' said Kelvin.

'Hmm,' said Gloria. 'And what did you disagree about? What was the "right thing"?'

'You know. Acknowledge the shame she'd brought upon the family by having a bastard.'

Gloria frowned. 'I can see why she felt the need to be firm.'

'Kelvin wanted her to shave her head and wear a sign round her neck.'

'I never did!' said Kelvin. 'But if she'd had the decency, she might've done it without being asked.'

Gloria frowned again.

'We were wondering where Mandy was going to get her crown from,' said the commander.

'That's easy enough. I brought over my mother-in-law's tiara. She used to appear at court a lot during the twenties.'

'A tiara?' said Kelvin. 'One of those little crown things?'

'That's right. It's really rather grand. Diamonds, rubies and emeralds.'

'Must be worth a bit,' said Kelvin.

'I suppose so. According to the story, my father-in-law exchanged it for the winner of the Derby.'

'A Derby winner's worth £10 million! Do you keep it at home? The jewels, I mean. Not the horse.'

'No. In the bank.'

'Cor!' said Kelvin. 'Ten million! Are you not worried about it? Where is it now?'

Gloria turned. 'Jackson! Where's the tiara?'

'How should I know? I've decided to give a month's notice,' said Jackson, who had been pouring out her woes to Lindy.

Her employer laughed. 'You can't, you silly goose. You resigned last time. It's my turn. You know the rules. You can't resign again till I've sacked you again.'

'I might cheat.'

'You do that and you're fired!' cried Gloria.

'Then I could resign!'

'Damn your eyes, woman!' Gloria turned back to the two men. 'What can one do with servants these days?' she said with a helpless shrug of her shoulders which lifted the hem of her dress to reveal strapping calves.

'What happened to the tiara?' asked Kelvin in some agitation.

'Oh yes, Jackson! My tiara. What have you done with it?'

'I gave it to the old man in the horse blanket.'

'I imagine that must be the Earl of Church Lane,' said the commander.

'Jimmy!' said Kelvin. 'You couldn't trust him with something like that.'

'I don't suppose he knows what it's worth any more than I do,' said Gloria. 'From what I understand the original horse was a ringer. The tiara may have been one as well.'

'A fake?'

'Well, there was a lot of it about in those days. D'you remember the Blue Water? That was a ringer. When it disappeared, all the Gestes had to join the Foreign Legion.'

'But don't you know?' asked Kelvin.

'No. I don't want to sell it. It's supposed to go to some cousin or other when I'm dead.'

'But you must have it insured.'

'What's the point? If it was real, I couldn't afford the premiums. It's quite irreplaceable, you know.'

'Bugger me!' said Kelvin.

Jimmy appeared in the door. 'Ladies and gentlemen, we are now ready for the ceremony. If you'd all go through to the lounge, Her Majesty is ready to be crowned.'

'Where's the crown?' demanded Kelvin as the crowd surged forward.

'Prince Keith's got it, I suppose,' said Jimmy. 'Either him or the archbishop.'

'I have never been to a coronation before,' said Sodov as they squeezed through the narrow passage towards the lounge and the sound of the organ. The route was further obstructed by a veneered telephone table at the foot of the stairs. The apparatus itself was gold with a white porcelain hand-hold.

'I doubt many of us have,' said Kelvin. 'Who's the archbishop?'

'Search me,' said the commander with a shrug. 'I've no doubt all will shortly be revealed.'

The lounge had been emptied of furniture, save for a dark brown ecclesiastical chair in front of the fireplace and the electric organ, now playing *Trumpet Voluntary* by itselt under the wary supervision of Mary Mowbray who played in the Bethesda Bible Chapel each Sunday. The usher, the Earl of Church Lane, split the guests into two groups on either side of the room, keeping a central passage to the fireplace. The commander opened one of the double-glazed aluminium windows to allow smoke from the earl's cigarette a convenient exit.

With a nod to Mary who pressed a switch silencing the organ in mid note, Jimmy hobbled to the doorway and the audience stilled. He cleared his throat. 'Oyez! Oyez!'

'For heaven's sake, Jimmy!' said Lindy. 'There's no need to shout.'

Chastened, Jimmy began again. 'Oyez, oyez,' he said. 'In the name of Queen Mandy the First, I command all her subjects to foregather hither to bear witness to the coronation of the aforesaid Mandy the First, heir to the Plantagenets as rightful Queen of Moorcombe.' He beamed round the room, proud to have managed his speech without a fluff. 'She also wanted me to say that she was rightful Queen of England, too. But I made her leave that bit out.'

'Quite right, Jimmy,' said Kelvin. 'Foreign policy and wars of conquest against other states is the business of the government, not of her.'

'Oh yes!' said Jimmy. 'You're also commanded to show proper respect by keeping your mouths shut.'

'Bloody cheek!' muttered Kelvin as Mary switched on *Trumpet Voluntary* once more. 'Who the hell does she think she is?'

'The queen?' said the commander.

'Ah, but who made her queen? It was me.'

'True. In fact few men could say they created an entire nation. History will remember you. Garibaldi. Simon Bolivar. Bismark. Kemal Ataturk. Kelvin Morchard.'

In cassock, surplice and brown suede shoes, the archbishop suddenly appeared. The Rev Richard Alworthy was the plump, unctuous priest-in-charge of Moorcombe and five surrounding parishes. The bishop showed considerable perception in his choice of spiritual shepherd for the community as Alworthy had had a career in the City ending in his bankruptcy and a fraud charge. The judge, a member of the General Synod, had been impressed by the prisoner's remorse

126

and his provisional place at a theological college and given him probation.

'Archbishop!' Kelvin's derision was obvious and audible.

'Yes,' said Alworthy, turning his head. 'Her Majesty appointed me this morning. She's decided to amalgamate all the churches and put me in charge.'

The organ stopped. 'I'm a Methodist,' said Mary Mowbray. 'Are you saying she's put you in charge of us, too?'

'I'm also a cardinal,' said Alworthy. 'I'm not very happy about that, either.'

As a buzz of conversation filled the room, Kelvin elbowed his way to Alworthy's side. 'What gives you the right . . .' The rest of the complaint was lost as the royal couple, preceded by the Earl of Church Lane, came into the room.

Bearing a red velvet cushion, lace frilled, on top of which sat the crown, Jimmy entered with stately dignity. The Royals were less successful. A brief scuffle, a smack, 'Do what you're told!' and Keith spilled into the room. Lowering his eyes, he scuttled to the fireplace, taking his position on the left-hand side of the throne as the archbishop joined Jimmy on the right. The organ broke into a fanfare as Mary adjusted a knob and Mandy entered.

She had been at the hamper in which were stored the costumes used by the Moorcombe Dramatic Society for their infrequent productions. In many yards of white net overlaid by satin, she was recognisably the Fairy Godmother.

'Cor!' whispered Kelvin. 'The Abominable Snowman!'

Mandy's black eyes flickered towards him and her glossy scarlet lips narrowed, but she continued her stately progress towards the throne, her backside touching the embroidered hassock at the moment the fanfare ceased. Her eyes darted round the room as the organ switched to soft background music in the style beloved by crematoria.

'Dearly beloved,' began Alworthy. 'We are gathered here in the sight of God and in the face of this congregation of her subjects to crown this woman as our lawful wedded queen. If any man have cause to speak, let him now speak or forever hold his peace.'

Kelvin stuck up his hand.

'Yes, Kelvin.'

'That's the marriage service. Not a proper coronation at all.'

'And what the hell do you mean, Mandy, by saying that the

vicar is head of the Methodists?' demanded Mary. Murmurs of support came from many of the farmers. In theory, Nonconformity claimed the adherence of half the population – just as the rest were supposedly C of E. In fact, the combined congregations of St Wilgeforts, the Bethesda Bible Chapel and the Ebenezer Bible Chapel on an average Sunday would scarcely overload an office lift.

'Be quiet,' said Mandy. 'In our speech from the throne after the ceremony we shall outline the themes of our reign.'

'But . . .' began Kelvin.

'Shut up,' said Mandy. 'Otherwise our bodyguard shall throw you out.'

The heads of the audience wimbledoned towards the door which was filled by Parrott. 'I'll damage you, too, Kelvin. After I've kicked you out.'

Mandy's subjects held their peace.

The ceremony was short. There was a hiatus when Keith had to hurry into the kitchen to retrieve a bottle of sunflower oil for the annointing and Alworthy nearly lost his nerve when the ferocity of Mandy's setting lotion caused her bottle-black hair to crackle and snap as he lowered the tiara into place, but a massed choir, concealed somewhere in the chips of the organ, broke into *Vivat Regina* followed by *Zadok the Priest* as Alworthy backed from the throne and bowed to his monarch. The rest of her subjects burst into spontaneous applause and turned towards the exit beyond which, they surmised, refreshments might be concealed.

Her Majesty slapped the arm of her throne. 'Pay attention! We shall be holding a meeting of the Privy Council immediately after this ceremony. Everyone who's not been appointed can wait in the garden. When we have concluded our consultations, a buffet is available in the dining room.' She smiled. 'Lumpfish caviar on cheese biscuits and sausages on sticks.'

'Have you been made a privy councillor, Kelvin?' asked the commander, as the mob surged towards the door.

'No.'

'Oh? Isn't that a little odd? I should've thought the Prime Minister ought to be.'

'What the hell for? I don't know what she's on about anyway. Let 'er play with the trappings of power if she wants. Good sort of ceremony, I thought. Nice and short. Where's the grub? D'you think there'll be drinks, too? We have to be able to toast the new queen.'

'We have to wait till after the meeting.'

'You can. I'm not!'

Pioneering a path for the locust horde, Kelvin pushed open the dining room door and entered. With fingers skilled in the subtle intricacies of midwifery, Lindy rapidly coaxed the three boxes of British Wine into yielding their dubious contents and a heavy silence fell over the room as the guests, realising the lumpfish roe biscuits covering the glass-topped table were in limited supply, concentrated on consuming their share.

Gloria Field-Hay bulldozed her way through the crowd.

129

'Spffl?' she asked, sandblasting the commander with crumbs.

'I beg your pardon?'

She swallowed. 'I asked whether you enjoyed the service.'

'You didn't,' said Kelvin. 'You said something like spiffle and spat crumbs all over me.'

'If you must know, I spat them all over the commander, not you,' replied Gloria loftily. 'I thought it went very well, didn't you?'

'Yes,' agreed the commander. 'I admired your tiara.'

'Nice wine,' said Kelvin, chomping his way through his latest biscuit.

'Hmm,' said the commander.

'Preposterous farrago, just the same,' said Gloria.

'I wouldn't shout that view,' said the commander.

'Ah! Here's Keith,' said Kelvin. 'How's our new queen?'

Gloria managed to take the last two biscuits. 'Is there any more food?'

'I don't remember Her Majesty giving permission for the buffet to be opened.'

'She didn't,' said Kelvin. 'But I had better things to do with my afternoon than wait till she's sorted out her privy.'

'She's not going to be very pleased.'

'If we'd've waited, there'd've been no food left,' said Kelvin. 'You didn't put out enough. The wine's like pig's piss, too.'

'Oyez. Oyez,' said Jimmy. 'Pray silence for Her Majesty.'

HM, as her consort had predicted, was pissed off. 'I told you bastards to wait! You haven't left any at all. What about me?'

'I bet you guzzled dozens when you were making them,' said Kelvin.

'I did no such thing! Too many give me hives. Brings me out all over and I certainly didn't want hives today of all days. I want a word with you, Kelvin. Come here!'

'Ask nicely,' said Kelvin. 'You can't order people round like that.'

Mandy frowned. The tiara quivered. 'I command your presence in the sitting room. Immediately.' Turning on her stiletto heel, she rustled her way out of the room.

'Huh!' said Kelvin, holding out his glass to Malcolm, on his way to fill his own. 'She's got a long wait coming. Nobody talks to me like that.'

Parrott materialised by his elbow, making Kelvin jump. 'Didn't you hear what she said?'

'What? About the grub?'

'No. About going next door.'

'I would've done if she hadn't been so rude. Did you hear her? She bloody well tried to order me around. Nobody orders Kelvin Morchard around. Never. Particularly now I'm Prime Minister.'

'If you don't get through there at the double, my old son, you'll need to call the vet to glue you together.'

Kelvin thought about it and looked at the commander, who gave a little shrug. 'I suppose I might as well. Just 'cos I feel like it.'

'You come too, Commander,' said Parrott.

'Say "please".'

'Please.'

Mandy was adjusting the tiara in the mirror above the fireplace as Kelvin ambled in, trying to make it look as if he had just been out for a stroll and felt like dropping by, rather than answering a Royal command.

'Let's have a look at that thing,' said Kelvin.

'What thing?' asked Mandy.

'Your crown.'

'It's very becoming, isn't it?' Mandy patted the base of her hair with pudgy, aquamarined hands.

'Gloria was saying it could be worth ten million if it was real.'

Mandy's hands stopped patting. 'How do you know?'

'I've just told you. She said so. She says she doesn't know if it's real or not.'

'If she doesn't know it's real, how does she know it's worth ten million?'

'Because that's the value of a Derby winner. Take it off and let's have a look.'

'I can't do that! It's my crown.'

'Think about it,' said Kelvin. 'It's Gloria's and she doesn't mind if it's worth £10. Why even one stone from it could be worth a fortune! She'd never notice if one went missing.'

'You're an absolute rogue, Kelvin,' said the commander.

'Isn't he?' said Parrott. 'Why not let him have a look, Your Majesty?'

Mandy considered. 'Shut the door, Parrott, and make sure

131

nobody comes in.' Reaching up, she unpinned the tiara from her hair which fought like a mating porcupine to retain it. 'I haven't really had time to look at it,' she said, dragging it from a few tenacious tendrils. 'It's really most pleasing. It looks genuine. How do you tell?'

'Give it to me!' demanded Kelvin. Putting on his spectacles, he took the tiara. It was a mixture of blue, green and white stones in an art deco setting. 'It's genuine,' he announced.

'How do you know?' asked the commander.

'It's obvious, isn't it? The jewels sort of sparkle and have hidden fires in their depths.'

'Gosh,' said the commander, impressed in spite of himself. 'Are there really?'

'Bullshit,' said Parrott. 'You haven't a clue.'

'There's one way to tell for sure,' said Kelvin. 'The glass test.' He walked to the mirror above the fireplace and swept the tiara across the glass, the grinding screech putting teeth on edge throughout the room. 'Hmm.'

'They're real!' said Mandy. 'Look what's happened to my mirror.'

'You could almost say Kelvin ruined it,' said Parrott.

'If we take one of the jewels – we could call it tax or

something – I could turn the whole wall into a mirror. And put one on the ceiling of the bathroom.'

'You couldn't do something like that,' said Jimmy. 'It would be embarrassing. Imagine having to look at yourself with no clothes on when you're having a bath! I wouldn't know where to look.'

'Blast it!' said Kelvin, who had been working on the tiara with a pocket knife. 'One of them's broke. It's a diamond, too. I reckon that horse must've been a ringer.'

'It's not real?'

'No.'

'My coronation crown was a fake?'

' 'Fraid so.'

'And you ruined my mirror.'

'You shouldn't've told me to test the jewels on it.'

'I didn't, you fool.'

'Yes, you did, you stupid cow.'

'Don't you dare call me a cow!'

'It was your fault. You were calling me a liar!'

'Parrott!'

'Oh dear,' said the commander. 'I don't think you should've said that. Particularly since she didn't.'

'Didn't what?' asked Kelvin.

'Didn't tell you to scratch the mirror.'

'Didn't she?' said Kelvin with a nervous glance over his shoulder at Parrott. 'I'm sorry, Mandy. I didn't mean that.'

'Get down on your knee before your queen,' thundered Mandy, pointing a forceful forefinger, only a slight ridge marring the smooth line of the artificial nail, towards the pink acrylic carpet.

'But . . .'

'I wouldn't argue,' said the commander.

'Heh-heh,' wheezed Jimmy.

'Go on,' said Parrott. 'I had to do it.'

Kelvin did it.

'You'll be interested in what the Privy Council decided,' said Mandy.

'No, I won't,' said Kelvin, on his knees but not about to crawl.

'We dismissed you as Prime Minister and appointed Keith to take your place.'

'You can't . . .'

133

'Stay on your knees, serf,' said Parrott, as Kelvin tried to struggle to his feet.

'You were right, Kelvin. Might is right,' said Mandy with a smirk. 'I'm taking over your job which means Percy reports to me and Jimmy's Chancellor of the Exchequer.'

'The Earl of Church Lane,' said Jimmy.

'Sorry,' said Mandy. 'I mean the earl.'

'You dirty little sheep-shagging shit!' said Kelvin, shuffling round on his knees towards Jimmy. 'You're a traitor to your own kind!' He shuffled back towards Mandy. 'You can't overthrow the democratically elected government of Moorcombe like this. You've forgotten the Emergency Volunteers.'

'A few old men with pitchforks,' said Mandy with a dismissive wave of the hand.

'The people won't have it!' said Kelvin.

'The people're out there scoffing my food and my drink. You wouldn't get one of them on to the barricades with you.'

'We'll see,' said Kelvin.

'Now listen to me, Kelvin,' said Mandy, towering over him. 'You're my first outgoing Prime Minister. You'd be entitled to an earldom . . .'

'That's not fair!' said Jimmy. 'You've just made me one!'

'How about a duke for Jimmy?' suggested the commander.

'Yes, I like that,' agreed Jimmy. 'I'll be a duke. I don't think any of my family's been a duke before.'

'A marquis,' ruled the monarch, firmly. 'As I was saying, Kelvin. You'd normally get to be an earl but I'm not sure you're a loyal enough subject, so I'll wait till my birthday honours.'

The commander corrected her. 'Our birthday honours.' He was skewered by a steely gaze from the throne. 'Sorry.'

'However. If you ferment rebellion, alarm or despondency or plot against the Queen's Grace.' She smiled. 'That's me. I read it in a Barbara Cartland.'

'It is beautifully put,' agreed the commander.

'Your arse won't touch the ground till you're banished from this realm and Prudence gets Northcott on condition you never set foot on the place again!'

Shrugging off Parrott's hand, Kelvin struggled to his feet, his face livid. His plastic teeth squeaking as he ground them. 'The last person who crossed me's dead, Mandy.'

A shadow crossed her face. 'Who?'

'Henry Burdock. He reported me to the War Agricultural Committee in 1942.'

'Henry Burdock!' said Jimmy. 'He died last year in his bed at ninety-six!'

'You're a fraud, Kelvin!' said Mandy.

'I've eaten better men than you before breakfast!' he replied, thrusting out his jaw.

'Even Keith's a better man than you!' Mandy hurled back. Keith blushed at the unexpected compliment.

Kelvin staggered back. 'I know when there's no point in continuing with reasonable discussion. We know when we're not wanted. Come on, Commander!'

Before the commander could work out the implications of being forced to take sides, Kelvin grabbed his elbow and hustled him out of the room and out of the house, jeers from the royalists ringing in their ears.

'There was still some wine left,' protested the commander as he was hustled down the path.

'We've more important things to think about than Mandy's wine, Commander,' said Kelvin, grimly. 'Might is right. We'll see.'

135

Chapter Eight

'ARE YOU DOING anything for the next couple of hours, Commander?' asked Kelvin, a couple of days after the coronation.

'That depends,' replied the commander cautiously.

To his surprise, Kelvin had discovered the commander still at work, even though it was late afternoon. Pullover discarded, he was planting out bean seedlings on the far side of the two-acre field he had turned into the market garden.

'I want to have a chat with you, and the squire wants me to shoot some rabbits and I wondered if you'd come along.'

The commander was tempted but still wary. 'What do you want a chat about?'

'What do you think?' said Kelvin. 'I want your advice about something. It's national business.' After looking cautiously behind him, he lowered his voice to a hoarse whisper. 'You could even say it affects the security of the state.'

'What?' said the commander.

'I said it could affect the security of the state.'

'I can't hear you,' said the commander, somewhat exasperated. 'Why are you whispering?'

'Because I'm concerned about secrecy,' Kelvin bellowed.

'There's no need to shout,' said the commander. 'There's nothing wrong with my hearing. You can speak perfectly normally. There's nobody lurking beneath the rhubarb.'

'They use directional microphones these days which can pick up conversations in skyscrapers a block away from a parked limo,' said Kelvin. 'I saw it on *Miami Vice*.'

'Fortunately we neither have limos nor skyscrapers in Moorcombe so we have nothing to worry about.'

'That's true,' admitted Kelvin. 'Are you coming to shoot rabbits, then? The squire's paying for the bullets.'

The commander looked down at his tray of seedlings. 'All right. I've just about finished here anyway. I can tidy up in the morning.' He led the way along the beaten earth path which wound its way through beds of neatly regimented rows of baby carrots, broccoli and courgettes.

'They say they're setting up a border post on the bridge the day after tomorrow. Are you going to be there?' asked the commander.

'Of course. I wouldn't miss it. It should be a nice morning, too, though they're promising rain later in the week.'

'What was it you wanted to talk about?'

'The security of the state.'

'Oh. Can't you tell me now?'

'I'd rather wait until we're away from prying eyes and ears.'

'Hmm. I'm not sure ears can pry. Whose ears and eyes are you worried about anyway?'

'You can never tell,' replied Kelvin, peering round suspiciously. Along one side of the commander's land ran the river from which he pumped water to his marrows and courgettes in high and dry summer. On the other, the back gardens of the cottages on the main street of the village bordered Frank's main hay fields.

'What time'll we be back?' asked the commander. 'I'd better tell Elfrieda.'

'Why?'

'Why? Well, she's my wife. She'll want to know what time to cook supper.'

'Does she still cook you supper?' Kelvin's voice held a wistful note.

'Of course,' said the commander.

'Really? A full proper meal?'

'Yes.'

'Funny that,' said Kelvin.

'Can't see why,' said the commander. 'I mean that's what wives are for isn't it?'

'Yes, but I heard her telling Maud in the post office how she's nearly got you house trained. She's getting you a little apron all your own for your birthday.'

The commander stopped. 'She's been saying that?'

'Yes,' said Kelvin happily. 'And more.'

'You don't believe it, do you?'

'Oh no,' said Kelvin. 'I know you're the sort of chap who still has his wife under proper control.'

'Of course,' said the commander.

'I'm sure you don't have to wash your own clothes, get your own supper and things. It's going to have little flowers on it.'

'What?'

'Your new apron. You've got to be more careful when you iron it and not burn a hole in it like you did the old one.'

'I don't know what she was talking about. Still, I don't suppose I do have to tell her where I'm going,' said the commander. 'We won't be particularly late?'

'No, just a couple of hours. You'll be back in time. Fried liver isn't it tonight? Elfrieda said you were good at that.' They had come through a stone wall and into the small yard in front of the house where Kelvin's battered green Land Rover was parked. 'Get in.'

They drove out of the village for a couple of miles, between fat, billowing hedgerows splashed with pink campion, yellow buttercup and the fine white filligree of cow parsley. Kelvin turned off the thin ribbon of tarmac and on to a crude forest track with deep wheel ruts cut into the yellow clay subsoil which climbed through the trees. Half a mile later, he turned again and the oak and beech thinned into a valley with steep, grass-covered sides rising a couple of hundred feet to the horizon. Kelvin took the vehicle off the track and they stopped, its bonnet pointing uphill against a new sheep fence, topped by a couple of strands of barbed wire.

'Up there,' said Kelvin, pointing up the hill before leaning over the seat to pull his rifle from the back.

The slope was dotted with small patches of gorse in full yellow flower interspersed by hummocks, bumps and excavations created by generations of badgers, foxes and rabbits. The rabbits were in residence at the moment. Through the windscreen, the commander could see half a dozen white tails bobbing about on the slope and a glance through Kelvin's binoculars showed more nibbling the grass by the mouths of the burrows, round many of which the grass had been worn away to show the grey, shaley soil.

Leaning across the commander, Kelvin scrabbled amongst the baler twine, wisps of hay, rusty bolts and expended cans of aerosol sheep-markers in the glove compartment and found a plastic box containing a hundred bullets. He pulled the magazine from his .22 and stuffed in five of the hollow-nosed shells. Poking the rifle out of the window, he peered through the telescopic sight. 'I'll go for that big bugger just beneath that lone thistle in the middle. Mark the drop of the bullet.'

The commander swivelled the binoculars. 'The windscreen's so damn filthy, I can hardly see a thing. Which one? Oh yes, I see it. What about that one by the fence? It's a lot closer. The other's a good 150 yards away.'

'I might get a richochet off the wire.' Kelvin expelled his breath.

Crack!

A spurt of soil flew up a yard below the target which continued to chew the grass with insouciance.

'A long way below,' said the commander.

'I know. I'm not blind,' said Kelvin, pulling back the bolt to reload.

'You asked me to spot,' said the commander.

Crack!

'I didn't see that,' said the commander. 'But it must've been close. The thing jumped.'

'I was aiming a yard over the top,' said Kelvin

Crack!

The rabbit twitched its ears in irritation and withdrew unhurriedly towards the mouth of its burrow.

139

Crack!

The rabbit disappeared. 'I got it!'

'Nonsense,' said the commander. 'It just went down its hole. Give me a shot.'

'I've still got one left. I'll go for the one by the hedge.'

Crack!

The thwack of the striking bullet came back a full second after the crack of the rifle. 'Nice one,' said the commander, watching as the rabbit rolled over without a twitch.

'It was a baby, too. Much smaller and more difficult to hit.' Taking out the magazine, Kelvin loaded it for the commander and handed the rifle across. 'Careful. The safety catch is broken.'

The commander sighed. 'I'll go for the ones by the big yellow bush.'

Pulling a pipe from his pocket, Kelvin struck a match, filling the cab with clouds of acrid smoke. 'The security of the nation. That's what I want to talk about.'

'But you're no longer Prime Minister. It's nothing to do with you anymore.' The commander wriggled in the seat, trying to get a view through the sight.

'I talked to Prudence and Sodov. They think it's all to do with Parrott. Rasputin was what Prudence called him. He's got Mandy under his thumb. If I'm to preserve Moorcombe from the tyranny of dictatorship by Parrott, we have to act.'

'We?'

Crack!

'Blast! Just above.'

'I had a word with Sodov. He's willing to help. He reckons it wouldn't be in his country's interests if Mandy's regime gets established. Undemocratic, he called it.'

'Is that right?' said the commander, quartering the slope in search of another target.

'Did you ever have anything to do with nuclear bombs? I'm thinking of getting one.'

'Don't be silly, Kelvin.'

'Sodov might get us one, but I don't like being too dependent on one supplier. Especially him. He's trying to say he meant a million in Bulgarian stotinki or something and not pounds.'

'It doesn't surprise me. What's a stotinki worth?'

'Dunno. What about an atomic bomb, then?'

'Have you tried Harrods? They claim to be able to supply anything,' said the commander.

Crack!

'Got 'im! I'm very good.' A grey cloud, as thick as phlegm, rolled across the cab. The commander coughed. He lifted his head from the stock of the rifle. 'For heaven's sake, will you blow your smoke out of your window!'

'Harrods eh? I hadn't thought of them. They're up in London, aren't they? I wonder if they deliver down here.'

'I wouldn't know. Kelvin . . .'

'How much are they?'

'How much? Over how many months would you want to pay?'

'How am I supposed to know that, you fool? Until I know how much one would cost, I won't know how I'll want to pay. Get on with it!' Kelvin waved the stem of his pipe at the rabbits who were taking only minimal interest in the demise of their associates.

'Are you serious?' asked the commander.

'About what?'

'A bomb.'

'Why not? We're a free country. I don't see why we're not entitled to proper protection.'

'And Sodov's said he'll give you one?'

'I haven't asked him yet, but I'm sure he would.'

The commander snorted. 'Don t be absurd! People don't go around offering nuclear bombs. Anyway, the Bulgarians haven't even got any of their own.'

'There's a fat one just come out up there,' said Kelvin, pointing through the glass.

The commander returned to the telescope, resting the barrel on the driving mirror outside his window.

Kelvin put the binoculars to his eyes.

Crack!

'You should've hit that one. You were well to the left. It didn't budge. Sodov should be able to borrow one from the Russians.'

Crack!

'What's wrong with you? That was half a mile the other way.'

'I'm not finding this conversation conducive to accurate

141

shooting,' said the commander. 'The trouble with you is I never know when you're serious.'

'Well I'm serious now. I think Moorcombe should have its own independent nuclear deterrent.'

'Why?'

'Why? Why? It's obvious, isn't it?'

'No, it isn't. It's probably the most stupid idea I've ever heard you express, and you've come up with some extraordinarily stupid ideas in your time.'

'There's no need to take that attitude.'

'On the contrary. What would you do with it?'

'I thought we could hide it in Arnie Bladderwick's barn until we needed it.'

'I see. And how will you know if you've got one?'

'What kind of a question is that?'

The commander squinted along the barrel. There was a click. 'Blast it! That one would've been a goner.' Taking out the magazine, he began to fill it with bullets. 'Just suppose Sodov takes some thousands of pounds off you and delivers a bomb, how will you know it's not a dud or a fake? I certainly wouldn't be able to tell you.'

'Hmm. Perhaps we could buy two and test one out.'

'Not a good idea. Quite apart from the test ban treaty, facilities for letting off a nuclear bomb in Moorcombe are limited. There's a really fat one near the top of the hill.'

Kelvin trained the binoculars on the skyline. 'I've got it. You'll need to allow for a lot of drop. I'd aim at the level of the top of that thistle.'

The commander concentrated. 'Damn! I can't quite line up on it. Would you back the Land Rover?' Releasing the handbrake, Kelvin twisted the steering wheel. The vehicle rolled back on the slope a few yards, presenting the commander more broadly to the hill. 'That's better.'

Crack!

'I didn't see it,' said the commander.

'Nor did the rabbit. It's a hell of a long way.'

Crack!

'Bugger me! Nice shot. I thought you were aiming at the big one. I didn't even see the little one.'

'Nor did I,' admitted the commander. 'This is rather good fun.'

'Isn't it?' said Kelvin with a quick grin. 'Different from a shot gun. Sort of cold and calculating and precise. We ought to have one.'

'One what?'

'A bomb.'

'You still haven't told me why,' said the commander, taking a handful of bullets.

'It stands to reason . . .'

'I've learned that when you say that it never does.'

'What?'

'Stand to reason.'

'I don't know what you're talking about. It's my turn to shoot.'

'But I've just loaded it!'

'Thank you very much.'

Muttering, the commander handed it over, but Kelvin showed no immediate coneyphobia. 'If you look at it calmly,' said Kelvin, 'we're in a very vul... vul... dangerous position. The nation's defence in the hands of Mandy. If we get a bomb, it'll defend us against aggressors and make me Prime Minister again. Parrott's only got his pistol. He wouldn't be able to do much if I had an atom bomb. But the main thing is we're a tiny country surrounded completely by a much larger and more powerful one. Britain. Our army . . .'

'Our army? We haven't got an army.'

'Yes, we have. I checked with Percy and we've got twenty-six shotguns in the parish and eleven rifles. The squire's got a .375 Remington which he uses when he goes stalking in Scotland. And Jason has a crossbow.'

'Christ!' said the commander.

'But even with that number of guns, we'd be no match for them if they invaded.'

'Assuming they agree to the independence of Moorcombe, why should they invade?'

'History teaches us the hard lesson that if one nation can subjugate another with little cost to itself, then it will do so. Look at Hitler and all the places he took over in the thirties.'

'Who told you all that?'

'Nobody told me. Well . . . I was talking to Prudence and Sodov again. But we need our own independent nuclear deterrent.'

'No, we don't.'

'Yes, we do. It's vital to preserve peace and guarantee our

143

independence. It's not so much the English government I'm worried about. It's the Russians. If they decide to invade us, there's nothing we could do to stop them.'

'Join NATO. Then Moorcombe'd be protected by the American nuclear umbrella. You could send Jason with his crossbow as our contribution to annual manoeuvres in Germany. Although he might hit problems with the standard-isation of equipment.'

'Ah!' said Kelvin. 'But do you think the Americans would risk a global thermonuclear war just to protect Moorcombe?'

'If we were in NATO and we were invaded, yes.'

'Balls! The English government's not stupid and they don't trust the Americans. That's why the Prime Minister's got a button all of her own. She can start a war without asking some bloody Yank for permission, even if they would nuke us first if they thought she might press it.' He poked the rifle out of the window. 'You can never trust the Yanks. One of them asked Maisie Appleyard to dance with him in the war and he went and married her. Terrible waste. She were a fine maid, Maisie. Fertile and a good worker.' He aimed the rifle.

Crack!

Although the moor seemed to crawl with tourists for much of the year, most of them never dared to venture more than a hundred yards from their cars. Even the few who tramped the bogs and heather, wearing stout boots and earnest expressions, would stick rigidly to the limited web of marked paths and bridleways. For weeks at a time, the narrow valley in which they sat would never see a human visitor.

'How would you deliver the bomb?' asked the commander.

'Deliver? What do you mean?'

'You know,' said the commander impatiently. 'Missile, aircraft, submarine, etc.'

'Oh I see. Yes, I hadn't considered that. Hmm. We could get a missile. Yes, that might be best.'

'A missile? Stick it in Arnie Bladderwick's barn, I suppose.'

'Could do. They've all got to go somewhere.'

'And you fire it when we're invaded?'

'Of course.'

'And who do you fire it at?'

'Dunno. The Russians? Yes. Moscow. We'd fire it at the Kremlin. They're the buggers who'd've ordered the invasion.'

'How?'

'How what?'

'How would you fire it?'

'Light the fuse, I suppose.'

'You turn a key or press a button these days.'

'Do you? It'd be bound to come with an instruction manual. I'd press the button. I wouldn't be afraid of the responsibility.'

Bang!

'Didn't see it.'

'That must have been a dud or something.'

'You missed it, Kelvin. Bad workman and all that.'

'You heard the noise it made. It was completely different. That one went "bang". All the other shots went "crack".'

'That's undeniable,' agreed the commander. 'They're guided missiles, Kelvin. They need to be programmed so they land within a hundred yards of the target. It's not like shooting rabbits.'

'Oh. P'raps, it isn't. Hmm.'

Crack!

'That's better. Well, we obviously can't use a submarine and none of us can drive an aeroplane. I think there's only one thing left.'

'Oh? And what's that?'

'The obvious. It won't be as quick as a missile or a plane, but it'd get there sure enough, provided it was a small bomb. We'll send it airmail. Now, look what you've done!'

The commander's shout of laughter had achieved what the crack and subsequent thud as the hollow-nosed slug shattered flesh and bone, had not – scared the rabbits. Those protected by the dangers of ricochet from the fence, thumped their back legs, flashed their scuts like can-can dancers and disappeared down their burrows. In a chain reaction, their neighbours spotted the disturbance and followed suit. Soon not a rabbit remained above ground.

'It's a very good idea,' said Kelvin. 'If there's a threat of invasion, we just put it in the post.'

'And how will you explode it?'

Kelvin thought for a few moments. 'A timing device!' he said with triumph.

'And what about Customs?'

'Oh, we'll just write on the outside "unsolicited gift" and they won't bother.'

'I see. And how would you know when to set it to go off?

CRACK

Would it be delivered by the first post or the second post?'

'You're just trying to create problems.'

'I think it's worth considering all eventualities when planning the use of nuclear weapons. What happens if there's a postal strike? Or it got lost?'

'It would turn up again when it went off.'

'Make an awful mess of Mount Pleasant sorting office. Just forget this whole stupid idea.'

'Perhaps you're right,' said Kelvin. 'Look! There's a fat rabbit up there. You can have the shot.'

'Thank you,' said the commander.

Targets were beginning to re-emerge from a great bank of gorse and brambles alongside the wood, although nothing had yet lifted its head above the trenches and bunkers of the warrens in the middle.

Crack!

'Nice one,' said Kelvin. 'Harrods, eh? I'll ask Prudence about it.' He chuckled. 'I'd like to hear Mandy pretending she was in charge once I get a bomb! Incidentally, if you breathe a word of this to anybody else, I'll have you shot when I'm in charge again.'

'You are a berk, Kelvin.'

Crack!

'Damn it!'

When Kelvin and Sodov returned from the Hunted Hind that evening, Prudence made them cocoa.

146

'Now we're alone, I can talk,' said Kelvin. 'I've got a plan.' They were sitting round the kitchen table, nursing their hot mugs beneath a dingy bulb which hung from the ceiling in a tulip-shaped glass shade.

'Yes?' said Sodov.

'You see what's happening here, don't you? Mandy's taken power and that Parrott has got her twisted round his little finger.'

'Yes, I fear you are right.'

'I doubt if the interests of Botograd on Vit are going to be high on the agenda of Parrott and his chums, do you?'

'I agree.'

'Therefore it's up to you to help me to regain the initiative. In fact it's your duty to your country, particularly if you want to build an embassy in the flat field.'

'What are you driving at, Dad?'

'I want something from you, Sodov.'

'I had gathered that.'

'I want a bomb. I got absolutely nowhere on the telephone. I don't think the commander can've known what he was talking about. I asked him where I could buy one and he said Harrods but they said they didn't stock them because there was no demand. So I thought you could get me one.'

Prudence snorted. 'Really, Dad. What kind of a bomb did you have in mind?'

'A proper bomb. One of those nuclear ones.'

'That's plain daft!'

'No, it isn't. If I had one, I'd be Prime Minister again. Parrott wouldn't dare try to stop me. Then we could have proper democratic government in Moorcombe again and put Mandy in her place. How about it, Sodov? Will you get me one? You can use some of the million stotters.'

Sodov spread his hands. 'I understand your need, Kelvin. But, alas, I cannot help you. You see even our glorious defence force has no nuclear arms.'

'You could ask the Russians for one. You're supposed to be allies and they've got them, haven't they?'

'Yes, but I fear they are unlikely to give them away or even sell one.'

'Damn!' said Kelvin, taking a sip from his mug. 'That rather mucks up that idea. P'raps it's for the best. The commander said I wouldn't know one if I saw one anyway.'

'I don't think that matters,' Prudence was drying the dishes placed at the side of the stone sink after washing them up.

'What do you mean?'

'None of these bombs are ever let off. So how does anyone know whether they work or not? All you need is something that looks like a bomb and tell everyone it is a bomb and they won't be able to risk that you're bluffing.'

Sodov frowned. 'But surely nobody would believe him? What kind of man would have his own nuclear bomb?'

'The locals'd believe it of Dad.'

'That's true,' acknowledged Kelvin. 'I'm known as a man of my word hereabouts. And if I got a real one, I wouldn't be all that happy if I had to let it off. I'm a peaceable man, really. I think you may have solved our problem, Prudence. Well done! Sometimes you think almost as well as a man. I suppose it's because you're my daughter.'

'You are very fortunate in your daughter,' said Sodov. 'In my country a woman so strong and so intelligent would have a man of fire to protect her.'

'Gee, thanks,' said Prudence.

'So,' said Kelvin, turning to Sodov. 'Your lot must at least know what a bomb looks like. You can get me a fake.'

'But . . .'

'You can telephone them from here tonight and go up to London tomorrow to pick it up.'

'But . . .'

'Mind you listen for telephone tappers. I don't trust Mandy.'

Sodov looked at Prudence for assistance, but she looked back with a sardonic smile on her lips. 'Bet you didn't think you'd have to do this to pay for your B and B.'

Chapter Nine

'I DON'T LIKE being up this early in the morning,' said Kelvin, scraping idly at the lichens on the grey stone parapet of the bridge with a horny thumbnail.

With his elbows on the wall and his backside jutting into the road, he watched the mist twisting through the fresh green leaves of the willow and hazel lining the banks of the river. The dawn chorus was in full throat and the swifts, arrived in Moorcombe only a day or two earlier, were screaming through the arches of the bridge, ignored by the early brood of ducklings who peeped with concern as their mother flirted with a trio of gang-banging drakes, their breasts plucked naked by days of ritualistic combat.

'I thought you farmers were used to it,' said the commander. 'The number of times I've stood on the bridge and watched the sun climb up over the horizon.'

'What are you doing always standing here at that hour?'

'No, the bridge of a ship. Seeing the flying fishes . . .'

'I read about those in a book.' The commander shot a surprised glance at Kelvin. 'Well . . . not read exactly. It was one of Brett's. *Natural Marvels in Colour*, it's called.'

'They're fascinating creatures. They leave the water to escape . . .'

'They've got another thing in the book. A great big monster called Tyrannosaurus Rex with lots of teeth which'd gobble you up. They used to live on earth a long time ago and were all killed by a comet.'

'Really? Flying fish can travel quite long distances, a hundred yards or so. I remember once . . .'

'I don't believe that.'

'Why not? Their fins have developed . . .'

'Well, it's stands to reason. If a comet killed them all, why didn't it kill us too? And we had that comet a few years ago. Halley's Comet and that didn't do any harm to anyone.'

'God! You two are boring!' said Parrott.

Kelvin and the commander turned mildly disapproving eyes towards him. 'And what do you talk about first thing in the morning, Rasputin?' asked Kelvin. 'Interesting ideas like us? Or how thick the traffic is and what was on telly the night before? I'm telling you, you're very lucky I said I'd come out and give you a hand this morning. I'd like to see you or Mandy trying to organise something like this, let alone the Marquis of bloody Church Lane.'

A heron, flapping its way sedately upstream suddenly saw those on the bridge at an hour when it expected the world to itself. It churned its wings in an abrupt change of direction, lost height and landed clumsily in the shallows.

'Look!' said Parrott. 'A flamingo!'

'Where is the bugger?' said Kelvin irritatedly. On cue the sound of an approaching tractor came roaring up the valley on the opposite side of the river from the village. Black smoke jetted above the trees from the exhaust funnel. It came into view round the corner just before the bridge, Frank Mattock at the wheel and a trailer loaded with bales of straw behind.

Straightening up, Kelvin raised his arm and waved Frank across the bridge, his load only inches below a saggy loop of telephone wires. Frank switched off the engine as the heron, its composure regained, launched itself into the air and retraced its flight path back down the river in search of a more peaceful place to fish.

' 'Morning Frank.'

'Who's going to pay for these, Kelvin?'

'You hang around for an hour or two and you'll have your money Frank.'

'I will, will I?' said Frank, stepping down from the cab. 'And what do you want the bales for?'

'We're going to build a barrier here. The world's going to find out Moorcombe's an independent country from this morning. We're fixing up a Customs and immigration barrier here.'

'But half the parish's on the other side of the river,' said Frank. 'I am and so are you.'

'We only need one barrier and to get round this, you'd have to go all the way to Swinehanger and cross the bridge there. It's about the middle of the parish.' He gestured to each side of the bridge. 'We want the bales, two deep and two high to block the road, leaving just enough room for one vehicle and we'll have a gate across the gap. You've brought a gate?'

'No.'

'You can get one after you've dropped the straw.'

'Oh yes?' said Frank. With fair thinning hair and a red complexion, his vacant blue eyes and slack jaw gave him a sheep-like look, but he was the most successful farmer in Moorcombe. While others had watched the fat years of Common Market agriculture drift past, Frank had exploited every advantage of the system, raising barns, ploughing moorland for wheat, appealing against milk quotas and even buying shares in a company which stored surpluses. His peers did not mind. Although fond, perhaps even inordinately fond of money, they were not prepared to work hard enough to accumulate large quantities of it.

Frank wandered over to the parapet. The sun had yet to break through the mist but Frank had the top three buttons of his shirt open to show golden hairs on his fleshy torso and a cross nestling in their midst between his large pectorals. A decade earlier he had been to Torremolinos on a Club 18–30 holiday which had been the most significant cultural experience of his life.

'Well, don't just stand there,' said Kelvin irritably. 'Get the bales out.'

Frank continued to contemplate the water below. Operating a shuttle service with its mate to feed its chicks in a nest under the arch of the bridge, a dipper whirred down the river for fifty yards before landing on a stone. After a couple of dips, it plunged into the shallow rapids bobbing up for air every few seconds before ducking beneath the surface once more. Flying back to the stone, it gave a few more dips before setting off again, skimming a few inches above the surface, back beneath the bridge to its chicks which wheezed and piped their enthusiasm as they were fed the insect larvae their parent had winkled from crevices and gravel on the river's bottom. 'Right pretty,' said Frank, straightening up from the parapet. 'You're going to need more than bales. Some people are not going to take too kindly to the road being blocked.'

'Huh!' Kelvin sniffed contemptuously. 'I don't care what they think.'

'And it's not going to be much good just hitting them for 20p on their way through. You won't be a foreign country or anything. Just a toll road.'

'We're going to have Customs, police and immigration.'

A duck, with a couple of drakes in hot pursuit, arrowed its way downstream. It feinted as if going beneath the arches and then skimmed above the parapet to make an untidy landing in the middle of the bridge. In perfect formation, its would-be lovers made height, banked round the chimneys of the commander's house before cupping their wings and dropping their landing gear to plonk down beside her, a few yards from the men. 'Bloody tourists,' muttered Kelvin. 'If they didn't feed those damn birds, they wouldn't dare come so close.'

A door slammed up the street behind them.

'About time,' grunted Kelvin, as Malcolm, pulling a sweater over his head, shut the gate to his postage stamp front garden and walked the hundred or so yards down towards the bridge.

'Morning all. A bit too early for me,' said Malcolm.

Having already milked a hundred cows, eaten his breakfast and loaded his trailer before driving down, Frank looked at him without sympathy.

'You're just in time to help Frank set out them bales,' said Kelvin.

'I haven't much time. I've got to go in to College this morning for a meeting,' replied Malcolm.

'I don't need to know your problems,' said Kelvin. 'We've all got to make sacrifices at a time like this. Why, I was talking to Prudence this morning and she said when Israel was founded they were invaded immediately by Arabs. The same thing could happen to us.'

'There aren't any Arabs round here,' said Frank.

'No, it doesn't have to be Arabs, you fool,' said Kelvin. 'In our case it would be the English.'

'How did Prudence know about Israel?' asked Frank.

Kelvin scowled. 'She's not the daughter she was. Her head's full of the most extraordinary rubbish these days. She's still a good worker, mind, but she doesn't treat me with the proper respect any more, especially now I'm the Prime Minister.'

Malcolm tutted, but without much enthusiasm. 'I thought you were ex-PM. I thought Mandy had taken over the reins of government.'

'Not for long,' said Kelvin grimly.

'Now, now,' said Parrott. 'Remember I'll have to banish you if you talk sedition and treason.'

'That law wasn't ratified by the Parish Council.'

'Might is right, Kelvin. Remember? We're in a dictatorship now. Mandy's, not yours.'

Kelvin ignored him. 'She'll finish the chores and put Brett to bed but does she cook me a proper tea? She gives me salads and frozen stuff. Not proper man's food like stews and plum pudding.'

'Shame,' said Malcolm.

'Yes, and then she's off at her studies or feeding Brett and leaves me to do the washing up! I put it down to not having a mother who'd teach her the proper way for a woman to behave. She talks about getting education! Education! What the hell does she want any of that for? It's not as if she were a man and there's her duty to me to consider.'

'And to Brett,' said Frank.

'Yes. Him, too.'

The group stood contemplating the shortcomings of Prudence for a few minutes. A crow landed heavily on a thin branch jutting across the river from a willow, provoking a frenzy of scolding chinks from the dipper perched on its stone beneath. No unguarded duck's nest or, dream of dreams, a ripening lamb, drowned further up the valley and floated down to become becalmed in the Moorcombe shallows, met the crow's searching glance, so it spread its wings and cruised unhurriedly down the centre of the river, following the flight path of the heron.

'I've had a busy night,' said Malcolm.

The others looked at him eagerly. Stephanie was hard to admire as she gave short shrift to natives whose eyes appraised her as they would the hams on a pig or conformation of a bullock.

'I've got some things here.'

'Things?'

'Yes.' Malcolm dived his hand into a plastic supermarket bag. 'These are stamps.'

'Stamps?'

'Yes, Stephanie actually made them from lino, but I think they should work fine. I've got an ink pad too.'

'That kind of stamp. What're we supposed to do with them?' asked Kelvin.

'Stamp people's passports, of course.' He retrieved some sheaves of paper. 'Stephanie and I drew these up and I ran them off on my photocopier.'

'What are they?' asked Kelvin.

'The passports. Mandy wanted them. Until we have some proper documents drawn up, we can issue them to citizens so that we know who's who.'

'But we know who's who already and we're not going to start spawning bureaucrats. So you can stuff them and help get the barrier built. Rasputin, don't just stand there. Get to work.'

'I'm not a bloody labourer.'

'You may be Mr Big at the palace but Mandy's not here. Get to work, you idle bugger!' Kelvin leant back with his elbows resting on the parapet as Frank climbed to the top of the trailer and kicked bales down to Parrott. 'We should've gone independent years ago. When you tell people to do things, they do them.'

'You take good care of these bales!' shouted Frank. 'I'll be wanting them back when you're finished with them.'

'We should get something more permanent.'

'First customer!' exclaimed the commander from the middle of the bridge. The others turned to look.

'It's Vic!' said Kelvin.

Barrelling down the narrow road towards the bridge and Moorcombe, was a blue milk tanker. Moving at about 60mph, its air brakes puffed and sighed as it approached to stop in the middle of the bridge, its engine idling. 'Morning, Commander,' said the blue-overalled driver, a man in his forties with white hair slicked back from his forehead and a cats cradle of laughter lines round his eyes.

'Hullo, Vic,' said the commander

'What's going on here?' Vic leaned forward and the engine died.

'You've got to go through Customs and immigration,' said the commander.

'Oh, aye,' said Vic.

'Kelvin'll explain to you.'

Kelvin strutted across the bridge towards the lorry.

'Kelvin,' said Vic, with a nod.

' 'Morning, Vic,' said Kelvin, looking up at the cab. 'I'd forgotten about you. You're a bit late.'

'Stopped off for a cup of tea at Mudford.'

'Well, things are a bit different this morning. We've declared independence. The other side of the bridge is a new country, Moorcombe. You'll have to go through Customs and immigration.'

'Oh, aye,' said Vic. Turning to the commander, he raised his eyebrows and lifted his hand to make a clockwise motion to his temple.

'He actually means it, Vic,' said the commander.

'He does, does he? I hope it won't take too long. I'm a bit late this morning. What exactly do I have to do, Kelvin?'

'You get out of your lorry and go to immigration and pay for your entry stamp and meanwhile we'll search the lorry for contraband.'

'Oh, aye,' said Vic. He gestured towards the wall of bales which was still growing ahead of him. 'And how am I supposed to drive through that?'

'Through the border checkpoint? We'll move some bales to let you through.'

'It's a narrow bridge this,' said Vic. 'You'll have to move the whole lot.'

'We've just finished putting them up! Can't you squeeze through if we just take out the middle?'

'No,' said Vic. 'Use your eyes.'

Kelvin walked across the front of the lorry and checked clearance on the off-side. He came back. 'Blast! Why did the first have to be you?'

'That's the way the cookie crumbles,' said Vic. 'Who's that?' He nodded towards the one face he did not know.

'That's Rasputin. He's from Scotland Yard. He's the queen's bodyguard, really.'

'Oh, aye,' said Vic. 'Got a queen, have you?'

'Yes. Mandy.'

'Bloody hell! Why choose her?'

'She turned out to be the real queen of England. She's the heir to the Plantagenets.'

'Ah! I see.' Vic shifted in his seat above them.

'Will you get down then?' said Kelvin.

'No,' said Vic. 'I haven't got time for pissing about. I've got to pick up from another three farms before going back to the factory.'

'You have no choice,' said Kelvin. 'You have to cross an international border here or else go round by Swinehanger. And that's another twenty miles.'

Vic sat in thought for a few seconds. The commander, interested in the outcome of this confrontation, hoisted his backside on to the parapet of the bridge.

'You know I've already been to Northcott, don't you, Kelvin?' said Vic. 'And I've got Frank's milk on board as well.'

'I know that, Vic.'

'You wouldn't want your milk to go off sitting here in the back of the lorry, would you?'

'No, Vic. So the sooner you're out of the cab, the sooner you can get on your way.'

'I work for the Milk Marketing Board. I can't allow any unauthorised persons on to my tanker and I can't pay any sort of toll to you. Not without proper authority.'

'I have the proper authority.'

'Oh aye?' said Vic, drumming his fingers on the steering wheel. 'I've got Frank's milk on board.'

'I know.'

'Frank's got a lot of milk. Couple of thousand litres. Not like you – just a couple of hundred.'

'I know that, too,' said Kelvin.

'What would you do if I decided to pump your milk into the river?'

'You couldn't do that!'

'Oh aye?' Vic disappeared to delve round in the glove compartment of the lorry. Re-emerging with a booklet, he thumbed it through, but the author had not foreseen the situation in which he found himself. He opened his cab door and stepped down to the road. 'I think I'd better telephone the office for instructions.'

'You'll have to go through the frontier if you want to use the phone box,' said Kelvin. 'You'll have to pay for an entry permit.'

'Are you part of this too, Commander?'

Vic received a noncommittal shrug in reply.

'One thing I've learned in twenty years coming to pick up milk in Moorcombe,' said Vic, going round to the side of the lorry and picking up a pair of leather gloves from a wooden box below the curve of the tank. 'When you people get a bee in your bonnet about something, arguments have to be pretty persuasive. I reckon your milk was contaminated, Kelvin.' He took hold of one end of the hose and screwed it on to the outlet of the tank. He pulled the other end from its reel towards the parapet.

'What are you doing?' asked Kelvin.

'What does it look like?' said Vic. 'If you're going to make me drive an extra twenty miles, I'm going to take the weight off the back of the lorry. I'll have to give it a bit of wellie and I don't want all this contaminated milk sloshing round in the back. It's a twisty road, you know '

'But my milk's on there,' said Kelvin. 'You can't do that.'

'Frank's milk's on there too. £300's worth,' said Vic. 'Don't forget that. I won't be able to pick up Ivor's either or anyone else's on the other side of the village. Think of that, too.'

'We'll soon put a stop to this!' said Kelvin, grasping Vic's arm. 'Commander, seize the other side. You're hereby under arrest.'

Vic looked mildly down at Kelvin's hand. The commander

stayed where he was. 'For God's sake, Kelvin. Don't be silly. Let me go.'

'No,' said Kelvin. 'I'm arresting you.'

'Let him go,' said the commander. Reluctantly, Kelvin obeyed. 'It's a bit dicey, Kelvin. You see Vic's not in Moorcombe and he's not breaking any laws. The river is the parish boundary. You can only arrest him once he's across.'

'I could sue for wrongful arrest,' said Vic. 'I could get thousands.'

'We could kidnap him and drag him across the river.' suggested Kelvin.

'That'd be a serious breach of international law,' said the commander.

'Quite right!' said Vic. 'I'd certainly take you to the European Court.'

'Moorcombe's not in the EEC,' said Kelvin.

'Really? In that case it won't matter about your milk. The MMB only deals with English milk. We don't want any of that foreign muck. All tastes like Long Life, doesn't it?' Dragging the hose over to the wall, he draped it over the parapet beside the commander before returning to his cab to start the engine.

'Here!' shouted a voice from the frontier. 'What are you up to, Vic?'

Vic paused, his foot on the step of the lorry. 'Hullo, Frank,' he called. 'I'm just pouring your milk into the river.'

Kelvin was mainly interested in sheep and beef and milk was merely a sideline, but Frank was a professional dairy farmer, intent upon winning the last penny of profit from his milk quota. 'You're doing no such thing!' Hopping hurriedly over the bales, Frank trotted across the bridge. 'What are you stopping here for anyway?'

'Ask Kelvin,', said Vic.

'He refuses to go through Customs and immigration,' said Kelvin.

'What the hell are you about, Kelvin?' asked Frank. 'I thought this independence thing was supposed to make us rich and free. It won't work if our milk gets chucked away. D'you think you're going to get the farmers' vote?'

'It's the principle. We can't be independent just when it suits us.'

'Oh, I don't see why not,' said the commander. 'I mean

what are you going to do when the beer lorry tries to get through to deliver to the Hind? Are you going to turn him away because he won't fill in a form?'

'That's different,' said Kelvin.

'No, it isn't.'

'Yes, it is. Beer's not the same as milk. Everybody knows that. And it'd be an import, not an export.'

Frank began reeling the hose back in. 'I don't care what it is. All I know is that my milk is not going into the river. So let Vic through.'

'I can't do that,' said Kelvin. 'It would mean we shirked the very first test of our independence. Future generations would curse us.'

'My bank manager would curse me if I don't sell my milk.'

'Don't worry about him. We'll repudiate our foreign debts,' said Kelvin.

'Get into the lorry, Vic. I'll clear the road for you,' said Frank.

'I forbid it,' said Kelvin.

Frank had twenty-five years, six inches and three stone on Kelvin. He gave Kelvin a stony look and the latter understood.

'Stop him, Commander.'

'No,' said the commander.

'Here! Rasputin' shouted Kelvin. 'Come here and put Frank under arrest!'

'No,' said Parrott, still sitting on his bale.

'See you tomorrow morning, Kelvin,' said Vic, starting up the lorry. Preceded by Frank, the lorry throbbed forward to the frontier.

'Bastards!' said Kelvin viciously, standing legs apart, hands on hips in the middle of the bridge.

'You begin to see the limitations of power, Kelvin,' said the commander, as they watched the tanker ease through the gap that had been cleared in the frontier. 'You can only act if you carry the people with you.'

A shrill 'beep' from a horn forced Kelvin to leap for safety as Father Loosemire swept across the bridge in the post office van. Without pausing, he speeded through the frontier in the wake of the milk tanker. Frank raised a hand in salute as he passed.

'Did you see that?' cried Kelvin. 'He wasn't even stopped!'

'He was bringing our mail from town,' said the commander.

'It's like the milk and the beer. It's in our own interest not to impede the progress of people like that.'

'We can't do that!' said Kelvin. 'Ah!' A car was coming along the road towards the bridge. 'This one we'll get. Come on, Commander!'

The frontier was rebuilt in a matter of seconds. Having shifted three bales, Kelvin was breathing heavily as he turned, arm upraised, to stop the car. 'Damn! It's Sodov!'

'Good day, Mr Kelvin,' said Sodov.

'I told you to come round by the other road,' said Kelvin. 'Let him through.'

'No,' said Parrott. 'I'm going to search him. Strip search him and then dismantle his car.'

'You can't do that. He's my adviser.'

'That might have been important when you were Prime Minister, but you're just a commoner now and he's just a foreigner,' said Frank. 'Search him.'

'No,' shouted Kelvin.

'It's all right, Kelvin,' said Sodov. 'I have diplomatic

immunity.' He smoothly produced a diplomatic passport from his pocket.

'You think you have an answer to everything, don't you?' said Parrott.

'More so than you,' said Kelvin.

'Don't you believe it,' replied Parrott. 'You're not an officially accredited diplomat here. You may have presented your credentials to the court of St James, but you haven't presented them at the court of Queen Mandy.'

'Don't forget I was a guest at the coronation. I was the only foreign ambassador.'

'Mandy doesn't trust you. At the palace, the opinion is you're scheming and plotting with Kelvin at Northcott. Where's this million pounds you promised?'

'The exchange rate between the pound and our lev is difficult at the moment.'

'Aha! Now he tells us! You're all talk. Get out of that car. I'm going to take it apart.'

'Here's another car!' said the commander.

Kelvin looked up eagerly. 'It's the vet! We'll have him. Let Sodov through.'

Being regularly in transit across the bridge, the vet treated it as would a native. Once round the corner at the far end, he accelerated over the hump and was in mid air before he noticed the obstructing bales barring his progress at the frontier.

The border guards scattered as his car slewed across the road, its back end slapping into Sodov's boot with a crash, followed by a tinny rattle as a hubcap spun on its axis for several seconds before subsiding noisily on to the tarmac.

'Oh God!' said the commander. 'I've had enough of this. I'm going home for breakfast.'

The vet, a man of fifty with wild eyes and a tongue notorious throughout ten parishes, opened the door of his car. He was wearing brown trousers, green wellingtons and a checked shirt.

'You ******* ******** *****s.'

Sodov, his car several hundred pounds worse off, was equally comprehensible. 'Datieba maikata!' he said, springing from his vehicle.

'What the **** do you think you're ******* well ******* about here for?'

161

'Well, see you around,' said the commander, moving hurriedly up the road towards his house less than fifty yards away.

'Hoy!' shouted the vet. 'You're the commander, aren't you? You're a witness! I'll be wanting a statement from you!'

'Must fly!' said the commander over his shoulder.

The vet turned his glowering eyes to his car. '****! Look at the car! I bet all my bottles are broken.' He went round to the back of the vehicle and, after a struggle managed to haul open the buckled boot lid where he examined his supply of medicines and equipment. 'Oh ******* ****!'

'You were going too fast,' said Sodov, going round to the back of his car and hurriedly slamming his own boot which had sprung open at the impact.

'What you got in there?' asked Parrott.

'Diplomatic baggage,' said Sodov, having difficulty in keeping the lid shut.

'Here!' said Kelvin, unknotting the piece of baler twine from his pocket and handing it over. Sodov secured the boot lid to the bumper before straightening up. 'That's better!'

162

'What the **** were you doing parked in the middle of the road? And what the **** are all these bales doing here? I've got a cow in trouble out at the squire's. If it's a bull calf it's worth a couple of hundred. Oh what a ******* **** up!' He returned to his car, unhooked a microphone from the dashboard and spoke into it.

The others watched guiltily until he had finished.

'The ******* squire's on his way down here to pick me up. I suppose this is your doing, Kelvin?'

'No,' said Kelvin.

'Bloody is,' said Parrott.

'Yup,' agreed Frank. 'Kelvin's responsible. He wanted the barrier put here.'

'I hope your insurance covers this,' said the vet.

'Mine?' said Sodov. 'This is nothing to do with me. It is I who am the injured party. Anyway I am a diplomat. I do not need insurance.'

'I'm not talking to you,' said the vet. 'You, Kelvin.'

'You were driving too fast,' said the sullen Kelvin. 'It wasn't my fault. I don't owe you a penny.'

'Oh yes! That reminds me. I'm glad I caught you, Kelvin. You owe the practice nearly five hundred pounds. You haven't given us any money for over a year.'

'That last bullock you came to died,' said Kelvin. 'That was worth a couple of hundred at least.'

'If you stick a beast in a field and give it nothing to eat but ragwort, you can hardly blame me for not saving it. Particularly since it was dead before I got there.'

'You took too long to arrive.'

'You shouldn't've left your roller across the top of your lane. It makes access difficult. Are you going to be at Northcott later on this morning?'

'Why?'

'So's I can pick up a cheque.'

'A cheque. Well, I might be.'

'I wouldn't take a cheque off him,' said Frank. 'Not unless you want to play tennis with it. He keeps cash in a brass milk churn in his hall at Northcott.'

'How the hell did you know?'

'Jason Looscmire told me.'

'What? Jason? How did he know?'

'Everybody knows, Kelvin.'

163

'Ah!' said the vet. 'Here's the squire. You're in charge of my ******* car, Kelvin. I'll see you later.' Taking his bag, a couple of fearsome looking clamps and a pair of overalls from his boot, he walked across the border to where the squire's Range Rover had drawn up. As soon as he was in, the vehicle roared off back up through the village towards the patient.

'Come on, Sodov. It's time we were off home for breakfast,' said Kelvin.

'What about the vet's car?' asked Frank.

'I've got more important things to do. Matters of national business.'

'You'll have plenty of time to move your money later,' said Malcolm.

'No, I've got to see a man about a bomb. Come on, Sodov!'

'Silly ass!' said Frank, as Sodov's car backed across the bridge before turning towards Northcott. 'A bomb! What's he talking about?'

The commander would have had an inkling, but he had already preceded Kelvin home for breakfast.

Chapter Ten

FROM THE VILLAGE, the road towards Northcott ran alongside the river. A thin screen of spruce and larch protected travellers from the unsettling sight of the water awaiting them, should drink, senility, inexperience or mechanical malfunction cause them to veer off the tarmac. On the right, bracken sprouted amid the beeches and oaks, clinging to the thin soil on the hillside which rose a hundred feet to the lip of the valley.

A mile downstream from Moorcombe bridge, Sodov turned left on to the muddy track towards the farm. An ancestral Morchard, serendipitously in occupation during the prosperous years of the Napoleonic wars, had thrown a single-arch stone bridge across the river at this point. His descendants had cause to bless him as it cut half an hour from the walk to the Hunted Hind. With Kelvin's Land Rover on his tail, Sodov delicately negotiated the crossing, built when a packhorse was the widest vehicle, before trying to avoid the worst of the potholes in the lane, threading a path between the six-foot hedge banks.

Sodov drove into the concrete yard in front of the limewashed cob farmhouse with its corrugated iron roof. Given central heating, white paint, stripped pine and double-glazed windows, any estate agent would have put it on his books at a couple of hundred thousand pounds but, in its present condition, it was scarcely fit for human habitation – rotten window frames, missing lengths of guttering and holes in the roof where the tin had rusted through. One gap was covered by a blue tarpaulin, itself torn and rotten.

From a spring in the hillside behind the house, Prudence had brought running water. Black alkathene pipe snaked its way into the kitchen and upstairs to the avocado bathroom suite in a corner of her bleak lino-floored bedroom. Kelvin still preferred to patronise a small wooden shed at the bottom of the garden, its seat directly above the cess-pit which seethed and grunted through the summer months. This early in the season, only a faint hint of its dramatic late-summer potential curled the hairs in Sodov's nostrils as he stepped out of the car, but he had put it down to the aroma from the cattle sheds on the opposite side of the yard.

Kelvin pulled up alongside, the baldness of his tyres betrayed by the track through the film of wet slurry lying on the concrete. 'Have you got it?' he asked eagerly, tugging ineffectually at the twine securing Sodov's boot.

'Yes,' said Sodov.

'That was a near one at the bridge!' said Kelvin. 'It'd've spoilt everything. Prudence! Prudence!'

Startled by the noise, a few shiftless pigeons, occupying the hay barn until Kelvin got round to shooting them, clapped noisily into the air from some spilled barley and wheeled up to perch on the branch of a large oak, used as a gate post at the entrance to the yard.

Prudence appeared in the doorway of a barn, her sleeves rolled up and covered in black smears of oil. 'What d'you want?'

'Come here and look at this!'

'I'm replacing a piston ring on the tractor. It'll have to wait!'

'We've got the bomb!'

'I'll come and look when I've finished . . .' She turned back and disappeared into the blackness of the barn's interior. The forlorn bellow of a cowless calf greeted her return.

'No romance in her!' said Kelvin. He stopped wrestling with the twine and plunged his hand into the pocket of his jacket, pulling out a single-bladed knife and sawed through the string. He flung open the boot. 'Where is it?'

'It's in the box, Kelvin. I think you'll be pleased.'

'In the box?' Kelvin frowned at the modestly-sized cardboard carton. 'It's not very big.' He tore off the tape which sealed it to reveal a polished metal cylinder about the size of a beef wellington. Picking it up, he hefted it in his hand. 'It's quite heavy. How do you set it off? Is there a timer inside it?'

'It's not a real bomb, Kelvin. Remember?'

'I know that, but it's got to look realistic.'

'It does look realistic. I asked for a model of a device of

166

about one hundred thousand kilotons which could be carried by one man. Belchev made it last night.'

'But it don't look anything like a bomb.'

'Belchev is more used to adapting umbrellas than making bombs, but he is very good. He makes engines for model aeroplanes for a pastime. He copied the bomb from *Startrek*, an episode when an agent of the Klingons put such a device upon the Enterprise.'

'Huh!' said Kelvin, unimpressed. 'I don't recall that one and I bet nobody else in Moorcombe does either. It was probably only shown in Bulgaria. We're going to have to have something better than this.' He strode off across the yard, boots squelching across the slurry, and disappeared into the dark interior of the barn, still carrying the bomb. 'Prudence! Prudence!'

Starting off with an empty forty-gallon oil drum, Kelvin built an atom bomb to his own specifications. With help from Prudence, he welded on sections of steel piping, normally used to ferry milk round the milking parlour, before painting it yellow. On top, he glued a multi-buttoned calculator, given by a cattle feed company when Kelvin once paid a bill without the need for a solicitor's letter.

After a midday break to eat, plan and give the paint time to dry, he returned to add some authenticity. He painted a black skull-and-crossbones, several radiation warning signs, an assortment of letters and numbers – some Arabic script and some Cyrillic, provided by Sodov and, as a final touch, the letters USA on one side and CCCP on the other.

'It looks very good,' said Sodov as they stood back to admire the drum. It had been built in situ on the bed of a hay trailer. 'However it is less subtle than my bomb.'

'Mine's not supposed to be subtle. It's meant to convince Moorcombe, not the Klingons. But it'd be a pity if you'd been all the way up to London for nothing.' He rubbed his jaw, making a sound like frying bacon against his stubble. 'What we could do is have yours on the trailer too. How about that?'

'A good idea,' said Sodov.

'Mind you, we'll have to clean up the yellow paint drips on the trailer.'

'Just scatter some straw on top.'

'And when I move the thing the straw'll all blow off and

show the splodges again,' said Kelvin. 'There's a can of petrol over there,' he pointed into the dark recesses of the barn. 'You can clean it up.'

With a sigh, Sodov plodded off in search of the can while Kelvin turned to Prudence. 'I think we've earned a cup of tea. That's a good day's work.'

'What happens now?'

'I'll go to the pub while you do the milking,' said Kelvin.

'Yes, I know that, but what're you going to do with the bombs?'

'Take the trailer down to the bridge tomorrow morning. It's time the government of Moorcombe was back in safe hands.'

' 'Twas on a Monday morning,' sang Kelvin as he laced his boots in the kitchen. 'That I beheld my darling. She looked so sweet and cha-arming ta-tumty tumty tum. She looked so sweet and charming-o a hanging out the linen-o. Washing away with a smoothing iron. Washing away with a smoothing iron. She stole my heart away.' He stood up from the bench by the kitchen table and went over to the stove, moving the heavy iron kettle from the simmer plate to the hot. Pausing with a frown, he opened up the door to the firebox and slammed it shut as a billow of yellow smoke escaped into the room. 'Oh what a beautiful morning . . .'

It was, too. Outside the early morning sunshine was already burning wisps of steam from a landscape glistening after a night of heavy rain. The sky was a cloudless blue with that technicolour intensity which comes when the air has been scoured clean of dust. Even through the grime covering the window, a hard bolt of sun cut across the smoky room like a searchlight through mist.

Kelvin hummed his way through his tea, whistled his way down the garden path to the privy and then sang his way to the barn. 'The sun has got his hat on. Hip, hip, hip, hip, hoorah!'

Inside, squat and menacing, the great yellow bomb sat contentedly in the centre of the hay trailer. Pulling himself up beside it, he ran his finger across the paint, giving a grunt of satisfaction when it rubbed dry against his thumb. A small sound from the far side of the barn caught his attention.

'What are you doing, Prudence?'

'I told you yesterday, Dad. I'm replacing the piston rings

168

on the tractor. I'd've finished too, if you hadn't got me painting that thing.' Wearing blue overalls, she had a smudge of oil across one cheek.

'But I need the tractor now. I want to take the bomb down to the bridge.'

'It won't be finished for another couple of hours and then I need it to haul a cow out of a ditch. Three Tits's been stuck in the bottom field all night.'

'The cow can wait,' said Kelvin roughly. 'This is much more important.'

'She's only been calved a fortnight and she needs milking, Dad. You can have it when I'm finished with it.'

'Look . . .'

'No. You look.' Prudence slammed a spanner against the back tyre of the tractor. 'I've said you can have the tractor to play with when I'm finished. The longer you stop me working, the longer it'll take. If you want to speed things up, you can get Brett up, change him and give him his breakfast.'

'I'm not doing a woman's work!'

'In that case, take over this spanner and do a man's.' She turned back to the tractor.

Irresolute, Kelvin looked between his bomb and his daughter. 'I'll take the Land Rover.'

'You can't. The trailer hasn't got brakes.'

'Aha! You forget we're making our own law now. Percy's not going to stop me.'

'Do what you like, Dad. I could really do with the tractor all day. I'm a bit behind with the slurry spreading.'

'You're a good girl, Prudence. I won't take your tractor away from you.' He waved a magnanimous hand. 'You just enjoy yourself. I'll make do with the Land Rover.'

Demonstrating his generosity of spirit restored Kelvin's upbeat mood. 'All things bright and beautiful,' he carolled, raising his face towards the sky to allow better egress for the sound. Terrified by his tuneless boom, the pigeons clapped out of their barn and headed off towards the river. He stomped back into the house. 'Sodov! Sodov!' he roared from the bottom of the stairs. 'I'm taking the bomb into Moorcombe. Are you coming?'

At the top of the stairs, Sodov appeared wearing a lugubrious expression and striped flannel pyjamas which swelled across his abdomen. Behind him, peering through his

169

legs with a loose nappy trailing on the threadbare landing carpet, stood Brett. 'What do I do with your grandson?'

'Do with him? You don't have to do nothing. Prudence'll give him his breakfast, soon.'

'I was asleep fifteen minutes ago. I wake up and he is in my bedroom, trying to climb through the open window. I have to stop him.'

'What were you up to, boy?' asked Kelvin. 'Anyway, get your clothes on, Sodov. It's time we were off to the village.'

'I cannot. When I catch the boy, he has already thrown my clothes out of the window.'

'Tsk, tsk,' said Kelvin. 'Let's have a look.' He clumped up the stairs towards the bedroom occupied by Sodov at the back of the house. It contained a brass bed, a marble-topped washstand on which stood a jug and basin and a pine chest of drawers. As in much of the house, the floor was covered by cracked brown linoleum which had settled over the years to show the uneven outline of the boards beneath. The window overlooked a steep, cow-filled grass field rising to a straggly hedge. 'Hmm,' said Kelvin, looking through. 'Brett must've been after your jacket. It's stuck over the telephone wires.'

'I know,' said Sodov.

'But I don't know how your trousers got away out there.'

'They landed on the back of one of the cows. Then they fell to the grass which is exceedingly wet and the cow has since dropped faeces upon them.'

'I'll lend you some trousers,' said Kelvin. 'I've got an old pair in my cupboard.'

Sodov looked at Kelvin's current pair. Even the grease, cow dung, mud and sweat which enriched the garment had failed to protect the turn-ups from fraying and Kelvin's shiny knee-caps from peeking through. 'Unfortunately, I would be too large for your trousers. I shall wait for Prudence. It is not good to leave a child so young by itself. She can clean and press my garments and I shall admire her bosoms.'

'You keep your admiring to yourself, you dirty bugger. Don't worry about Brett. We just have to chuck him in the calf pen as we go. He doesn't need a nappy 'cos he can piss on the straw.'

'No. I shall wait. You go ahead.' Not a fool, Sodov was relieved to have an excuse to avoid the actual moment of Kelvin's *coup d'état*.

170

'Well, I can't wait. You'll miss all the fun.'

'I shall try to withstand my great disappointment.'

Kelvin shrugged. 'Suit yourself. Stoke up the Aga when you make a cup of tea.'

'Yes, I feel like a beverage.'

'The wood's in the shed to the left of the back door.'

'Right.'

'There's an axe and saw hanging behind the door. That trunk needs to be cut into nine-inch lengths before you split it. Half a dozen logs ought to be enough.' Kelvin whistled his way happily down the stairs and out to the barn where he adjusted the height of the hay trailer's draw bar. Returning to the yard, he started the Land Rover, backing it expertly up to the trailer which jerked as the ball married with the socket. He wound up the jack on the trailer.

'You'd better put a rope round the oil drum, Dad,' said Prudence, deep in the bowels of the tractor.

'It won't need it.'

'The trailer's light; the drum's empty. It'd bounce off into a puddle before you got fifty yards down the lane.'

'Oh, all right. I'll put on some baler twine.'

'You want it to look heavy. Can't you bolt it on?'

'I'll use a rope and some cow chains.'

'That'll do.' Cow chains tied cows into stalls for milking before the advent of the milking parlour, but they had a myriad of other functions. They could be used to tie gates, to stuff down and block rat holes, attach implements to tractors, block gaps in hedges and patch chain harrows. A step up in strength and durability from baler twine, they were nearly as ubiquitous.

It was nigh on 11 am before Kelvin was ready and the Land Rover, a flashing red torch tied to the bonnet, eased its way carefully down the lane towards Moorcombe.

To Kelvin's disgust, the checkpoint at the bridge was deserted. He had to wait while two cars, unquestionably tollable, nosed over the hump of the bridge above the brown water of the rain-swollen river, their drivers believing they had passed through a sleepy rural village rather than the latest addition to the family of nations. Rather than park right on the bridge, he nosed across and turned left down River Lane to leave the bomb in front of 'Pixies Laughter'.

He pressed the bell on the palace door but the first dozen

171

notes of *Home Sweet Home* failed to elicit a response, so, leaving the trailer, he walked the 150 yards up the village to the pub. The tap, as he expected, was full.

'Where've you been, Kelvin?' asked the Marquis of Church Lane in a high good humour. 'We had some good fun at the bridge yesterday. I can tell you.'

'I've been busy,' said Kelvin, going behind the bar to pour himself a beer. Although it was early, the dull roar of conversation was accompanied by a heavy fog of tobacco smoke.

'Rain's forecast tonight,' said Jimmy.

'It often is,' replied Kelvin. 'I see you've lost your chair.' Mandy, with Keith and Parrott alongside her, was sitting in the Windsor chair normally occupied by Jimmy.

'Mandy had to have a throne.'

'You had no right to let her. That chair's for the oldest regular customer in the pub.'

'And if I decide to let Mandy sit there, then I can do. She's made me a marquis after all.'

'When you die and the chair's mine, she's out.'

'I'll outlast you!'

'I wouldn't put money on it if I were you,' said Kelvin, looking appraisingly at Jimmy. 'If you were a beast of mine, I'd send you to the abattoir before the hunt came to take away your carcass.'

'You're just trying to get me cross!'

'No, I'm not. If I was trying to get you cross, I'd be taking the piss out of you by calling you a sheep-shagger.'

Turning red with rage, Jimmy drew his breath to riposte but broke instead into an alarming coughing fit as he inhaled the half inch of ash on the end of the cigarette adhering to his lip.

'I'd sit down,' said Kelvin solicitously. 'You don't want to go down in history as the old bugger who croaked in the pub.'

'Bastard!' spluttered Jimmy, his chest wheezing.

'Are you all right?' asked the commander, coming over to thump Jimmy on the back. Unusually, his wife, Elfrieda, was with him. In her mid-fifties with a long horsey face and long unkempt grey hair, she had embraced feminism, pacificism, animal rights and ley lines in recent years.

'Thank heaven's you're no longer in charge, Kelvin,' said Elfrieda which whom he had only cordial dislike in common.

'Huh!' Finally satisfied with the trembling plenitude of his glass, Kelvin raised it to his lips and took a cautious sip.

'We may not have to be independent for much longer. Malcolm had a call from the council. He thinks we could reach a compromise. If we don't put on the crenellations and the portcullis, they may let us go ahead with the hall.'

'You can't compromise on principles,' said Kelvin. 'Anyway what about Botograd on Vit?'

'Bugger Botograd!' said Jimmy with a regal wave of his cigarette. 'I haven't seen much of this money yet and I've got my pension to consider.'

'You're a gutless lot. What about you, Rasputin?' asked Kelvin, spotting Parrott. 'Can't say you've been keeping much of an eye on Sodov over the last day or two.'

'He's with you, isn't he? With a fool like you telling him what to do, he's not going to be able to do much harm, is he?'

'That's what you think,' said Kelvin grimly.

'Off with his head!' shrieked Mandy. Parrott, obviously in as celebratory a mood as she, put his hand on her knee and guffawed. Mandy had a laugh like Woody Woodpecker. Even Jimmy wheezed into his glass.

'You lot are doing a grand job!' said Kelvin. 'There're streams of cars crossing the bridge without anyone there to check them.'

'Oh, blow the cars!' said Mandy, waving her beringed hand at him. 'Here! Guess what?'

'What?'

'No! You've got to guess.'

Kelvin ducked out of the way as she aimed a slap at his back. Experience had taught him the metalwork on her fingers acted like a knuckle duster. 'I didn't come here to play games!'

'Ooh!' Mandy lurched back against Parrott. 'Who's a little crosspatch today?'

Kevin snorted in disgust. 'You're drunk, woman!'

Mandy leaned towards him and waggled an uneven finger under his nose. 'Now that's treason, isn't it?' She turned to Parrott. 'Isn't it?'

'It's something, certainly.'

'Look . . .' began Kelvin.

'Shall we cut off his head?' said Mandy. 'Or shall we lock him up in the squire's cellars for years and years so's his hair grows long and his toes are nibbled by creepy crawlies and rats?'

'Make him buy a drink!' said Jimmy.

'Now that's why you're the Marquis of Church Lane and Kelvin's just a peasant.'

'No longer!' said Kelvin dramatically. 'I . . .'

'Oh shut up, Kelvin,' said Mandy. 'I'm talking. I say you buy us a drink or we'll . . . we'll . . .' She turned to Parrott. 'What'll we do?'

'We'll banish him,' said Parrott. 'And Sodov. He's an undesirable alien. So you'd better buy a drink, Kelvin.'

'Right,' said Mandy. 'That's settled. Mine's an advocaat and coke.'

'I've a bomb outside,' said Kelvin.

'Oh have you, now?' With a slight effort, Mandy focused her eyes upon Kelvin's face 'A *bombe surprise*?'

'Ooh! That's a good one!' said Parrott.

'What did you say, Kelvin?' The commander frowned slightly as Mandy and her bodyguard put their heads together and giggled.

174

Kelvin turned to him with relief. 'I said I have a bomb.'

'What sort of a bomb?'

'One like we were talking about.'

'From Harrods?'

'No, from Sodov.'

'Really?'

'Yes. Really. Two bombs in fact. A big one to use locally and a little one we can send through the post.'

'Oh, shut up, Kelvin,' said Mandy. 'Where's my drink?'

'What sort of bombs are we talking about?' asked Jimmy. 'Are you going blasting salmon in Ash Pool? Even if we are independent, we can't have that sort of thing.'

'I'm not talking about blowing up salmon,' said Kelvin, scornfully. 'I'm talking about power.' He faced square on to Mandy and Parrott. 'You two've had your chips. I'm taking over in Moorcombe again.' Puzzled, Mandy blinked at him. 'I've got a bomb outside your house, Mandy and I'll let it off unless you appoint me Prime Minister again.'

Mandy rocked back on her throne. 'Well, set the bloody thing off, then! See if I care.' She turned to Parrott. 'He's a real bore, Kelvin, isn't he?'

'Oink! Oink!' said Parrott.

'What? Oh! I see. Boar as in pig!' The machine gun cackle of royal mirth brought indulgent looks to the faces of her subjects round in the rest of the bar.

'Right!' said Kelvin. 'Right! If that's what you want. Right!' He turned to go to the door. 'You've asked for it!'

Fortunately the commander intervened before Kelvin was forced to destroy the world. 'Er . . . Kelvin. Hang on a minute.'

'No,' said Kelvin. 'They've had their chance.'

'Kelvin!' The urgency in the commander's voice silenced the cackles of Mandy and made Kelvin pause. 'Think what you're doing, man!' Kelvin stopped and thought. The commander, beads of sweat starting on his brow, continued. 'Let's just make sure we all know what you're talking about. You've got an atom bomb outside Mandy's house.'

'No,' said Kelvin. 'I haven't. I've got two atom bombs parked outside Mandy's house.'

'You're a daft old bugger, Kelvin,' said Jimmy. 'People like you should never be allowed to have atom bombs in the first place.'

Grunts of agreement came from many other patrons.

'How did you get hold of them?' asked Mick.

'I was thinking about it for a while,' replied Kelvin. 'I thought Moorcombe deserved the best we could get. Sodov got them for me. He brought them in yesterday. We were lucky they didn't go off when the vet crashed into him.'

'What's he talking about?' asked Parrott.

'Dunno, ducky,' said Mandy. She hiccuped. 'Pardon me.' She put an apologetic hand to her lips.

Ignoring Mandy, the commander addressed Parrott. 'Kelvin says he's been given two nuclear bombs. He has put them outside Mandy's house.'

'Two nukes!' Parrott turned to look at Kelvin. 'You stupid jerk! Santa came early this year, did he?'

'Er . . .' said the commander, glancing nervously at Kelvin. 'Kelvin was talking to me about it a day or two ago. It appears Mr Sodov may have had something to do with it.'

'Don't be daft. Not even the Bulgarians would go round dishing out nuclear weapons.'

'They did to me,' said Kelvin.

'Oh yes? And where did they get them from? And even if they had them, how would they get them to you and why? You must think I'm an idiot!'

'I do,' said Kelvin. 'I'm off to do what has to be done. A man's got to do what a man's got to do.' He began to move towards the door once more, but slowly, giving the commander time to stop him.

'Stop!' said the commander.

'Let him go!' said Parrott, but Kelvin had stopped.

'I think it would be wise to take a look at what Kelvin has,' said the commander.

'While you lot have been carousing and whoring,' said Kelvin, 'I've been preparing for the survival of Moorcombe. Mandy, it was me who made you queen. It is I who can depose you. The squire should be our monarch, not you. I'll see you down at River Lane.' He exited.

'The squire?' said Mandy. 'Off with his head!'

A rumble of disapproval came from Jimmy. 'I don't think we should be disrespectful to the squire.'

'Eeeh! Listen to the marquis, there,' said Mandy. 'Who's side are you on?'

'I'm just saying the squire's been in Moorcombe a damn

sight longer than you and done a damn sight more for the community than you. He and his family'll still be here long after the worms have shat you out in the graveyard!'

There was a second's pause before Mandy's face cracked, slabs of powder shedding from her face like rendering from a building. 'Keith! He's being horrid to me. Do something about it!' But Keith was working on the village hall.

'Shut up, Mandy,' said Parrott. 'You think Kelvin might actually have something sinister down there, Commander?' he asked, the mists of alcohol clearing more rapidly from his mind than from his liege-lady's.

'Let's put it this way. Kelvin can sometimes spring some extremely unpleasant surprises.'

'Shit! I suppose we'd better take a look.'

'What about me!' wailed Mandy as her court followed in Kelvin's footsteps. Only Jimmy, as was his custom, stayed behind for a few seconds to drain the glasses.

'I don't believe it' exclaimed Parrott, as he turned the corner into River Lane.

Not wishing to encourage too close a scrutiny of his deterrents, Kelvin was busy hanging cow chains between the high timber ends of the trailer. 'What do you think?' he asked proudly as the establishment of Moorcombe paced silently down the lane towards him.

'I don't think I want to get too close,' said Jimmy, stopping twenty yards away.

'It's going to make a frightful mess of Mandy's cottage if it goes off,' observed Elfrieda, stopping alongside Jimmy.

'It'll make a frightful mess of southern England,' said the commander, grimly.

'What've you got there, Kelvin?' asked Parrott, his voice betraying some strain.

'It's my bomb,' said Kelvin with pride. 'Nobody'll dare attack Moorcombe now we've got this.'

'Christ!' whispered Parrott, coming to a dead stop, his eyes wide.

'I see you've solved the problem of delivery,' said the commander gesturing to the trailer.

'No,' said Kelvin. 'The trailer's just to bring it here. The yellow one stays here in case we're invaded. I've got a little one for foreigners. It's in the box.'

177

The commander and Parrott walked warily forward to the trailer and peered into the box. Sodov's steel cylinder lay enigmatically on a bed of crumpled newspaper. They withdrew the few yards to Kelvin.

'Tell us about them,' said Parrott, a tremor in his voice.

'Certainly,' said Kelvin, importantly. 'The one over there,' he waved his hand at the oil drum, 'that's yellow. The other one's not. They're a hundred killer tons, you know.'

'Kilotons,' corrected the commander.

'That's lots, isn't it?' asked Kelvin.

'Yes,' confirmed the commander. 'That's certainly lots.'

'What've I got into?' said Parrott. He was actually wringing his hands.

The commander gripped his elbow. 'Don't lose control. I'll handle this.' He turned to Kelvin. 'How are they armed?'

'Armed?'

'Yes. Fused.'

'Fused,' said Kelvin, his eyes turning towards the fishing gnome in Mandy's garden for ideas. 'The usual way, I suppose.' Inspiration suddenly struck. 'No! They're electronically fused.' He pointed towards the oil drum on top of which was glued the calculator. 'See?'

They looked and they saw.

'They can't be real,' said Parrott.

' 'Course they're real! Do you want me to let one of them off just to show you? Look! See the symbols on the side of the yellow one? That means it's radioactive. Giving out death rays like all the sheep on the moor after that power station blew up in Russia. Them rays'll make you sterile.' Like footballers facing an indirect penalty, both the commander and Parrott crossed their hands over their loins. Kelvin noticed and approved. He pointed to the bomb. 'And look lower down where it says CCCP. That's Russian for Russia.'

'Where did you get them?'

'I've told you,' said Kelvin. 'From Sodov. They were in his boot when the vet bashed into him by the bridge.'

'Nonsense! As I told you, even if he had access to the things which he hasn't, he wouldn't give them to you.'

'Look,' Kelvin gestured to his bombs. 'They're there, aren't they? D'ya think I made them myself?'

Parrott looked. 'Oh dear.' He wrung his hands again.

'Kelvin,' said the commander. 'You say they're electronically fused. They're not dangerous at the moment, are they?'

'That's for me to know and the enemy to find out!' said Kelvin.

'Silly old fool!' said Jimmy rather loudly. He, along with the others from the bar, had seated themselves on the low stone wall running alongside the river from where they could watch, a safe twenty yards from the bombs.

'It's you who's a silly old fool!' said Kelvin, striding angrily across the lane towards him.

'Not half as silly as you!' replied Jimmy. 'If Prudence can't trust you to do the milking without cocking it up, she shouldn't let you out in charge of a couple of atom bombs.'

'Atom bombs?' said the late-arriving Stephanie, turning pale. 'I'm sorry. What are you talking about?'

'Those are my atom bombs,' said Kelvin gesturing proudly towards his trailer.

'Oh, I didn't know,' said Stephanie. Closing her eyes, she slid from the wall to land in a crumpled heap on the tarmac. Her cotton skirt rode up her leg to mid thigh. Tiny golden hairs were lit by the sun against the brown of her skin.

'Quick!' shouted Kelvin. 'Loosen her clothing! She's fainted!'

'Get away from her!' shouted Malcolm, as Jimmy and Kelvin scrabbled for the privilege of undoing the bottons on her blouse.

'Let's have a butcher's while he's trying to look up her skirt,' said Parrott. He and the commander moved towards the trailer. 'Can you take down the numbers on the big one? They may help us to find out what exactly they are.'

'I haven't got a pencil and paper,' replied the commander. 'D'you see? It's got American markings on it as well as Russian. It was bound to happen, I suppose. The super-powers must be jointly developing bombs now under the free exchange of information.'

'You're right! That's important intelligence. I'd better get to a telephone and get help.'

'Use Mandy's,' said the commander.

'You keep him busy,' said Parrott as he crossed the concrete front garden.

'How?' called the commander.

'Humour him until the experts get here. Or see if you can defuse them.' He disappeared beneath the rose trellis at the side of the house.

'Defuse them!' muttered the commander. 'Does he think I'm James Bond?' He walked back to the trailer and leaned over the cow chains to examine the bomb.

'Darling! Get away from there!' The argument over Stephanie's figure stilled as the rest of the villagers, along with the commander turned in astonishment towards Elfrieda as she stood, face clouded with concern. 'You could get hurt.'

The commander hurried over. 'You haven't said something like that for twenty years! I thought you'd stopped caring!'

'Only because I thought you'd stopped caring.'

'Dearest Elfie!'

'Darling Snuggle Buggle!'

'Snuggle Buggle!' snorted Kelvin, as the commander gingerly put a tweed-clad arm across Elfrieda's shoulder in a rough hug.

'Isn't that sweet?' said Jimmy, a sentimental smile cutting unaccustomed wrinkles across his leathery cheeks.

'Bloody disgusting at their age!' said Kelvin. 'Anyone'd think they weren't married.'

Stephanie suddenly revived. 'If you touch my leg again, Kelvin, I'll kick you in the crotch!'

180

Kelvin snatched his hand away in alarm. 'I was only trying to help. You fainted.'

'Malcolm will give me all the help I need,' she said, climbing to her feet. 'It's more important that you get rid of those bomb things immediately.'

'I couldn't do that,' said Kelvin. 'They're here for our protection.'

'You're quite right, Stephanie,' said Elfrieda, untangling her headscarf from the wrist-band of her husband's watch. 'This is quite monstrous! It's the most terrifying and irresponsible act I have ever heard of!'

'Oh, I don't know,' said Kelvin. 'I'm sure worse things happen at sea.'

'The sinking of the *Titanic*', said Jimmy. 'That was worse.'

'Exactly! There's no comparison. Nobody's been hurt and nobody's going to get hurt.'

'But they could go off!'

'And you might get lumbago or the sun not come up tomorrow morning.'

'That's not very likely!'

'It's not very likely these here bombs'll go off either . . . well, not unless I want them too.'

'Ha!' The shout made them all turn. Parrott crouched in the roadway between them and the trailer.

'What's with you?' asked Kelvin, puzzled.

'You swine! I'm not going to give a raving maniac like you a chance to set these things off. You can wait there 'till some help arrives.'

'I could go through Mandy's garden and come round the other side,' Kelvin pointed out.

'No. I'm putting you under arrest. Enough of this pissing about,' said Parrott, advancing menacingly towards Kelvin. 'You're going to be thrown in jail and then we'll chuck away the key.'

'Here!' said Jimmy. 'You watch yourself! He may not be Prime Minister any more, but he was Chairman of the Parish Council. He deserves proper respect.'

'You keep out of this,' said Parrott. He pushed Jimmy roughly out of the way.

'Be careful!' said the commander. 'There's no need for violence.'

'I said keep out of this!' snarled Parrott. 'Or you'll join

him!' Pushing his way through the natives, the policeman took hold of Kelvin by the arm and twisted it behind his back.

'Ow!' said Kelvin, dancing awkwardly from foot to foot. 'That hurts! What do you think you're doing?'

'Now look here, Parrott!' The commander strode forward. 'You can't behave like a hooligan.'

'Leggo!' yelled Kelvin.

'I'll teach you to threaten to blow up the world,' said Parrott, his mouth a few inches from Kelvin's ear. 'You disgusting old peasant!'

'That's enough. You heard my husband!' said Elfrieda, grasping Parrott's elbow. The effect was immediate. With a gasp of pain, Parrott released his prisoner and clutched his elbow.

'Cor!' said Jimmy. 'That was good. What did you do to him?'

'Pressure point,' explained Elfrieda with crispness. 'I learned about it in acupuncture.'

'Whose side are you on?' asked Parrott, the hot blood of his righteous anger beginning to cool. 'It's imperative we keep him away from the trailer till help arrives. We can't have him triggering those bombs and he's daft enough to do it.'

'They're on timing fuses,' said Kelvin. 'They don't need me to go off.'

'When have you set them for?' asked the commander.

'Dunno. I forgot. Sodov set them.'

The commander sighed. 'You will really have to do better than that, Kelvin. If you have charge of a nuclear device, you know how and when it'll go off, otherwise it's just not credible.'

'True.' Kelvin considered for a few seconds. 'Unless I fiddle with the buttons every hour, they'll go off. How about that?'

'It'll do, I suppose.'

'The more I think on it, the more I'm sure they're fake,' said Malcolm. 'I mean, is it likely?' He gestured to Kelvin. 'Look at him! We're expected to believe he's got two bombs there? Half a dozen countries in the world have spent millions for decades and still haven't got them. Kelvin Morchard, achiever of the terrorist's dream? The whole idea's absurd and we're fools to even think of taking it seriously.'

'That's the nice thing about these things.' said Kelvin. 'You have to take them seriously.' The crowd had let him free and closed in on the trailer. He leaned over and stroked the yellow cylinder. 'If there's even a chance they're real, then you have to assume they are. You can't afford to take the gamble, can you?'

'There's another thing, too,' said Jimmy, 'if he set them off, he'd go up with them.' He jerked his head at Kelvin. 'You wouldn't get him risking something like that.'

'But I might,' said Kelvin, looking smug.

'Kelvin,' said Stephanie. 'What do you want?'

'Want? I don't want anything. Just to be treated with respect due to my position as head of this community.'

'So if we depose Mandy and make you god-king or whatever, you'd get rid of these bombs?'

'Well . . . If I did that, what's to stop you ganging up on me again? I think it'd be better if I just kept them safely hidden away somewhere. Just in case of emergencies.'

'That won't be allowed,' said Parrott.

'I don't think it's up to anyone except us to say what's allowed in Moorcombe. We're independent now.'

'Ever heard of the Cuba missile crisis?' said Malcolm. 'If the Americans wouldn't allow them on Cuba, can you see the government allowing them in Moorcombe?'

'They ain't got no choice,' said Kelvin.

'That's what you think,' said Parrott.

'You've got somebody coming to sort me out, have you?' asked Kelvin.

'Wait and see,' said Parrott.

'Are they going to be coming soon?' asked Jimmy. 'I don't want to have to wait here all day.'

'I expect they'll be coming soon.'

'Where's Mandy, then? She could at least give us a cup of tea while we wait.'

'I could get some of my elderflower wine,' said Elfrieda.

'That'd be nice,' said Kelvin. 'We could have a nuclear bomb party. That reminds me. I'd better go and reset the fuses. With all this excitement, I nearly forgot.'

'Bullshit or not,' said Jimmy gloomily, as Kelvin climbed on to the wagon and punched away at the calculator on his oil drum. 'When you say things like that, it don't half put a bit of a damper on things. Those things are dangerous, Kelvin. You ought to show more care.'

'Sorry,' said Kelvin, hopping back to the ground.

183

'What about the other one?' said Parrott.

'That one's different.'

'In what way?'

'Well, it's in a cardboard box, for a start.'

'No. In what way is the fuse different?'

'Er,' said Kelvin. 'It's a secret.'

'A trembler? Is that it?'

'Yes,' said Kelvin. 'It's a trembler. I remember now.'

'And you bounced it up on the back of that trailer! I'd better get on the phone again. We'll have to evacuate the South West. Then I'll go down and arrest Sodov.'

'You do that and Prudence'll clobber you', warned Kelvin. 'She's taken a bit of a shine to him.'

'Panicky sort of a bugger, i'n'e?' said Jimmy, as Parrott disappeared back into 'Pixies Laughter.'

Elfrieda and the commander brought bottles to the road from their wine cellar and the natives spread themselves across the concrete patio of 'Pixies Laughter' to await events. The first event was the telephone. 'It's for you, Kelvin,' said Mandy, coming out of the house.

'Me?' asked Kelvin. 'Who is it?'

'I don't know.'

'But how did they know I was here?'

'I don't know.'

'Where's the phone?'

'Here,' said Mandy, thrusting out her cordless telephone. Kelvin looked at it with alarm. 'What's that?'

'It's a telephone, you fool.'

'Huh! I hope the electronic signal doesn't set off the bomb.'

'Oh shut up, Kelvin!' said Stephanie. Having enjoyed a couple of glasses of wine, she was sitting beside the garden pond, dabbling her fingers in the water.

Mandy looked over. 'I'd mind the bleach.'

'Where?' asked Stephanie.

'In the water. It keeps it clean.'

Kelvin suspiciously took the phone. 'Hullo? Who is it? Oh, hullo.' He put his hand over the mouthpiece. 'It's Cattermole. He's the county emergency officer, meant to be in charge of the emergency volunteers.'

'Perhaps you'll take orders from your boss,' said the commander.

184

Kelvin returned to his call. 'How did you know I was here? ... You rang Northcott ... No. That was Mr Sodov. He's a Bulgarian and then you rang the pub. I see. Well, what can I do for you? ... Parrott? yes, of course I know him. He's gone off somewhere.' He listened for a few seconds. 'I'll ask.' He looked to the commander. 'D'you think Parrott's potty?'

'I wouldn't've said so.'

'No,' said Kelvin, addressing the telephone. 'I see.' He looked up. 'Did anyone actually see his identification?'

'Parrott's?' said the commander. 'Yes. I did and so did you.'

'So I did,' said Kelvin. 'Yes, he's genuine.' He listened again. 'Is that right? It does sound a bit of a funny story, but it's true ... No, not just one. There're actually two of them.' Putting his hand over the telephone, he winked massively at the commander. 'Yes, yes. It is a great opportunity for the volunteers. Can I handle it? Of course I can handle it. I give you my word. I'm in charge here. Don't you worry. Thank you. You reckon you can get us walkie-talkie radios? Good ... good. Hang on, I'll borrow a pencil. I'd better take this down.' Kelvin clicked his fingers. Malcolm produced the paper and pencil. 'Yes ... yes ... I got that.' He scribbled furiously. 'Yes, you can count on me. Thank you.' Kelvin handed the telephone over to Mandy.

'Well?' said the commander.

'That was Cattermole.'

'We know. What did he say?'

'He wanted to know if Parrott was mad. Apparently he was phoning the police saying there was a nuclear bomb here in Moorcombe and someone was threatening to set it off.'

'Huh!'

'Anyway,' Kelvin consulted his list, 'he's coming out. So's the police.'

'Oh yippee,' said Malcolm. 'Don't you think this is getting a bit silly?'

'Principles are at stake, here,' said Kelvin. 'It might be quite a good afternoon. I wonder if they'll send a helicopter?'

Chapter Eleven

THEY DID SEND a helicopter, or one certainly came over. A green Lynx, it clattered up the valley and did a circuit of the church, the bridge and the lane in which was parked Kelvin's trailer. The wine was taking a hold and the guests at the bomb party waved enthusiastically before the helicopter continued on up the river.

The next arrival was a police car, a white Ford Sierra, drawing up at the straw bales which were still strewn across the road. 'Who's going to go?' asked the commander.

'Let them come here. It looks like that Inspector Parsons. He's a right prat,' said Kelvin.

'Do you notice that's the first car that's come here for half an hour?' said the commander.

'What's so strange about that?' said Jimmy.

'I think they've put a road block somewhere.'

'No,' said Kelvin. 'They wouldn't do that.'

With his hands behind his back, the policeman walked a measured tread along the centre of the cul-de-sac towards the natives. He looked bleakly at the trailer behind them. 'So it's true then.'

'It depends what you mean,' said the commander, for whom the day was beginning to take on its accustomed rosy hue.

'Where's Constable Green?'

'In bed, I should think,' replied the commander. 'Now he reports to himself as Chief Constable, his hours are not onerous.'

The inspector looked from the trailer to the commander and then swept his eyes over the remainder of the party. 'And Sergeant Parrott?'

'Now that I'm not so sure about. He may have gone to Northcott to arrest Sodov.'

'Yes, that's where he said he was going,' confirmed Kelvin. 'But he may have a bit of trouble 'cos Prudence's there too. Anyway, what can we do for you? I'm in charge here.'

'What are those?' The inspector walked through the party and stood beside the trailer.

'Those are the bombs,' said Kelvin with pride.

'Bombs?' said the inspector. 'I can only see one of them.'

'There's another in the box.'

'Is there? May I look?'

'Be my guest,' said Kelvin with a wave of the hand.

Still with his hands behind his back, the policeman leaned forward and peered into the box at the cylinder nestling inside. 'Hmm. Got an explosives permit?'

'Yes,' said Kelvin. 'I issued one myself.'

A collective groan was silenced by the inspector with an imperious wave of his hand. 'I see. This is part of the fantasy that this village is an independent state?'

'Correct, but it's not a fantasy.'

'And you are claiming these to be nuclear devices, Mr Morchard?'

'Yes.'

'And you refuse to dismantle them?'

'Yes. Not until our just and legitimate demands are met.'

'Can you do anything about him?' asked the inspector turning to the commander.

'What had you in mind?' asked the commander cautiously.

'Execution?'

'He says he's the only one who knows how to change the combination on the electronic fuse.'

'I see.' With a final careful examination of the trailer, he turned and strode back through the party.

'Aren't you going to do something?' cried Stephanie.

'I'm afraid it's out of my hands,' replied Parsons, pausing. 'But I'd advise you all to clear the street.'

'Clear the street?' said the commander as the policeman passed out of earshot. 'What's that supposed to mean?'

'Perhaps he's concerned about our safety if there's an explosion,' said Stephanie.

'Don't you worry, my dear,' said Kelvin. 'I'd make sure not a hair of your pretty head came to any harm.'

'Patronising sod!' snorted Stephanie.

'Don't take it like that,' said Kelvin, rather hurt. 'I only meant to be reassuring.'

'Reassuring? You're the loony with the bombs! It's like being reassured by Jack the Ripper.'

'If I let you into a secret, Stephanie,' said Kelvin hoarsely. 'Will you promise not to tell anyone?'

'It depends,' said Stephanie with caution.

'Oh, go on,' said the commander. 'Say yes.'

'But it might be something awful. Like he's going to murder Brett or something. Then I'd have to tell.'

'I wouldn't do something like that!' exclaimed Kelvin.

'It's true,' said Jimmy. 'I wouldn't put much past Kelvin, but I reckon even he'd draw the line at murdering his own grandson.'

'Oh well,' said Stephanie, grudgingly. 'I promise I won't tell anyone.'

Kelvin bared his immaculate teeth with their salmon-pink gums in a triumphant smirk. 'I've fooled everyone. They're not real bombs!'

'What! You mean . . .'

Kelvin nodded his head vigorously, a beam still splitting his face. 'Yes. I made it all up. The yellow one's an empty oil drum which I painted and the other's a model that Sodov had made. They've worked a treat though. Everyone's taking us seriously now!'

Jimmy broke through the babble of voices. 'Wait! Kelvin, how do we know you're telling the truth? If you say you were lying when you said you had them, how do we know you're telling the truth when you say you haven't?'

The frown of concentration which had momentarily over-shadowed Kelvin's grin cleared. 'That's right!' he exclaimed in delight. 'This whole deterrent thing is marvellous! Once you've said you have them even if you haven't, then everyone thinks you have them whether you have them or not. Even if you never had them at all! Ho, ho, ho!'

'For God's sake, shut up, Kelvin!' snapped Stephanie.

'Keep your hair on!' said Kelvin. 'I was only trying to make you feel better. Have another drink and we'll wait to see what happens next.' He topped his glass from the wine box containing, instead of the advertised Chablis, Elfrieda's parsnip *ordinaire*. Since her vintage parsnip was considered pretty *ordinaire* by most wine critics, her *ordinaire* was extremely *ordinaire* indeed. Kelvin held his glass to the watery sunlight. 'This was commended at the horticultural show?'

'Nobody's forcing you to drink it!' said Elfrieda.

'Yes, they are,' he growled. 'There isn't anything else.' He returned to sit on the white garden bench against the front of the house. 'Lot of rain last night.'

'It's forecast to be warm and dry over the next few days,' said the commander. 'High pressure drawing warm air across Spain and up here from the Sahara.'

Jimmy wrinkled his nose. 'I don't much like the sound of that. It's not right our air should've been breathed already by foreigners. It'll stink of camel fart and garlic.'

'Don't be silly, Jimmy,' said Stephanie, idly.

'Hoy!'

'What?'

'I didn't say anything,' said the commander.

'Hoy!'

'It came from over there,' said Kelvin, gesturing across the wall towards the other bank of the river.

'Hoy!'

'See?' said Jimmy.

'No, I don't,' said the commander. 'There's nobody there.'

Jimmy shivered. 'A bit spooky, if you ask me. When nobody shouts "Hoy" at you like that.'

'Help!'

'Now that was different,' said Jimmy. 'Nobody said "Help" that time. I think it's coming from the trees over there. They're trying to lure us into an ambush.'

'The trees?'

'No, Stephanie. The police.'

'It seems to be a pretty silly place to set a trap,' observed the commander. 'I mean we're not likely to wander into a sopping wet wood on the wrong side of the river.'

'Here!'

'That was clever,' said Jimmy. 'It seemed to be coming from behind us that time.'

'It did, didn't it?' agreed the commander. 'It must be some quality of the echo across the valley.'

'You! Commander! Do something!'

This time they turned round to see Mandy leaning out of the bedroom window, gesticulating violently towards the opposite bank of the river.

190

'What's she got on?' asked Jason.

'It's a corset,' said Jimmy. 'My missus used to wear one, but you don't see them much these days.'

'Do something!' yelled Mandy. 'Quick!'

'What's she talking about?' growled Jimmy. 'What is it you want us to do?'

She flapped her arm again. 'In the river!'

'In the river,' repeated Jimmy. 'Does the woman want us to jump in or something?'

'Go and rescue them! Quick!'

'Ah!' said the commander, striding swiftly to the wall and looking down into the river. 'I thought so.' He waved his arm. 'Hullo! Do you need any help?'

The rest of the natives moved over beside him.

A boulder, still above the rushing brown spate, was host to a rubber dinghy. Two men were leaning over the edge of the vessel, clutching to a conveniently shaped spur which jutted from the lee side of the rock. White-faced, sodden hair plastered to their heads, they looked most unhappy.

'Bloody tourists,' said Kelvin, dispassionately. 'They'd

better watch themselves. If they let go of that rock, they'll probably be dashed to pieces against the buttresses of the bridge. They should've had more sense than to go down the river when it's as high as this. I reckon they'll probably get killed.'

'What can we do for them?' asked Stephanie.

'Throw stones at them,' suggested Kelvin. 'Get it over with.'

'Kelvin!' protested Stephanie, 'for heaven's sake!'

Kelvin cupped his hands. 'Jump into the river! It's only a couple of feet deep! You can wade to the bank!'

'That's nonsense!' said the commander.

'It's a couple of feet deep when the water's low,' replied Kelvin.

'I'd agree with you there, but it's not low. It's in full spate.'

'It is, isn't it?' said Kelvin. 'There must've been a hell of a lot of rain up on the moor last night. I reckon it's Nature's way. Tourists as stupid as them shouldn't be allowed to live to breed to pass on their stupidity. The river's culling them.'

'Get on with it!' shouted Mandy from her window vantage point.

Kelvin waved a hand above his head in acknowledgement. 'I suppose we'd better do something,' he grudgingly admitted. 'Jason, you go in and rescue them.'

'Why me?'

'It's well known you're the bravest man in Moorcombe. Isn't that true, Commander?'

'Well, er . . .'

'I'll hold your jacket for you, Jason. The leather'd get spoiled if it got wet and you wouldn't want it to be ruined if you get drowned. Commander, you must have some rope across the road.'

'I have, but I don't think it'd be a very good idea if Jason just plunged in. He'd be rather worse off than those chaps out there.' He lifted his voice. 'Hang on! We'll have you out of there in a jiffy.'

'Please hurry!' came the reply.

'Isn't that Winston Venn?' asked Kelvin

'I've no idea. I don't know Winston Venn,' said the commander.

'It is, too,' said Jimmy. 'What's 'e doing in the middle of the river?'

'He's Gold Top,' said Kelvin.

'Sorry?'

'That's his call sign with the Emergency Volunteers. Gold Top. He's got a herd of Jerseys, see? Down at Marshmead. Winston! Is it you?'

Winston who was not going to let go of his rock in order to wave, roared an affirmative.

Kelvin cupped his hands. 'What are you up to?'

'Trying to survive,' came the returning yell.

'I think we ought to hurry,' said Malcolm. 'The river's still rising and the sky's black above the moor.'

'We need a float of some kind. Something like a life belt which we can tie Jason to,' said the commander.

'The bomb!' said Kelvin. 'My bomb. That's tied on with rope. We could chuck it in upstream and play out the rope and it'd land up by the rock.'

'Will it float?' asked the commander.

'Course it'll float. It's just an empty drum, isn't it?'

'Really?'

'Really?'

The commander snorted. 'If we chuck it in the river, you're going to have difficulty persuading people it's a bomb again.'

'No problem,' said Kelvin. 'We've still got Sodov's and his is the real nasty one.'

'I see. Well, go and get the drum, then,' said the commander. 'Help him Jason. You too, Malcolm.'

'Right!' said Kelvin.

As the would-be rescuers hurried up the lane, the commander leaned over the wall to sweep a professional eye across the torrent beneath. 'When you get a man overboard at sea, you've got to hurry, but you have to know exactly what you're doing.' He pointed upstream. 'I should think we'd best launch the rescue from up there. We can chuck the drum in and play out the rope as we go. If Jason strikes diagonally across the flow, he should make the rock quite easily.' He cupped his hands and shouted across to those in the river 'We're going to get a rope out to you!'

'Hurry up! It's damn cold!'

'Poor things!' said Stephanie. 'I'll go and get some cocoa ready for them inside "Pixies Laughter". I'll see if Mandy has some towels ready.'

'Good idea!' said the commander. 'Is there any way we can help those men if something should go wrong and they're swept away? Kelvin is quite right about what'd happen if they hit a buttress. Look at that!'

In times of spate, the river made the most of the opportunity for its future comfort by re-making its bed. Rocks poking uncomfortably up would be removed, wrinkles of gravel or sand formed over the year would be flattened and the accumulation of rubbish – branches, trunks, twigs, fertiliser bags, beer cans, empty plastic drums of agricultural chemicals and dead sheep – would be swept downstream to the sea. The commander had seen a plank snap in two as it hit the pointed stone buttress.

'I think we should pray,' said Elfrieda.

'Look what I've got!' said Kelvin with pride, approaching the wall. The other turned. 'It's brandy! I got it from Mandy.' He took a swig from the bottle. 'It's good stuff. She brought it back from Majorca. Jason's to have some before he goes in the water.'

'Is the drum ready?' asked the commander.

'Yes. We're about to launch.'

'Well, let's go then.' He shouted across to the rock. 'Hang on! We're just about to send you a rope!'

'Get on with it, then!' came the reply.

The commander frowned across the water. 'I've just said we're coming!'

'Well, bloody hurry up!'

'Ill-mannered lout!' said the commander to Jimmy. 'Anybody would think it was him doing us a favour rather than the other way round.'

'He's got a point,' said Jimmy. 'It can't be too nice sitting there in that thing waiting to be swept away if you let go of the rock.'

'Even so,' said the commander. 'I don't think much of his manners. Let's get things under way.'

Moving up River Lane, they climbed over the barbed wire fence at the end and walked towards the point where a small subsidiary stream joined the river. It too was swollen with rain water and a couple of disintegrating members of Kelvin's flock were snagged in the drooping branches of a stunted oak which trailed into the swirling brown water. On the bank was laid the bomb and a couple of coils of rope, one looped round the drum and the other ready to be attached to Jason's waist. 'We'll chuck the drum out into the river and the current from the stream should take it into the middle so it should get close enough to their dinghy,' said Jason.

Now they had come down from the lane to the level of the river, it looked even more formidable than before. Instead of the usual soothing babble as water danced over the pebbles, the predominant sound coming from the water was a deep bowel-crunching rumble as boulders rolled down the bed towards the sea.

'You wouldn't catch me going into that,' said Kelvin.

'Me neither,' agreed Jimmy fervently. 'I reckon even a salmon'd be turned into fish cakes.'

'You two are just spineless,' said Stephanie. 'Two lives are at stake. Any man worthwhile would be prepared to put his own at risk.'

'They're not even our own people,' said Kelvin. 'Well, Winston Venn's nearly local, but I dunno who the other is.'

'They say that ladies are often better in the water than men,' said Jason. 'Their fat keeps them warm and their breasts help keep them afloat.'

'You'd do all right, Stephanie,' said Jimmy.

'I'm sure she would,' said Malcolm, before Stephanie could work out a suitable response. 'But Jason is so desperately brave and my wife isn't.'

'Exactly,' said Kelvin. 'Let's get on with it.'

'But . . .' began Jason.

'Grab the drum,' said Kelvin. The commander, Malcolm and Jimmy obeyed. 'Right. One . . . two . . . three.'

The drum sailed out and landed with a little splash. Immediately the current seized it and carried it downstream. It looked to be dead on target to the rock.

'Who was supposed to be holding on to the rope?' asked the commander, as the last couple of feet uncoiled and slid into the water.

'I don't think we'd decided,' replied Kelvin.

The commander sighed. 'That was a pity.' Rather sadly, the spectators watched the drum bob down the river towards the rock. Winston Venn, relying on the strong right arms of his colleague, let go his handhold on the rock to grab the loop of rope round the drum as it bobbed past. A murmur of relief ran through those on the bank.

195

'A fat lot of good that's going to do them,' said the commander.

'They might be able to throw the rope to the bank and we could grab it,' said Jason.

'Look!' exclaimed Jimmy. 'What's up with them?' Something indeed was up with them. Winston had attached the rope to the dinghy, then uttered a hoarse cry and cast the drum back into the river. His passenger who had been holding on to the rock, flung himself to the floor of the craft.

'Oh dear,' said the commander.

'Aagh!' said Winston.

'That's not going to help them much,' said Kelvin. 'Winston's supposed to be trained to handle emergencies, but it's just as well his volunteer group has not been put to the test if that's how he copes. Perhaps they'll choose somebody better to replace him. We might be able to amalgamate his group with ours. They've nobody else qualified to take over.'

'I should've thought your duties as Prime Minister might lead to conflict,' said the commander.

'I hadn't thought of that,' acknowledged Kelvin.

'Shouldn't we do something?' said Stephanie as the dinghy spun out of the eddy behind its anchorage and joined the current of the stream.

'Not much point in getting wet now,' said Jason, cheerfully.

'Lucky sods!' exclaimed Kelvin as, at the last instant, the flow of the river took the dinghy to the right of the central buttress and through the arch of the bridge.

Jimmy heaved a sigh. 'Ah well, I suppose that's it then. They'll be at the weir in a couple of minutes and that'll be the end.'

'I'd forgotten about the weir,' said the commander.

'I hope they have too. It'll mean their last few minutes might have some hope.'

'They may be all right,' said Stephanie.

'We might as well get down there,' said Kelvin. 'The bodies'll probably be washed up on that bend about quarter of a mile down. That's where sheep end up. We'd better make it quick. There're a lot of foxes and crows in that wood and they don't leave the carcasses alone for long. I'm not quite sure of the best way of dealing with this tragedy. It has all the makings of a diplomatic incident.'

'I think it'll take second place to them worrying about

whether you're about to annihiliate southern England,' said Stephanie.

'Yes, that's true,' agreed the commander. 'Come to think on it, I'm surprised that policeman hasn't come back.'

'We'll worry about that after we've recovered the bodies,' said Kelvin. 'Jimmy, go get your gaff. We might need it. Particularly if Jason's frightened of getting his feet wet.'

'We'll need to get Lindy so's they can be pronounced dead,' said Jimmy. 'It's Saturday. She'll be changing Granny Gabb's truss about now. We could pick her up on the way down.'

They walked back across the field and down River Lane towards the bridge, Stephanie peeling off to inform Mandy of the tragic events. 'If Winston Venn was an emergency volunteer, d'you think it could've been anything to do with us?' asked Kelvin.

'What do you mean?'

'Well, Cattermole's involved and he could've told Winston to invade us.'

'I doubt it,' replied the commander. 'Let's get the bales out of the way. What's that?' Faint cries made them turn in the direction of 'Pixies Laughter', but Mandy was not hanging from the window ululating her grief. The sounds were coming from the river, on the far side of the bridge. 'It's them!'

Rushing to the parapet, they looked over. A dozen feet beneath was the dinghy, its flat bottom planing against the current. Adjacent to it was the oil drum. For a moment the commander stared down in perplexity. 'The rope! The oil drum must've gone one side and the dinghy the other and the rope must be round the buttress. What's wrong with them?' The crew was still clutching itself on the rubber floor of their craft, uttering moans of fear and distress. 'What's wrong?'

At the sound of the commander's voice, Winston Venn looked up. 'Damn lunatics!' he yelled. 'Get away from here!'

The commander frowned. 'What a strange fellow! You'd think he'd be quite pleased to be still alive. Jason, pop across the road and get another rope. I've got one hanging in the garage on the left.'

Grudgingly, Jason departed and the others leaned back over the parapet. 'Don't worry!' called the commander. 'We'll have you out in a jiffy! Jason's just gone to get another rope!'

'What about the bomb?'

'The bomb?'

'Yes. That damn thing!' Winston Venn risked a hand over the swollen gunwales of the inflatable to indicate the yellow drum thumping cheerfully against its side. 'If it goes off, we haven't a chance!'

'Ah!'

'We'd've made it too, if the river hadn't been so high. We surrender and expect to be treated by the rules of the Geneva Convention.'

'What are they on about?' asked the commander.

'They think your bomb's about to go off,' said Jimmy with a chuckle. 'They let go of the rock hoping to get away from it.'

'It's not that funny,' said the commander. 'You thought the bomb would go off a little while ago.'

'Did you hear him, though? Winston's saying he was

attacking us.' Kelvin looked back over the parapet. 'Here! You! Winston Venn! What were you doing on the river anyway?'

'I don't have to tell you!'

'I'll set off the bomb!'

'We were trying to capture the bridge.'

'And who's that with you?'

'He's a policeman.'

'It's your own damn fault!' said the commander as Kelvin pulled back from the parapet. 'This whole thing has gone well beyond a joke. It wouldn't surprise me if you end up in jail.'

'Ach!' said Kelvin. 'You're always belly-aching. Let's haul them out and take things from there. Hurry up, Jason!'

The rope was lowered and the dinghy's crew was helped up and over the parapet. Any aggression had been leeched out of them by the numbing cold and they stood, shivering, in the road. 'You're our prisoners,' said Kelvin. 'But we'd better get you out of those wet clothes before you catch your deaths. Mandy's got some towels and things.'

'What about the bomb?'

'You'll take care of it, Commander?' Kelvin winked.

'I suppose so.'

'Why were you attacking the bridge?'

'I don't have to tell you.'

'Yes, you do,' replied Kelvin. 'Here, Copper. What were you supposed to be doing?'

'Following orders.' Winston was in his late thirties and rather fat, but his companion was burly, blond and about twenty-five although he was suffering from premature baldness and a hank of hair, which used to cover his dome, now hung down to his right shoulder.

'What orders?' Kelvin waited for a response, but it was not immediately forthcoming. 'Come on! you're hostages now. Speak up, or we'll chuck you back in the river.'

'We were supposed to secure the bridge and then the others could come over and arrest you all.'

'Really? Go on . . . What was the plan?'

'Well. Once we had the bridge, then we'd've signalled to the others and they'd've come over and taken Moorcombe before you had time to do anything about it. Cattermole and Inspector Parsons wanted to re-establish authority before London was called in. Parrott told them about the bombs on

199

the phone so they've picked up Sodov. Once you've been taken out, the whole thing'd be over.'

'Taken out?' said Kelvin. 'They ain't got a sense of humour over there. And what's all this about Sodov?'

'He was arrested at Northcott. There was a bit of a struggle and he was hurt.'

'Exit Sodov,' observed the commander. 'Before things get too silly, I think I'll go and lock myself in until this is all over.'

Kelvin turned, his eyes ablaze. 'Victory is almost within our grasp. This is not the time to give up!'

'Victory?'

'Yes. Remember what this is all for.'

'The village hall?'

'Yes. That and Botograd.'

In full war paint and coronation gown, Mandy opened her front door. 'Aha! You poor things. It was me that saw you. It was me to whom you owe your lives.'

'Thank you, missus,' said Venn.

'I'm Queen Mandy, you know.'

'Is that right?' said Venn.

'Yes, but we needn't stand on ceremony. You're dripping on the carpet. Go into the kitchen and we'll get some hot soup into you.'

A crowd of curious natives followed those rescued into the kitchen as Mandy bustled round with towels.

'What was the signal to show you'd been successful in your mission?' asked Kelvin.

'We were going to use our radios.' Venn paused while Elfrieda put a mug of instant minestrone in front of him. 'Thank you. But the radios were lost when we nearly capsized upstream. Somebody ought to do something about that river. Terrible dangerous. We could have been killed.'

'It shouldn't be allowed,' agreed the policeman.

'It's the greenhouse effect,' said Elfrieda.

'What?' Kelvin turned towards her.

'That's why it's in flood. The cutting down of the Amazon forests and refrigerators. People like you with those coolers buzzing away to chill your milk. That's what's damaging the ozone layer and changing the weather.'

'Farting termites.' The policeman had recovered sufficiently to rearrange his hair so that his pate was half-hidden and only a few strands still hung down to the blue towel on his

200

shoulders. The others in the room turned to look at him. 'Termites,' repeated the policeman. A freckled hand came from beneath the towel and ran the last hairs into place. 'You know. They add to the greenhouse effect too.'

'That's right!' exclaimed Elfrieda. 'Aerosols, forest fires, cigarettes and methane. I think it's . . .'

'Had you got a contingency plan?' asked Kelvin.

'I was talking!' said Elfrieda.

'I know you were, but we've more urgent things to talk about.'

'The destruction of the environment is one of the most urgent issues we face.'

'Yes, but not just at the moment. I'll tell you what we're going to do,' said Kelvin. 'You're going to get on the phone to Cattermole, Winston, and . . .'

'But he's crouched behind a hedge on the other side of the river.'

'Where?'

'A couple of hundred yards down towards Northcott by a house with a rotten caravan beside it.'

'That's Mrs Beasley's,' said Kelvin. 'We can phone her up and get her to pass a message on.' Going through to the hall, he picked up the gold telephone. '121 isn't it?'

'Yes,' confirmed Elfrieda.

'Is that Bella?' bellowed Kelvin. 'It's me! Go look out of the window of your front room down by the hedge . . . Yes, do it and tell me what you can see . . .' Kelvin smiled through the kitchen door and cupped the receiver. 'I've asked her to look out of the window of her front room and tell me what she can see.'

'Ah!' murmured the commander.

Kelvin's eyes narrowed as he concentrated on the telephone. 'Yes, I'm still here. Well? . . . Nothing! What do you mean nothing! There must be something . . . I meant you should draw the curtains . . . Well it doesn't matter about getting the sun on the telly because you'll be looking out the window, won't you? Yes, I'll wait.' He cupped the receiver. 'She says . . .'

'Flatulence in cows,' said the policeman.

'Surely flatulence from cows?' said the commander.

'You know perfectly well what he means, dear. That's quite right, Constable. Cars too. Carbon dioxide comes from the exhaust, but we mustn't confuse the destruction of the ozone layer with the greenhouse effect. I find the Gaia theory most persuasive, don't you?'

'Huh!' snorted Kelvin. 'Yes ... Good ... yes, yes, but forget them. Is there a fat little man in his mid-fifties with a great big arse? Good. Well, go and get him because I want to talk to him ... You can ask him yourself what he's he doing after I've talked to him ... No, he won't hurt you ... Will you get on with it, woman!'

'What's he going to say?' asked Venn of the commander, jerking his head at Kelvin. 'Cattermole's not going to take it too well.'

'Nor's the inspector. I was hoping for promotion to the CID, but this isn't going to help.'

'I don't know what he's going to say. Kelvin, what are you going to say?'

'Hullo? Is that Mr Cattermole? Good. Morchard of Moorcombe here. Yes, that's right ... Never you mind about that. We've caught your invasion force and they're our prisoners and hostages ... Venn, Winston Venn from Marshfield and a policeman ... Of course I know what I'm doing ... No, before you do anything else, I suggest we have a meeting in the middle of the bridge ... No, we won't do that. No, honestly we won't. They're quite safe on the trailer ... No, *you* listen. In ten minutes or ... or ...' Kelvin looked at the ceiling for inspiration. 'Or we'll start torturing them ... I don't know ... er ... connect their balls to an electric fencer ... Yes. Ten minutes.' Slamming the phone down, he returned to the kitchen. 'According to Bella, there're some soldiers over there, too. Commander, you don't have an electric fencer, do you?'

'You are disgusting!' said Elfrieda. 'How could you suggest such a thing!'

'I just wanted him to take us seriously.' He turned his head to the prisoners. 'Don't worry. I won't really torture you. I shouldn't think we'll need to. Let's find some more of that brandy before we have to go out.'

Fifteen minutes later, the front door to 'Pixies Laughter' opened and Kelvin stumbled out into the sunshine. Shading his eyes and looking towards the bridge, he uttered a grunt of satisfaction. 'They're there. Three of them. Waiting for us. We'd better get down there.'

'I'm not sure I want to,' said the commander, hanging back inside the hall so that he was invisible. 'It could be most embarrassing if I've met any of them socially. Who are they?'

Kelvin looked again. The group on the bridge had noticed him and were staring back. 'Cattermole. That Inspector Parsons and a bloke in a green sweater and trousers. He's a soldier, I suppose.'

'Go by yourself.'

Grabbing the commander by the jacket, Kelvin pulled him out into the cruel daylight. 'There! Now stop pissing about trying to avoid your responsibilities. Come on!'

Jimmy followed the reluctant commander and Kelvin down

River Lane towards the straw bales marking the frontier post. The reception committee, chins high, hands behind their backs, watched bleakly from the centre of the bridge.

' 'Afternoon, Mr Cattermole,' said Kelvin. 'Nice drop of rain last night. Get the grass moving.'

Cattermole flared his nostrils and sneered, an expression which caused the tufts of hair he sported on his cheeks to climb upwards like a brace of woolly bear caterpillars. In his late fifties with heavy jowls and thick black hair which hinted at liberal use of Grecian 2000, he had been county emergency officer for the past five years.

The policeman acted as spokesman. 'Mr Morchard. This is very serious . . .'

'Aren't you going to introduce us to your friend?' asked Kelvin, looking enquiringly at the soldier.

'You can call me Captain Smith,' said the other. The gentle Scots precision of his accent belied the cold grey eyes which examined Kelvin as if he were a pork chop well past its sell-by date.

'He'll be SAS,' whispered Jimmy to the commander. 'I heard there were a few of them on the moor this week.'

'I'm Kelvin Morchard. This is Jimmy, Marquis of Church Lane and . . .'

'It's all right. We know who's involved. We've done our homework.'

'Percy?'

'Percy,' confirmed the inspector.

'Thought I hadn't seen him around for a bit. Anyway, what can we do for you?'

'These bombs. Where are they?'

'There's only one left,' said Kelvin.

'What happened to the other one?' asked Parsons. 'I heard there were two.'

'The other's over there,' said Kelvin, nodding towards the parapet.

The three men turned their heads and looked down river. 'Where?' asked the inspector.

'Beneath the bridge.'

Moving swiftly to the parapet, Captain Smith looked over. 'Is that supposed to be a nuclear device?'

'What do you expect?' said Kelvin. 'This is Moorcombe, not Greenham Common.'

'It's an empty oil drum.'

Still tied to the dinghy by the rope looped round the buttress, the drum had taken quite a pounding. Yellow flecks of paint had transferred to the stone and the top had come adrift, leaving the drum half filled with water, to lurch uneasily against the restraining rope. 'Hmm,' said Kelvin. 'It doesn't look much now, I must admit. But it was a damn good bomb earlier on. See the side there?' Kelvin pointed. 'It had CCCP on it. That's the way they spell Russia over there. It was good, wasn't it, Commander?'

'Not bad,' admitted the latter.

Smith laughed. 'I think we'd better get on to Hereford, Inspector.'

Parsons tightened his lips. 'It does seem that you were being excessively alarmist, Mr Cattermole. I should've thought we could've sorted this out by ourselves.'

'With all due respect, Inspector,' said Cattermole, an angry flush staining his dewlaps in turn. 'I was taking up a suggestion made by the police. In this case yourself.'

'What suggestion?' asked Kelvin.

'Well, this army lorry slowed down and he . . .' Cattermole waved his hand towards Smith. '. . . asked what was going on. It wasn't me who took up his offer to help.'

The inspector looked bleakly at his companions and sniffed. Kelvin came to his rescue. 'And the inspector was right, too. You know what's going on here, don't you?'

'I can't wait to find out,' said Captain Smith.

'We've gone independent, see? And because we . . .'

'Actually you, Kelvin,' interrupted the commander. 'Not we.'

'All right, but you'll get the benefit too. Anyway, we knew perfectly well that we'd get people like you coming along to interfere, so we had to be sure we could defend ourselves properly.'

'I see,' murmured Smith. 'Good idea!'

'Yes,' said Kelvin with a suspicious look at Smith. 'If a nation can't defend itself, foreigners don't have no respect.'

'So you went and got yourself an oil drum,' said Smith. 'Excellent scheme.'

'It worked very well,' said Kelvin. 'It only went wrong because we had to rescue those fools from the river. But there's no need to worry, we don't need it.'

205

Smith turned to the inspector. 'I'll put all this in my report.'

'Report? We only flagged you down!'

'You're a panicky wee man, aren't you? You're supposed to know these people.' Smith appraised the natives. 'Bunch of geriatric yokels, if you ask me.'

This earned him a battery of hostile glances, both from the inspector and the residents of Moorcombe. 'SAS thug,' responded Kelvin.

'How did you know that?' said Smith.

'Stands out a bloody mile. Anyway you lot are always playing cowboys and indians up there and scaring the sheep.'

Before Smith could escalate the slanging match, the policeman looked at Kelvin. 'You say you don't need the oil drum, Mr Morchard. Tell the captain why.'

'Of course. We . . .'

'Kelvin,' interrupted the commander. 'Don't you think it might be a good idea just to leave things as they are?'

Kelvin considered for a second. 'No.' He looked back at the inspector. 'We have another bomb, of course.'

Smith snorted his disbelief. 'This is a waste of time! Made out of yoghurt cartons to the *Blue Peter* design, I suppose.'

'I don't think I like your attitude, you cheeky young bugger,' said Kelvin. 'P'raps we should break off negotiations till you mind your manners.'

'What kind of bomb?' asked the inspector.

'Nuclear, of course. A hundred thousand killer tons. It came from Mr Sodov who sympathises with our struggle for freedom against oppression.'

'I see,' said the inspector, looking across at Smith. 'Well, we've got Sodov safely locked up so I suppose his weapon, for what it is worth, is neutralised.'

'I don't see what makes you think that,' said Kelvin. 'Sodov's just a foreign ambassador. You don't think we'd have his finger on our button, do you?'

'Hmm,' said the inspector. 'Will you excuse us for a moment, Mr Morchard?'

'Certainly,' said Kelvin, waving an insouciant hand.

The negotiating team retired to the end of the bridge where they addressed the hillside to keep their conversation confidential.

'Let's call the whole thing off,' said the commander. 'That Smith chap could be most unpleasant.'

'Ssh!' said Kelvin. 'Listen to them! There's a good echo from the hillside.'

'We have to take it seriously,' the inspector was saying. 'Quite apart from the threat of his bomb which, I agree, does not sound convincing, he has two of our men as hostages.'

'Your men,' said Smith. 'We could have them out of that house in a matter of seconds. These people are a joke. They're not your normal terrorists.'

'I agree,' said the inspector. 'They're not terrorists, but the situation, like them, is dangerously unstable.'

'Look at the one with the moustache,' said Cattermole. 'The one Morchard calls the commander. Classic psychopath, if you ask me. Extremely dangerous.' The three negotiators turned to examine the commander.

The latter glared back. 'I've never been so insulted in my life,' he spluttered.

'I bet you have,' said Jimmy. 'I bet your Elfrieda has said worse things about you in her time.'

'Even if she has, it'd be different.'

'Why?'

'Well, she's family.'

'Ssh! Listen!'

'I recommend we continue negotiations in an attempt to bring things to a peaceful conclusion,' said the inspector. 'But I wish I knew where Parrott had got to. That diplomat could be trouble. We really ought to get on to somebody in London about him.'

'They'd take the whole thing over,' said Cattermole. 'I wouldn't like them to think we couldn't cope.'

'Give me two minutes,' said Smith. 'There might not even be many casualties.'

'I don't think much of that fellow either,' said the commander. 'I hope you know what you're doing, Kelvin.'

'Don't worry,' said Kelvin. 'Everything's fine.'

'Probably gone beyond fine to jail by now,' said Jimmy.

'No,' the inspector was saying. 'We aren't quite at that stage yet, but keep your men ready. It might be our last resort before we hand over control. Leave the talking to me.' Pivoting on his polished heel, he walked back towards Kelvin.

The latter took the initiative. 'I suggest we end this whole business once and for all. Before somebody gets hurt.'

'And how do we do that?'

'Get hold of Mrs Biss.'

'Biss? And who the hell's Mrs Biss?' Parsons looked at Cattermole who shrugged.

'She's our district councillor, the cause of the whole thing,' said Kelvin. 'Isn't that right, Commander?'

'That's right.'

'She lives over at Puddlewick. If you send a car, you should be able to get her here within twenty minutes.'

'But . . .'

'While you're getting her we could show the others the bomb. You'd like that, wouldn't you, Rambo?'

'Yes, I go along with that,' said Smith.

Kelvin beamed. 'You're a smart boy. For a Scotchman. We'll give you a good look round, don't worry. Show you the defensive positions and the like.'

'It sounds like a first-class idea.'

'Well then,' said Kelvin, 'you can run along, Inspector.'

'Don't worry, Parsons,' said Cattermole. 'It's the right thing to do.'

'We'll look after them,' said Jimmy.

'That's what I'm afraid of,' said the inspector. 'Take care. We don't want you to end up as hostages as well.' The inspector retreated across the bridge as the others walked through the straw bales into Moorcombe.

'Commander,' said Kelvin, 'could you show these gentlemen the bomb while I get back to our hostages.'

'And the brandy.'

'That's a consideration,' replied Kelvin cheerfully. 'Bring them into Mandy's after.'

As Kelvin scurried ahead down the lane, the commander turned to his guests. 'You'd like to see his bomb?'

'Oh yes,' said the captain. 'We wouldn't want to miss that. It's more sophisticated than the oil drum?'

The remaining bomb was inspected. In its box on the trailer, it did not look particularly impressive but its box had come from beside the kitchen Aga and was singed, a sign, as the commander pointed out, of radiation leakage. Smith noted firing positions, fields of fire and possible landing zones. The commander warned of the hidden obstructions in Kelvin's field in case he felt like a glider-launched assault and described the extraordinary delicacy of the trembler fuse.

Smith seemed sceptical. Wobbling his jowls in dismay since his home lay ten miles downwind of the fall out, Cattermole was less easy. When they had seen their fill, the commander led them to 'Pixies Laughter.'

With a sardonic grin across his face, Kelvin opened the door. 'Good bomb, isn't it?'

'It's a simple metal cylinder,' said Cattermole. 'Quite absurd to pretend it's anything else.'

'Lucky I'm not pretending, isn't it?' said Kelvin cheerfully. 'Come in and meet Her Majesty.'

'What?' Smith seemed not have been fully briefed on the more baroque aspects of the operation.

'She's been looking forward to her first audience with the likes of you. She's in the kitchen with the others. Come through. There's not much left in the way of booze,' said Kelvin apologetically as he led them through the shag-pile carpet of the hall towards the kitchen.

Inside, Mandy, Country Diary apron covering the taffeta dress, was frying a large pan of bacon. 'Heavens!' she shrieked. 'Look at me! More guests!'

'Sit down gents,' said Kelvin. 'That's the queen. She's making bacon rolls for the hostages.'

Huddled in towels round the kitchen table, the hostages considered struggling to their feet to stand to attention in the presence of their seniors, but settled for a rough genuflection performed from a seated position.

'There isn't any room,' said Smith.

'La!' said Mandy, waving a greasy spatula. 'Park your bottoms on the work surface and I'll give you some lunch. Isn't this exciting? Keith!'

'Yes dear?' Keith put his head round the kitchen door.

'See if you can find these gentlemen a drink. I think there's a wine box in the cocktail cabinet.' She vigorously stirred the hissing bacon. 'Ever so sweet, that young man.' She nodded her head at the young policeman. 'He was shy, weren't you, dear?'

'Where's the inspector?' asked the policeman, hugging his towel close to his curled up limbs.

'It's all right, he's not here,' said Cattermole.

'I'm sorry, sir,' said Venn.

'We'll talk about it later,' said Cattermole, stiffly.

'I said the river was too full but you wouldn't listen. We

were nearly killed! I didn't join the Emergency Volunteers to risk my life!'

'We'll talk about it later,' reiterated Cattermole.

'Now, now boys!' Mandy clattered the pan on the electric rings. 'I won't have cross words in my house. My home is an oasis of peace in a troubled world. Troubles just slide off peoples' shoulders in our home. Isn't that right, Keith?' Mandy looked over her shoulder and scanned the room. 'Keith! Where's the bastard gone? Sniffing round that Stephanie Jarrett like every other man in Moorcombe, I suppose! Keith! Keith!'

Keith's head popped round the door again. 'Yes, dear?'

'What are you doing?'

'Getting these people some wine, dear.'

'Where's Stephanie?'

'How would I know, dear?'

'Humph! Well, hurry up!' Mandy smiled at the new arrivals. 'He's a bit slow sometimes. I think he's a bit in awe of me now because I'm queen. You!' Her accusing spatula singled out Captain Smith who was looking through the window.

'Me?'

'Yes. Are you listening to me?'

'No,' said Smith.

'He's SAS,' said Kelvin. 'I reckon he was working out how to attack the house and rescue the hostages.'

'Attack my house! Is this true?'

'I hope it won't come to that, madam. And we'd do as little damage as possible.'

Slamming the pan down on the stove, Mandy undid her apron and dropped it to the floor, grinding it into the pink, patterned washable nylon carpet with her high heel. She glared round the kitchen. 'Get out of here! I slave my fingers to the bone, find my own towels for you and cook you lunch. And you sit there, drinking my drink, not lifting a finger to help. And now you're talking about damaging our little home! Get out!'

'Madam!' began Cattermole but, as Mandy picked up the still sizzling frying pan, Kelvin whisked him to his feet to join the rush to the exit.

'Stop' shouted Mandy. She indicated the policeman amid the frozen tableau. 'You stay behind. The rest of you. Out!'

210

'Poor fellow,' said Smith, as they made their safe escape to the garden. 'Is she often like that?'

'Yes,' said Keith who had been in the van of the retreat.

'Keith may not look much,' said Kelvin. 'But you've got to have guts to live with a woman like her.'

'Thank you,' said Keith. 'Are we going to the pub?'

'I suppose so.'

'Your bomb won't go off?' asked Cattermole.

'Not without my say so,' growled Kelvin. 'And I won't say so if you're buying the drinks.'

'Do they serve food?' asked Smith. 'That bacon smelled rather nice.'

'Helga does cordon blue cooking,' said Kelvin. 'So long as the microwave's been mended. Otherwise it's bread and cheese.'

It was bread and cheese, but the beer was good. Half a kilo of farmhouse cheddar and two pints of beer later, Cattermole leaned back and lit a cheroot. 'Glad we're not still crouched down behind the hedge, I see it's raining again.' Outside a sudden squall pattered rain against the windows as a small but angry black cloud trundled across the valley. 'What started it all off in the first place?'

'A front's moved in from a low pressure area west of Ireland,' said the commander.

'No, I mean this independence idea.'

'That was because we couldn't getting planning permission for the new village hall,' said Kelvin.

'Why?'

'Mrs Biss. A local mad woman. She persuaded the council to turn down our design. It's a castle, you see.'

'A castle? It sounds quite interesting.'

'There's a plan behind the bar. Jason, go and get it.' Clearing the clutter of glasses and ashtrays, Kelvin took the plan, unrolling it on the table. 'Hold down your end, Rambo.'

'Oh, I say. That's rather fun,' said Cattermole as he took in the design.

'You can't cover the gateway from the walls,' said Smith, pointing to the plan with a pickled onion on the end of a fork. 'The easiest solution would be to cut firing positions on either side of the door. Here and here. How thick are the walls?'

'A couple of blocks.'

'A couple of blocks! That won't keep out the rain, let alone a bullet. You might get somewhere if you filled in the gaps with concrete. Better still if the whole thing was reinforced.'

'That'd cost a fortune!'

'It'd have to be done, otherwise the thing'd be purely ornamental.'

'But . . .'

'In fact, I'd noticed that the whole village is in an excellent defensive position. With fortified points above the bridge, you could dominate all the approaches. It would be a real sod to take the castle without decent air support.'

'But . . .' said Kelvin.

'And if you put a missile position up on the lip of the valley, it'd be a real sod even with air support. Don't you agree, Cattermole?'

'It was the leat that gave me the idea,' said Keith. 'I could've piped it, but this seemed a better way. As a builder, I like to use the natural features of the terrain.'

The latch on the door creaked and the inspector entered. 'Ah! there you are!'

212

'We're having some lunch. Had it, actually,' said Cattermole.

'I see.' During the course of his career, the inspector had
developed a disapproving look and tone to his voice which
would have aroused feelings of guilt in a ewe lamb.

'Have a look at the plan for the village hall.'

'I'm more concerned about the small matter of a suspected
nuclear device. Mr Morchard.'

'Yes?'

'I've got Mrs Biss outside in the car.'

'So?'

'I was hoping you'd have a word with her so that we can
bring this whole matter to a satisfactory conclusion.'

'It took you long enough to get here. You've been away for
over an hour.'

'She didn't want to come.'

'Your charm wearing a bit thin, is it? Bring her in, anyway.
I'll chat with her. I don't bear grudges.'

'She won't come in.'

Frowning, Kelvin turned to Jimmy. 'She ain't dry, is she? I
know her Albert was, but she's not a Methodist?'

'It's nothing to do with religion. She's not in a very good
mood. A young man refused to let us over the bridge unless we
paid 50p and I had to ask her for some change.'

'You could've asked my lads to mount an assault rather
than pay,' said Smith.

'For an assortment of reasons I don't want to go into, I
decided against such a course of action. Mr Morchard, please
go out and talk to her.'

Kelvin winked at the locals. 'I will if you buy me a whisky.'

'Certainly not!'

'Then I won't go.'

'If you don't I'll arrest you.'

'If you don't I'll arrest you.' mimicked Kelvin. 'You stupid
bloody sod! Haven't you got it yet? We're the ones who can
arrest you, not the other way round. Go and get me a whisky.'

'I think I'll go on to brandy,' said Cattermole.

Parsons ignored him. 'A whisky. Then you'll go.'

'Yes. You can rely on me.'

'Right!'

Behind the bar, Jimmy silently poured the whisky into a
glass on the counter. The policeman handed over a fiver.

Jimmy placed it in the till and gave him a pound change. '£4 for a scotch!'

'The extra's tax.'

'Tax?'

'Tax,' repeated Jimmy firmly. 'And because we believe in the pursuit of happiness, I'll spend the tax on a drink for everyone else.'

'That's the spirit!' said Cattermole.

'Will you please go outside and speak to Mrs Biss.'

Kelvin grinned at the policeman. 'She's a difficult woman, I recall. I'll take a piss and see what we can work out. Commander, I'd be grateful if you'd come too. You might be able to help.' Heaving himself to his feet, Kelvin picked up his drink and tottered off in the direction of the bog.

With an embarrassed smile and a muttered 'Excuse me,' the commander downed his beer and followed.

Chapter Twelve

IN FRONT OF the Hind sat the police car, a white Ford Sierra bristling with antennae. A small covey of residents from the commune were milling in the street outside the post office. As Kelvin came round the edge of the pub, he frowned and waved his arms in an attempt to drive them away. One stood his ground. 'Hey Kelvin, man!'

'Oh, it's you Howard.'

Since he grew his hair and beard for six months before cutting both to the skin, Howard's appearance varied greatly and he was not always easy to identify. 'Maud won't cash our giro cheques because we're independent. And I think the drug squad might be around. Look! There's a police car.'

'Howard, go bugger a goldfish. We're busy.'

'But . . .'

'Don't say but,' said Kelvin, baring his pink plastic gums in a snarl. 'Just go away.'

'Commander . . .'

'You heard Kelvin. Haven't you been following what's going on?'

'Well, I know we're independent now . . .'

'There's an atomic bomb in the car park and it could go off at any moment.'

Howard and the half dozen communards rhubarbed their consternation. A plump woman in her thirties with lank green hair and a safety pin through her left nostil beat her breast and ululated like a distraught Taureg.

'Boom!' said Kelvin to encourage them on their way. 'Mushroom, mushroom.' He sketched the shape of a nuclear explosion in the air.

Losing their nerve, the communards broke, streaming back to their battered psychedelic camper which departed the

215

village in an explosive cloud of black exhaust fumes. From the back of the police car, Mrs Biss watched them go, her face a frozen mask of disapproval.

'I suppose we'd better get on with it,' said Kelvin, eyeing her with trepidation. 'I dunno what it is with women in this part of the world, but very few of them are what you might call the gentle sex.'

'True,' said the commander, gloomily. 'It might be something in the water. Elfrieda was perfectly amenable until I retired. And look at her now.'

Kelvin tapped on the glass of the police car. Mrs Biss turned her head to look at him. ' 'Afternoon, missus. Can I have a chat?' The angry black cloud had moved on up to the moor, but a close associate, following along behind, drew a hissing line of rain across the rooftops towards them. 'In fact, can we come in?' Kelvin went into the driver's seat and the commander to the passenger's. The doors clunked behind them just as the shower spattered against the windscreen. 'Cosy this,' said Kelvin, looking round the interior. 'Funny smell, though.'

'There wasn't before you came in,' said Mrs Biss.

'Essence of policeman, distilled through perspiration,' said the commander.

'Disgusting!' sniffed Mrs Biss.

''Tis, a bit,' agreed Kelvin.

The radio on the dashboard spat static, but the high sides of Moorcombe's valley kept out all but the most determined signals. It lapsed into silence again as they looked outside at the rain. Kelvin sipped his whisky.

'Gone too far, have you?' asked Mrs Biss.

'Oh, I don't know,' said Kelvin. 'It's been quite interesting.'

'As for you, Commander, or whatever you are, you should know better. It's not as if you come from the moor.'

'I've lived here for nearly ten years. It's difficult to retain one's perspective.'

'Atom bomb indeed! You're a silly old fool, Kelvin Morchard. And the rest of you are idiots to take any notice of him!'

'What are we to do, then?' asked the commander.

'What do you mean?' asked Mrs Biss.

'Well, I presume Inspector Parsons told you why he brought you here.'

'He did say something about negotiations.'

'Well, that's what you're here for then. To negotiate.'

'Why should I?'

'Ah!'

There was silence in the car once more as they looked at the rain. 'What's that for?' asked the commander.

Kelvin looked at the small video screen on the dashboard. 'It looks like a telly. Bit dangerous to watch when you're driving, I'd've thought.'

'It's a computer terminal,' said Mrs Biss. 'If you type in a car registration number, then it goes to the computer in Swansea and the name of the car's owner flashes up.'

'Don't be silly,' said Kelvin. 'It'd never do that.'

'It does,' said Mrs Biss. 'I've heard about it.'

'Let's try it then. What's your number, Commander?'

'Er . . . YOK 870T.'

'Right!' Kelvin found an on/off button and, breathing stertorously, with his tongue slightly protruding, he tapped the numerals on to the keyboard. 'Nothing's happening.'

'Hit it,' said Mrs Biss.

Kelvin's palm smashed the side of the screen. Obediently it threw up some letters. Kelvin leaned forward. 'Rear admiral J. Silver, The Oast House, Great Littleden, Kent.' He sat back. 'That don't sound much like you. I suppose it has guessed the navy connection.'

'Oh,' said the commander. 'I forgot. The car actually is in my father-in-law's name. That's him.'

'Rear admiral, eh?' said Kelvin. 'That's more important than commander, isn't it?'

'It's a more senior rank, if that's what you mean,' said the commander.

'That must've been a disappointment to Elfrieda,' said Kelvin.

'I don't think so,' said the commander, stiffly.

'I suppose her family reckoned to you being a bit of a failure.'

'And he gave you the car out of charity?' said Mrs Biss. 'I suppose the poor old man can't afford to buy you anything newer out of his pension.'

'We're here to negotiate,' said the commander. 'Not probe into my private life.'

'Huh! At least my Albert could support me.'

'He was a good worker, your Albert. A fine man. Methodie lay preacher, weren't he?'

'That he was.'

'I heard he could preach for three hours on a Sunday morning and hardly draw a breath.'

'The lion lay down with the lamb when Albert preached the Word.'

'He must've been awfully good,' said the commander.

'He was a sad loss,' said Kelvin. 'He had a worthy companion in you, though. Didn't he, Commander?'

'I'm afraid I never even met him.' said the commander.

'A worthy companion in Mrs Biss, you fool.'

'Oh . . . ah! I see. Yes. Most worthy.'

A curious sound, as if someone was trying to start up a chainsaw, came from Mrs Biss. She was laughing. 'You're trying to choke me with cream, Kelvin Morchard.'

'I wouldn't do that, missus. I respect you. You're a district councillor and one of the most important and famous personages on the moor.'

'It's true. And I'm Chairman of the Planning Committee.'

'Ah!' said Kelvin.

'Ah!' said the commander.

'Ah!' concurred Mrs Biss.

There was a short silence.

'Reckon this shower should soon clear,' said Kelvin, rubbing his hand across the window to try to clear the condensation. His calloused palm streaked a claw-mark over the glass.

'I hope so,' said Mrs Biss. 'I can't sit here all day.'

'I could do with another drink,' said Kelvin.

'Let's try to sort something out before we go back to the pub,' said the commander.

'It's all your fault, Kelvin,' said Mrs Biss. Her sudden venom making the other two jump. 'You trumped up that rule to deprive me of the Onion Shield. You should have thought ahead.'

'You have no right to allow personal feelings to affect your decisions,' said the commander.

'You just sit there and keep your mouth shut, Commander,' said Kelvin savagely. 'If you've nothing useful to say, don't say it.'

'I'm sorry.' The commander subsided into offended silence.

Kelvin sighed. 'Mrs Biss. We done you wrong.'

'Yes, you have. And now you can suffer. There's no point in looking to me to get you out of trouble.'

'Is that right?' said Kelvin. 'It's lucky then we're not in trouble. In fact we've a lot to be grateful to you for. If it hadn't been for you, we'd still be an ordinary village. Now we're a rich, free nation.'

'Not for long, judging by all them hiding behind the hedges on the other side of the river.'

'They won't do anything. We've got the bomb, you know.'

'I heard.'

'You know what they want, don't you?'

'What?'

'They want you to be a hero. They think you can influence me to change my mind and call off the independence thing and give up the bomb.'

'A hero?'

'Yes. I told the inspector he was wasting his time.'

'Why?'

'Well. I know you're a remarkable person, but even if you did give your blessing to the village hall and to the twinning, you could never make us give up independence. Wealth. Fame. Freedom from interference. No tax.' He shook his head decisively. 'We've got too much to lose.'

'Uh huh,' said Mrs Biss. Rummaging in her handbag, she furtively palmed something into her mouth. The odour of peppermints filled the car. 'Just suppose I did change my mind,' she said, shifting the mint from one cheek to the other with a slurping sound. 'Why should I?'

' 'Cos, you'd be a hero,' said Kelvin, offering his first inducement.

She savoured it, swallowed it and wanted more. 'Huh!'

'The only person in the whole world who could've sorted the situation out.'

She sucked her peppermint reflectively.

'We've got your nephew in there. We rescued him from the river. We could always torture him.'

'Which nephew? Winston Venn?'

'That's right.'

'Serve him right! Borrowed my billy goat last week and let it get out on to the moor. He says it'll turn up sometime. Ain't no damn good when I've got nannies to cover.'

219

'The commander'll give you free vegetables.'

'Here . . .' began the commander indignantly.

'His stuff is only good for compost!' said Mrs Biss with a sneer. 'I've seen his onions and lettuce.'

Kelvin drummed his fingers on the steering wheel. 'We'll change the name of the Onion Shield and call it the Biss Shield.' A grunt of surprise came from the commander, but, under the restraint of Kelvin's baleful eye, he held his peace. 'The Sheila Biss Shield. That'll be our way of saying sorry for the wrong we done you in the Horticultural Society Show.'

'The Sheila Biss Shield. Hmm. What else?'

'What else?' Kelvin sighed once more, puffing out his cheeks and staring through the windscreen. 'We could call the village hall the Biss Hall. The Sheila Biss Hall.'

'The Sheila Biss Hall. Painted black-on-white in letters at least eight inches high above the main entrance.'

Kelvin's thumb stole up to his nostril, expertly trapping a bogey between nail and flesh which he deposited beneath the driving seat. 'Right!'

'We could put up a stained glass window in the church,' said the commander. He actually put his tongue in his cheek, but neither of the car's other two occupants were looking.

'Good idea, Commander.'

'The chapel?' asked Mrs Biss.

'All right,' said Kelvin. 'A stained glass window in the chapel. Yes,' he said, cutting her off before she could speak. 'The Sheila Biss Memorial Window.'

'The Sheila Biss Memorial Window.' She rummaged in her handbag. 'Would you like a peppermint?'

'That's very civil of you,' said Kelvin taking one from the crumpled bag. She snatched it back before the commander could reach over. 'Of course, we'd have to wait till you were dead before we put it up. It would be dreadful bad luck to put it up while you were still alive.'

'We'll that's not much good. If I've gone before you install it, I won't be able to enjoy it.'

'You could look forward to it. If you go on holiday, they say the best part is looking forward to it. It'd be the same with the window. You'd look forward to being dead 'cos you'd know the Sheila Biss Memorial Window'd be going in. We'd double glaze it, too.'

The commander cleared his throat, uneasy about the logic of Kelvin's inducement.

'Hmm,' said Mrs Biss. 'I quite like that.'

'Is that it, then?' asked Kelvin.

'No, I need a billy goat. You get me one.'

'A billy goat! That could be difficult. I don't know anyone who keeps goats. Do you, Commander?'

'I'm afraid not.'

'Well, I want one.'

'Perhaps we could catch yours,' said Kelvin.

'We'd never find it,' said the commander. 'There's thirty thousand acres of moor up there.'

'I've got it!' Kelvin pounded his fists on the steering wheel. 'I know how we can find your goat!'

'How?'

Kelvin jerked his head towards the pub. 'Get them to take us up in a helicopter. We'll find your beast and take it back to your place. You'll be able to serve your nannies and still be back in time to watch *Neighbours*.'

She rolled her eyes. 'Ooh! I've never been up in a helicopter. I'd like that. D'you think we could?'

'Of course we could. So long as you withdraw your objections to the village hall.'

'Hold on,' said Mrs Biss. 'Just let's be sure we understand each other. The Sheila Biss Hall, the Sheila Biss Memorial Window . . .'

'That's after you're dead, mind.'

'Yes, I know. And the Onion Shield. Don't forget the Onion Shield. It's got Gilbert Bladderwick's name on it at the moment.'

'We just put a line through that and put yours there instead.'

'Here comes the inspector,' said the commander.

'Good,' said Kelvin, looking over his shoulder. 'What'll you have to drink, Sheila?'

'Mrs Biss to you. A milk stout.'

With the shower passed, Parsons was crossing the forecourt of the pub towards the car in the road outside. As he approached, Kelvin wound down the window. 'Good of you to think of us. I'll have a whisky. The commander's a barley wine and Mrs Biss a milk stout. And we'll want a helicopter.'

Rewinding the window, he returned to the business of

negotiation. 'Look, we have to trust . . .' Knuckles rapped authoritatively on the glass, Kelvin turned with a frown of annoyance to confront the white-faced policeman. The window came down again. 'Whisky, barley wine, milk stout. If you can't remember it, write it down in your notebook.'

'I did not come out here to be your waiter. I want to know whether we can end this without violence.'

' 'Course, we can. Just tying up loose ends.'

'And what's this about a helicopter?'

'We need one to find a goat.'

'To find a goat. What about the bomb?'

'Oh damn,' said Kelvin. 'I forgot about that.'

'You forgot!'

'There's no need to take that tone of voice with me,' said Kelvin. 'We were talking about the Onion Shield. When we've sorted that out, we'll sort out the bomb. The best thing you could do is just bugger off and leave us alone. Oh, and it would be a help if you brought the drinks. Whisky, barley wine and milk stout.' He shut the window. 'Useless sod! Now where were we?'

'The bomb,' said the commander.

'Oh yes. The bomb.'

Mrs Biss sniffed. 'I'm not at all happy about that thing. I thought it was the height of irresponsibility when I heard about it. Typical, I said. Typical of Moorcombe and Kelvin Morchard. You wouldn't get anybody on our side of the moor with a bomb. It's plain daft!'

'It's worked though, hasn't it?' said Kelvin. 'You're going to be a hero and we're going to get our hall and everything's going to be fine. We'll take it with us on the helicopter and get rid of it when we're well out of the way. 'Course you'll get all the credit, Sheila.'

'Mrs Biss,' said Mrs Biss, but Kelvin's blandishments were beginning to sweeten her sour expression. 'But you haven't told me what you're going to do about the Onion Shield. There isn't room left for my name, even if you do cross out the other.'

'We could stick a label with your name on it over the top of the existing inscription,' suggested Kelvin.

'I doubt if the Bladderwick family would be too pleased about that,' said the commander.

'I don't give a monkey's what . . .'

'If you'd change the name once, you'd do it again,' said Mrs Biss. 'I don't trust you. Anyway, I want a better trophy than that. If it's got my name on it, it's got to be something special.'

Kelvin suddenly gaffawed. 'I've got it! The bomb! It's a lovely shiny cylinder, Sheila. Once it's been officially defused, we can have it mounted on a nice bit of walnut and present it to the Grand Champion at the show. There'll be nothing else like it on the whole moor, or in the whole world, I suppose. The Sheila Biss Trophy.'

'What's it made of?'

'It's silver, isn't it, Commander?'

'Platinum or white gold, I believe.'

'Yes, that's right. 'Course there isn't a hallmark on it cos it's foreign gold, but it's terrible heavy. Worth a fortune. It'd be the most precious trophy. By far.'

Mrs Biss considered, a pink flush spreading across her weather-beaten cheeks. 'I agree. I'll withdraw the objections of the council to the hall and to that foreign place.'

'Excellent!' said Kelvin. 'I'll take the Land Rover back to Northcott and we'll meet the helicopter there. You stay here, Sheila, and we'll go and tell the others.'

'Mrs Biss,' said Mrs Biss.

Inside the pub, the inspector was standing by the bar with a milk stout, a barley wine and a whisky on the counter in front of him. He had a black leather purse with a velcro fastener out of his pocket and was painfully counting out coins under Jimmy's eagle eye.

'You can relax, Inspector,' said Kelvin, deftly pouring the whisky into the stout and taking a sip. 'I managed to work on her and get her to see reason. The crisis is over.'

'Can we bring in the bomb squad?'

'The bomb is flying out on the helicopter.'

'The helicopter?'

'Yes. She made that one of the conditions for stopping making trouble.'

'I can't get a helicopter.'

' 'Course you can,' said Kelvin. 'If I can phone up and get one to drop hay to my sheep in winter, you can get one to save the world. And if you can't do it, Rambo certainly can.'

'What do you need one for?'

'I told you. She wants to go home via the moor so's she can pick up a goat that's got lost up there.' He took a great slug from the glass. 'Thirsty work, doing your job for you. You're damn lucky to have had me to do the negotiating. If I hadn't been there to make her change her mind, there'd've been real trouble.'

'But . . .' began Parsons.

Kelvin raised his hand to silence him. 'No. There's no need to thank me. I just did my duty. I used to be a special constable, you know. You or Rambo there . . .' he gestured towards Captain Smith, '. . . can call up a helicopter and then take Sheila to Northcott to meet it. I'll finish my drink and me and the commander'll follow you in the Land Rover with the bomb.'

The policeman raised a questioning eyebrow at Smith. The latter shrugged. 'Okay by me. If the bomb's real, they're the only people who know how to deal with it. If it isn't, it doesn't matter anyway. The worst that could happen is that it goes off and that won't matter either because we won't be left to pick up the bits.'

Kelvin winked at the commander as they left the bar. 'We're not doing so bad, are we?'

'I'll tell you one thing you've forgotten,' said the commander.

224

'What?'

'Mandy. Who's going to tell her she's not queen any more?'

'McRambo, of course. He's SAS. Time he earned his pay. You can tell him after me and Biss are out of the way.'

The police car, Mrs Biss still in the back seat, was blocking the entrance to the yard as the nuclear convoy, containing Jimmy as well as the commander, lurched down the lane from Moorcombe. 'What the hell's he parked there for?' said Kelvin. Muttering with irritation, he halted the Land Rover and they splashed through the mud to the concrete yard.

An altercation was in progress by the barn, in the midst of which was Sodov, clad in a red boiler suit which Prudence had used during the latter stages of her pregnancy.

'What's going on?' asked Kelvin.

'Morchard,' said the policeman, turning to him with relief. 'Can you identify this man?'

' 'Course I can. What's he been up to?'

'What is his name?'

'He's Sodov, of course. Bulgarian ambassador to Moorcombe.'

Taking off his cap, the inspector shut his eyes and rubbed his temples. 'Who did your men pick up, Captain Smith?'

'What?' Neither Smith nor Cattermole were familiar with the rural slums of which Northcott was a typical representative and seemed distracted by the damp, moth-eaten hens picking over the rotting slurry in the corners of the buildings, the rusty coils of wire embracing ancient implements piled behind the barns and the hat-rack cows, their coats caked with dung, standing hock-deep in mud, at a gate at the edge of the yard.

'I asked who you arrested earlier on.'

'Er . . . Sodov, as we were instructed. This man's clearly an impostor. It's more of their silly games.'

Dressed for milking in filthy blue overalls and a dung-stained woolly hat with a bobble on top, Prudence, with Brett at her heels, emerged from the barn and crossed to a stack of bales of barley straw against the barn. 'I dunno what you all think you're up to, but I'm about to start milking.'

'Does the milk go for human consumption?' asked Cattermole, still looking round the yard. 'This is all a bit real, isn't it?'

'Da,' said Brett, pottering towards Sodov with his arms

outstretched and nappy trailing in the slurry which filmed the yard.

'He's not your da,' said Prudence as Sodov scooped him into the crook of his arm. 'I saw Sergeant Parrott being attacked in the lane by some soldiers before dinner. They took him away.' Slashing the string securing the bales, she broke the straw into wedges and shook them along the wall of the barn.

'I see,' said the policeman. 'Sergeant Parrott. Right. We've got that sorted out. Mr Sodov, do you admit to being Mr Sodov?'

'Why?' asked Sodov, in some difficulty as Brett was trying to stuff his fingers into his mouth.

'Because we take a dim view of aliens who supply nuclear weapons.'

'Supply nuclear weapons! Where could I get such things? I wish to marry Miss Prudence.'

Parsons screwed up his eyes as if in pain. 'I don't think your marital intentions are relevant.'

'He said he wanted to copulate with me,' snorted Prudence. 'And then tried to kiss me.'

'You swine!' said Kelvin, venturing towards him with upraised fist. 'You should be horsewhipped! My son-in-law's going to be rich. Not a Commie paid in stotties.'

'She has fierce eyes. Like the river in spate,' explained Sodov.

Prudence's mud-brown eyes looked at Sodov scornfully. 'Silly bugger! He wouldn't leave me alone. I don't think I hurt him.'

'You were magnificent!' said Sodov. 'She cast me to the ground when I grasp her by the . . .'

'Shut up!' said Prudence threateningly.

'Da,' said Brett, wrapping his damp nappy round Sodov's neck.

'She is fertile, you see and I have decided to defect. When I marry an English lady, I shall become English too, I think,' said Sodov.

'Not by marrying me you won't. You can bugger off,' said Prudence. 'What the hell do I need a man for?'

'You're under arrest . . .'

'No, he ain't,' said Kelvin. 'He hasn't paid for his board and lodging yet.'

226

'Look . . .'

'And we'll need his advice to help defuse the bomb. Remember? You don't want it to go off by mistake, do you? Now, where's the helicopter?'

'On its way. It should be here within five minutes.'

'Helicopter? I'm not having one of them coming here,' said Prudence. 'Not when I've got to go and get the cows in for milking.'

'It'll be out the way before then. Me and Mrs Biss are going off in it,' said Kelvin. 'We'll have it land out there. It's going to be quite exciting.' He pointed between the corrugated iron-roofed cowshed and the hay barn towards the slurry pit.

'It's flat, I suppose, but a bit small,' said Smith. 'What's the surface?'

'No,' said Kelvin scornfully. 'That's the slurry pit. The field alongside it.'

'Oh, I see. Well, I'll get on the radio and tell the pilot.'

'What's going on, Dad?' asked Prudence. 'Is that Sheila Biss in the car?'

'We've won!' said Kelvin gleefully. 'She's agreed to let us build the hall and twin with Botograd.'

'Can I come in the helicopter, too?'

'No,' said Kelvin. 'You've got to do the milking. Let's get the bomb off the trailer.'

'You haven't got the bomb on the trailer,' said Prudence.

'What?' Kelvin looked back at the trailer in alarm. 'Oh! You mean the oil drum! We lost that 'cos we had to use it to rescue some people in the river. I mean the little bomb. Sodov's bomb. It's in the cardboard box.' He walked round the police car to the trailer and carefully lifted the box from its bed. 'Keep back, now. Be careful of the gamma rays. In fact it'd be best if you get her out of the car.'

'But what about you?' asked the inspector, extracting Mrs Biss from the peppermint-filled interior of his car.

'I'm immune,' said Kelvin, stumbling over the ruts where the mud of the lane ended and the concrete of the farmyard began. The commander reached out a steadying hand.

'Be careful! For God's sake,' said Cattermole, putting Prudence between himself and her father.

With the others picking fastidious footsteps a few yards behind, Kelvin trudged across to the edge of the yard where the concrete ended and the ground fell steeply towards a small, flat paddock. Built into the slope was the slurry pit, its walls level with the concrete so that Prudence could push the muck from the yard straight in. Kelvin went through a gate in the barbed wire fence down into the field. 'Are you coming, Sheila?'

'Mrs Biss,' said Mrs Biss. 'I've got my good shoes on and the grass is wet.'

'Don't be silly. You've just walked across the yard.'

'I was looking where I put my feet.' She looked at Smith. 'You can carry me down there.'

'But . . .'

'Carry her down there, Captain!'

The rest of the party stayed safely back in the farmyard as, with Mrs Bliss clutching his neck like the Old Man of the Sea, he picked his way down through the damp tussocks of grass towards Kelvin. On cue, the thump of the approaching heli-copter echoed up the valley.

'Where is it?' asked the commander.

'In the clouds, I suppose,' said Parsons. Although it wasn't raining, the cloud currently overhead was snagged up in the trees lining the tip of the valley.

Travelling low and fast from the direction of Moorcombe, the helicopter came into sight. The cows which had been queuing up in a field by the house to come in for milking, scattered as it suddenly clattered over the farmhouse and descended swiftly towards the yard behind them.

'Hadn't you better tell him where to go?' shouted the commander as the wind of its approach ruffled his hair.

'Oh yes.' Parsons hurried back, beneath the descending helicopter, to his car and began to talk urgently into the radio. He came puffing back. 'He's out of radio contact,' he yelled. 'They say the hillside's blanking out reception and they can't get through.'

As Prudence balefully shook her fist at the helicopter hovering thirty feet above her head, the straw laid out at the edge of the yard for the cows to counter the laxative effect of the wet grass, was driven hither, thither and yon. Skeins of it wrapped themselves round the police car and drifts flattened against the fence alongside the slurry pit and round the legs of the spectators.

'Why don't you write him a note and hold it up for him to read?' suggested Jimmy.

'Point to where we want him to land,' shouted the commander, removing a handful of damp straw embracing his face. In response to their furious gesticulations, the machine suddenly dipped forward in acknowledgement and slid across the yard and the slurry pit to settle unevenly on the grass.

The helicopters which commonly clattered above Moorcombe, fighting for airspace with the jets which streaked over the lip of the valley like driven grouse, were Lynx or Sea King, both substantial machines. This was tiny in comparison, with skids and a perspex, doorless bubble at the front.

Kelvin, twenty-five yards away, clutched his jacket round his waist and hurried through the nettles and docks which thrived on the rich leakage from the slurry pit. 'Are you trying to get me killed,' he shouted. 'We're not going up in that thing! It's like something from a fairground. I want a proper one with wheels.'

'It's called a Sioux. It's the only one I could get at such short notice,' said Parsons. 'They don't sit around like fire engines waiting for me to call, you know. They have other duties.'

'Damn you,' said Kelvin furiously. 'Don't give them a drink when I'm gone, Prudence.'

'If you go up in that thing, I'll be too busy looking for your will.'

Scowling furiously, Kelvin opened his mouth to reply but could only come up with a snarl, compounded of rage and alarm. 'The things I do for Moorcombe! Why should I have to risk my life just to get a village hall?'

'Leadership carries grave responsibilities,' agreed the commander.

Kelvin gave him the benefit of a withering look, but the commander did not seem to be unduly withered. 'Huh! I hope the driver of that thing knows where he's to go.'

'He's been told to put himself at your disposal,' said Parsons. 'After you've defused the bomb, the fissionable material will be picked up by a truck from Mrs Biss's farm later this evening. Then we'll sort out what charges are to be laid.'

'Ha! Try to threaten me, would you? You're either an idiot yourself or you think I'm one,' responded Kelvin. 'And I promise you I'm not. If you bring any charges against me, I'll make sure you look a right idiot. Just you wait and see!'

'What an unpleasant man he is!' said Parsons.

'But he's quite right,' said Smith. 'If this comes out, you'll be a laughing stock.'

'Not just me,' said Parsons. 'You too.' Kelvin crabbed his way back to the bomb, lying on the grass by Mrs Biss. Picking it up, he ushered her towards the helicopter, both of them ducking to avoid the blades. Mrs Biss got in first, followed by Kelvin. They strapped themselves into their seats, Kelvin clutching the bomb on his lap. Under the gaze of the spectators, he donned a set of earphones and then had a brief conversation with the pilot. He pantomined tying a goat to the skids and then waved his hand over his shoulder in the direction of the moor.

The engine began to roar, the blades whacked the air as they picked up speed, Kelvin faced grimly forward, with his eyes shut, and the machine lurched into the air. Brett, his jaw agape and arms round Sodov's neck, gazed up with understandable wonder.

230

'I do hope it doesn't crash,' said Cattermole.

The policeman looked at him curiously. 'Why?'

'Oh come on, Parsons,' said Smith. 'What about the pilot? He's not done any harm.'

'It's the bomb I'm worried about,' said Cattermole. 'The risk of setting it off.'

'Blast!' said Parsons as the rotor wash caught his hat and carried it into a fetid puddle adjacent to the slurry pit. Retrieving it, he stood like the others watching Kelvin's ascent.

'Hallelujah!' said Jimmy as an errant ray of sunshine struck the canopy. 'Quite moving, isn't it? Just like M.A.S.H.'

'We should never have let him get away with it,' said Parsons, gloomily shading his eyes against the sunbeam to watch the helicopter as it rose vertically to get above the trees.

'We really hadn't got a choice,' said Cattermole. 'It was our duty to do everything to avoid the faintest risk of a nuclear explosion.'

'I agree,' said Smith. 'That silly old fool just might have been telling the truth.'

Now comfortably above the height of the few beeches and oaks round the farmyard which had escaped Kelvin's chain-saw, the pilot decided to point his frail craft in the desired direction.

It was not a manoeuvre that Kelvin had expected.

The machine banked at an angle of sixty degrees as it turned and, before the transfixed gaze of those beneath, the box on Kelvin's lap slid towards the open door.

'Oh, my God!' shouted Cattermole, clutching at Smith's arm.

The spectators were left with a vivid impression of the unexpected speed of Kelvin's reactions as he made a successful grab for the edge of the box, just as it was about to fall from the cockpit.

'Ooh!' shrieked Cattermole, letting go of Smith's arm.

But his ooh! was premature.

Kelvin had caught the box, but not before it had disgorged its contents. The errant beam of sunlight, about to be wiped out by the next cloud already looming above the valley, caught the gleaming polished cylinder of the bomb as it slowly tumbled to earth.

'Pretty!' said Brett, pointing a chubby arm.

'Aah!' screamed Cattermole, clutching once more at Smith, but the latter was no longer there. He and Parsons had flung themselves to the ground. Cattermole wasted little time in following suit.

But the natives just gaped as the bomb plummeted down.

A fraction before it landed, Cattermole, realising he was at ground zero, began to babble – possibly prayers, but his diction was unclear and the helicopter was still loud overhead.

The sound of impact, a soft thud like the landing of a clean-shot pheasant, was almost inaudible as the bomb landed in the centre of the slurry pit.

'Ooooh!' said Jimmy.

'Ah!' said Prudence.

'Oh dear!' said the commander.

'What's happening?' demanded Smith, his head in his hands.

'It's in there.'

'Where?' Unclasping their hands, the three visitors care-fully raised their heads. Not being in the midst of a boiling mushroom cloud, they got to their feet, Cattermole grunting with the effort. Their clothes were damp, stained by the mud and slurry on the concrete.

'Just look at you!' said the commander, wrinkling his nose in disgust. 'You are a mess.'

'You don't half stink,' said Jimmy.

'Oh, shut up!' said Parsons angrily. 'Where did it land?'

'Find it yourself, you rude man,' said Jimmy. 'And get down wind of us. Just 'cos you reek like a dog fox, there's no need to blame us.'

'Where's the ******* bomb?' asked Smith.

'It fell in the middle and disappeared,' replied the commander, gesturing helpfully towards the slurry pit.

'Oh.'

Moving over to the barbed-wire fence surrounding the pit, Smith and his colleagues examined the sinister brown surface crust, studded with half-submerged plastic fertiliser bags, empty tubes of antibiotic and lengths of baler twine. Catter-mole eased his sodden trousers away from his thighs with finger and thumb.

'Whereabouts?' asked Parsons, pulling a white cotton handkerchief from his pocket and fastidiously wiping his hands.

'Just in front of that dead lamb,' replied the commander.

'Oh. How deep is it?'

'Eight feet, I'd guess,' said Jimmy.

'Nearer ten, I'd've thought,' said the commander.

Parsons sighed, looking round at his colleagues. 'Are we agreed, gentlemen?'

'Agreed what?' asked Cattermole.

'That the bomb was a hoax.'

'What are you talking about?' said Cattermole, staring at the policeman in astonishment. 'Just because it didn't go off doesn't prove it's a hoax. The impact may have been too soft to trigger it. I'll have to give a full report.'

Jimmy snorted. 'You mean you'll be in the shit if you don't?'

'Well . . . er . . . I wouldn't put it like that myself, but yes, I suppose I would.'

'And where d'you think you'd be if you try to get the bomb back?'

'Er . . .' Cattermole looked at the slurry pit. Its surface shuddered as a bubble of gas erupted from the depths.

'I'll hold your jacket for you,' said Smith.

'Er . . . yes. Perhaps it was a hoax.'

'I think that's best,' agreed the commander, gravely. 'Let's go back to the Hind to celebrate. We're British again.'